I0685835

THE MYSTERY MISTLETOE BRIDE

Joanna Maitland

A woman with no name, no past, no memory—rescued by an earl with his own bitter secrets

Joanna Maitland Titles

THE MYSTERY MISTLETOE BRIDE

Joanna Maitland

Published by Joanna Maitland Independent, 2025

Published by Joanna Maitland Independent in 2025
LibertaBooks.com
The Mystery Mistletoe Bride
originally published as The Earl's Mistletoe Bride
by Harlequin Mills & Boon Ltd in 2010 by arrangement with
Harlequin Books S.A.

Copyright © Joanna Maitland 2010, 2020, 2025
Second revised edition 2020, 2025
Paperback: ISBN-13: 978-1-913915-16-2
Ebook: ISBN-13: 978-1-913915-15-5

The right of Joanna Maitland to be identified as the author of
this work has been asserted by her in accordance with the
Copyright, Designs and Patents Act 1988.

This book is a work of fiction. Names, characters, places and
incidents are the product of the author's imagination or have
been used fictitiously and are not to be construed as real. Any
resemblance to actual persons, living or dead, or to events or
places is entirely coincidental.

All rights reserved. No part of this publication may be
reproduced, stored in a retrieval system, or transmitted, in any
form, or by any means, electronic, mechanical, photo-copying,
recording or otherwise, without the prior written permission of
the publisher.

Cover Design and Interior Formatting: Joanna Maitland
Cover Images:
© PeriodImages.com/ VJ Dunraven/ Mary Chronis
© [Meowgli]/Adobe Stock; © [andersphoto]/Adobe Stock

Chapter One

London, September 1809

THE DOOR OPENED AFTER Jon's first knock. His cousin Ned Garway stood there in just shirtsleeves and breeches. The room behind him was a tumble of half-filled valises, uniforms and all the other paraphernalia of a military officer about to go to war.

"Jon! What a surprise. Come to see me off, have you?"

Jon stuck out a hand and they shook heartily. "May I come in, Ned? I hope you'll forgive the intrusion. You look, er, a trifle occupied." He waved in the direction of the baggage.

Ned laughed and called out to summon his batman. "Watson, make some space here so that his lordship may sit down." The batman began to carry heaps of kit into the next room, presumably his own domain. In the space of five minutes, Ned's room was clear enough for the cousins to sit down in front of the fire. "After so long in Portugal, I find I feel the cold," Ned said with a shrug, and added more coals. "I'll be glad to be back there."

"How soon do you leave?"

"Tomorrow."

"Ah. Then I'm glad I caught you. I need some advice. And, to be frank, you're the only man in England I can ask."

"In that case, Jon, I suggest we brew up some rum punch. Helps keep the cold out." Ned summoned his batman again and was soon stirring a steaming bowl.

Jon relaxed into his chair. The door to the batman's room was safely closed. They would not be overheard. Cousin Ned

1

was a very good friend, but it would still be easier to share confidences after a glass or two.

Having ladled the hot liquid into tumblers, Ned resumed his seat and looked across at Jon, waiting for him to speak.

Jon took a large mouthful of punch and savoured its spicy warmth. "You always were a dab hand with a punch bowl, Ned. Much better than I am, I must say."

Ned grinned. "Had more practice."

Jon chuckled. It was good to be with such an old friend. The two men drank in comfortable silence and Ned quietly refilled their glasses. Eventually, Jon took a deep breath. "I'm thinking of coming out to join you in the Peninsula."

Ned gasped. "Joining the army? But you're the Earl of Portbury. You have vast estates to run. And— Forgive me for being blunt, Jon, but you still have no heir."

Jon had come to Ned for frank advice and that was precisely what Ned was giving him. Jon swallowed hard and shook his head. "There's never going to be an heir, Ned, apart from my brother, George."

Ned made a face that showed precisely what he thought of Jon's wastrel brother.

"My marriage to Alicia is a failure. I can say that to you, Ned, but to no one else. Even after more than a dozen barren years, my mother continues to imagine there will one day be an heir. Like everyone else, she seems to have been taken in by the public performance Alicia and I put on. But it is becoming unbearable to live in the same house with her. She cannot stand the sight of me. She spends all her time with her companion, Miss Mountjoy. They even have, um, adjoining bedchambers."

Ned turned away to stare at the fire. "When you say there's never going to be an heir, Jon," he began quietly, "do you mean...er...?"

Jon took a deep breath. He had come this far, so... "That's the nub of it, Ned. There's no one else I'd trust with this, but I know I can trust you. Alicia will not share my bed. Or any man's. She shares her bed with Louisa Mountjoy."

Ned gulped and grabbed the poker to stir the fire. After a long silence, he turned back to his cousin. "Your father would have told you to throw the Mountjoy woman into the gutter and insist on your marital rights."

"That would be rape. Or as good as. I am not my father, Ned."

"No. And I am mighty glad of it. I thought you might become like him. Back then, you were trying so very hard to be the heir he demanded, to fill Henry's shoes, even though we all knew that no one could replace Henry in your father's eyes."

Jon sighed. "True. I was never going to be anything but a very poor second best after Henry died. I did learn that. In the end. When it was too late."

"You must not blame yourself for Alicia, Jon. Heavens above, you were only twenty years old and you had just lost the brother who was your closest friend. Your father presented you with a duke's daughter and insisted you marry her. What were you supposed to do? Run away and join the army?"

"God, I wish I had," Jon said, with feeling.

Ned ladled more punch into Jon's tumbler. "So is that what you're going to do now? Run away to join the army?"

Jon gave a shout of bitter laughter. "I hadn't thought of it like that. Fact is, Alicia and I need to live apart. But if we separate in England, the gossips will tear her reputation to shreds. No matter what she has done, she does not deserve a fate like that. It was not her choice to wed me. Her father sold her to the highest bidder."

Ned nodded. "Aye, he'd have sold her to an ogre for the right price."

After a long pause, Jon went on, "So, it seemed to me that joining you in the Peninsula was the solution. I will be doing my duty to my king and Alicia will be able to live the life she wants, with her reputation intact. What do you think, Ned?"

"Well...you'd certainly see action. But what about George? Do you trust him to run the estates in your absence? He hasn't been exactly trustworthy in the past."

"No, but my steward will refer important decisions to Alicia. She has a sense of duty. So does my mother. As heir, George needs to learn about the responsibilities of running the estates while I am away. I'm sure he'll accept that he must do so."

Ned looked sceptical but said only, "You seem to have thought of everything. And I can see that it could work, too, so why not? We could certainly use a man like you in the Peninsula. I do think that we have a better chance of chasing Boney's army out of Spain now that Lord Wellington is in charge, but it will take time. We need more men, more guns, more everything. You do realise, don't you, that it might be years before you could return to England?"

Jon laughed then, a real laugh, as though a great weight had been lifted from his shoulders. "You know, Ned, that is the most hopeful thing anyone has said to me in ages." He raised his tumbler. "Here's to the Peninsula. And years of freedom."

Chapter Two

England, December 1811

IT WAS COLD. SO VERY cold.

Sharp icy fingers were probing into the hidden crevices of her clothing and scratching at every inch of exposed skin. The sleet-laden wind was whipping across her cheeks like scouring sand, rubbing them raw. Every breath was a torment to her aching lungs.

But she had no choice. She must go on. Away from all those pointing fingers. To somewhere safe, hidden, somewhere she could breathe again.

She had no idea where she was or where this lonely rutted path might lead. She raised her chin to peer ahead, brushing aside the wet strings of her hair and screwing up her eyes against the sleet in an attempt to see her way. Overhanging trees, mostly naked against the onset of winter; an understorey of shrubs, some evergreen, but most of them bare and soggy black in the storm; a sodden path strewn with drifts of dead leaves that would soon be swallowed up by the deep, oozing mud. And beyond the trees, the path led into darkness.

She shivered, drew her thin shawl tighter around her shoulders and bent her head against the keening wind. If she stopped now, here, alone, the weather would win their unequal battle. She was not ready to yield. Not yet.

She plodded on, forcing herself to lift her weary feet, one step, then another, trying to ignore the freezing water in her boots and the squelching of the mud as it tried to hold her fast and suck her down. She was so very tired. If only—

5

For a second, the wind veered and whipped at her skirts from behind. She saw— No, she *fancied* she saw a simple fence, of posts and rails, of the kind that might border a country road, but it was gone in the blink of an eye. No matter how much she strained, she could not find it again. She had probably seen only what she longed to see—some sign of human habitation, of human warmth, of hope.

There was no hope.

The last light of the short December day was almost gone. Soon she would be alone, in the dark, in this strange wooded place, on a path that led to nowhere. Why on earth had she followed it?

At the time, it had seemed the most sensible course. What else could a woman do, abandoned at a lonely crossroads by the coach driver who had taken her up?

She had travelled many miles with him, naively believing that he was helping her out of the goodness of his heart. In truth, he was merely waiting to bring her to a suitably lonely place, where he could present his ultimatum: her money, or her person. When he discovered that she had neither money in her purse nor any willingness to pay him in kind, his bluff good nature vanished. He brought her even further from any chance of rescue, and pushed her out on to the deserted road, without even allowing her to take down her battered travelling bag. He would sell the contents, he said, to make up for the fare she owed him. Then he whipped up his horses, disappearing without so much as a glance at the woman he was leaving to the mercy of the storm.

She struggled to put the evil man from her mind. She must find the strength to go on. She must not give in to exhaustion. She *must* go on.

Beyond a huge oak tree, she found herself in an odd sort of dark clearing. It was edged with dense evergreen shrubs surrounding a broad area of churned mud and tussocks of grass. For a second, the wind dropped. In the sudden lull, she tried to tuck her hair back under her dripping bonnet. But the strings parted under the strain as the wind returned, howling around her. Her bonnet was torn off and disappeared into the darkness, leaving her unbound hair whipping her face like slapping fingers.

She was too tired to wonder why she should be suffering so. She knew only that she needed to find shelter soon, or the storm would surely best her.

There was that plain fence again. Or was it?

She took a few steps away from the path, trying to avoid the mud. The grass felt spongy beneath her feet, and treacherous, as though it might give way at any moment and plunge her down into some sucking void.

But those shrubs over there were thick and still densely green. Beneath them, she thought she could make out a kind of haven where they overhung a patch of more sheltered ground, full of dead leaves blown into heaps. It even looked fairly dry. She could take refuge there, for a while, until the worst of the storm was over and she had regained a little of her strength.

She moved more quickly now. Being out of the wet was a prize worth the effort. She focused all her remaining strength on gaining it. But, in her haste, she forgot to watch where she was putting her feet. Her ankle turned. The laces of her boot snapped with a loud crack. Before she realised what was happening, the boot was gone, sucked away, and her stockinged foot had taken one more unwary step, sinking deep into the mud.

She cried out in shock and fear. Slimy hands seemed to be trying to drag her down. She tried to tell herself that it was nonsense, wild imaginings, but her senses were bewildered. She could not make them obey her.

She tugged hard, desperate to release her foot, but she did not have the strength. Her flailing arms found one of the branches of the evergreen. Something to give her purchase. She hung on to it with both hands and pulled again. No use. Still she could not—

Suddenly, she was free. She stumbled forward a single step, then pitched head first into the base of the shrub and the pile of leaves. Her head and her right arm crunched against unyielding wood. Her nose and mouth filled with debris and dirt. She tasted decay and mould. She clawed at her face, desperate to breathe. It took her several moments to regain

7

enough control to force the terrors from her mind. Eventually, she spat out the last of the leaf fragments and forced herself up. Pain lanced through her injured arm. Was it broken? She could not tell.

The wind was howling even louder. The evergreens around the clearing bent before it with an angry but defeated hiss. Yet the branches above her did not swish away. They seemed to bend over her, caressingly, like a loving mother soothing her child to sleep. Soothing, soothing.

She let her body relax again into the leaf litter, pillowing her pounding head on her good arm, resting her cheek against her wet, ungloved palm. It would do no harm to close her eyes for a space. Until the storm abated. Then she would go on. She had to go on.

Closing her eyes changed everything. Soon she could no longer feel the pain or the cold seeping into her bones. The storm seemed less hostile. She could barely hear the wind or the beat of the rain on the leaves. Was she floating? She was beginning to feel as if she were weightless, drifting slowly up into the heavens. And in her heavens, the sky around her was a bright, fierce blue.

• • • •

Jon should have stayed at that last inn where there were good beds to be had for both man and beast. He had been mad to drive out alone in the face of the gathering storm. He knew that. And so did his horses. It had been unfair on them even to set out. They were a mettlesome pair, but the poor beasts had been slipping and sliding in the flowing mud on that last slope. Here the ground was flatter so they could be reasonably sure-footed, even in such appalling weather. He was thankful that there had been no lightning to spook them.

The first flash split the sky.

Jon swore under his breath, trying to focus on controlling his horses, afraid they might try to bolt.

The sudden light had shown him the simple rail fence dividing the narrow lane from the woods beyond. His woods. Even though he had not visited this estate for well over two years, he knew the layout intimately. The narrow lane had been skirting his land for a considerable distance now. Soon it would bring him to the village of Lower Fratcombe and, beyond that, to his lodge gates. Another mile and he would be able to give his straining horses into the care of the Fratcombe grooms and order a hot bath for himself. After he'd drunk a good stiff brandy.

His body began to relax a fraction, in anticipation.

A mistake. The lightning cracked again, more fiercely than before. The offside horse, eyes rolling and ears flattened, seemed about to rear. It took several seconds before Jon could bring his pair back under control and find the breath to curse his own failings. Stupid, stupid. No matter how tired he was, he should have been giving his attention to his cattle.

And yet something had caught his eye, yards back along the road, in that momentary flash of light. It had looked like—

It was impossible. He must have been seeing things. Tiredness, probably.

He spoke soothingly to his horses, trying to make himself heard over the storm. He should—

There *had* been something. Someone. He pulled back on the reins, easing his curricle to a halt. A Christian gentleman could not leave a man out here to die in the storm. It was Jon's duty to see what help he could offer.

He told himself he was being an utter fool. How could he possibly have seen anything at all in that fleeting moment? His attention had been all for his horses.

Yet his unruly conscience stabbed at him. It would not let him rest now, not until he had gone back to check. He had probably mistaken something else for a body. A fallen log, perhaps. Yes, that would be it.

But he had to be sure.

He sprang down and went to his horses' heads, automatically calming them with the sound of his voice and the stroke of his hand on their necks. Once he was sure they had quieted, he hitched the reins to the fence. "Wait there, my beauties, while I check out this odd fancy of mine. Then we'll soon have you in a fine warm stable."

He unhitched one of the carriage lamps and started to make his way back up the lane. Beyond the dim reach of the flame, the darkness was impenetrable. In order to check out what he thought he had seen, he was going to have to walk right into the woods. He glanced down at the riding boots he wore. They were muddy already, from that last inn yard and from walking these few yards back along the lane, but in the woods he would probably sink ankle-deep. He had played there as a child. He knew the area never dried out, even in high summer.

He sighed. He could well afford to replace a pair of boots. But he had so little of his leave left. He could not afford to delay his departure for something as trivial as new boots. They would have to be sent on after him.

He caught a distant growl of thunder, just as he reached the fence that divided the lane from the path to the clearing where he thought he had seen the crumpled body. The lightning storm was passing now, which was a blessing. There was unlikely to be any more to frighten his horses.

Leaning forward, he grasped the rail with one gloved hand and raised the lamp in an effort to see a little further. Useless. He could barely see five yards.

With a sigh of resignation, he lowered the lamp and ducked under the rail. He carried the lamp low to the ground so that he could pick his way between the soft mud and the tufts of slightly less sodden grass, but even after he had walked quite a distance, he still could not find the makeshift shelter under the evergreens. But there was no other clearing in this part of his woods, surely?

He raised the lamp once more and took another few steps, holding it high. The wind was still whipping at the tails of his driving coat, as if reluctant to concede that the storm was abating. It still sounded more like baying hounds than a force of nature.

Yes, there. That looked familiar. He could make out the shadowy shape of a great oak reaching its bare branches across the clearing. He vaguely recalled that it stood alongside the main path.

It was his nose that told him he had found the place. In a sudden lull in the wind, he smelt warm, wet wool. Astonishing. In among all the smells of decaying wood and leaves, he could smell warm, wet wool. Wet wool could only mean wet clothing. And wet clothing meant a human being.

10

Perhaps—God forbid—a body. He had seen far too many of those in Spain.

He pushed on more quickly now, swinging his lamp from side to side as he cast about for that elusive shelter he was now sure he had seen. And there it was—in the lee of the trees, where a group of tangled, overgrown evergreens nestled, their branches almost touching the ground. The wind must have whistled around this clearing even when there was no storm, for the dead leaves of autumn were banked up against the trunks and branches, making a welcoming mound. A relatively dry mound, too, for the shrubs were thick enough to keep out much of the wet.

Jon bent to pull back the branches. The smell of wet wool was very strong. Huddled against the trunks was a shapeless human body, its knees pulled up to its chest in an effort to keep warm. He brought the lamp closer and dropped to one knee, preparing to crawl in under the branches. But first, he dragged off one glove and reached out his bare fingers. Would the body be ice-cold? Dead?

The head and face were hidden by lank, dripping hair. With gentle fingers, Jon pushed it back in order to touch the skin beneath. It was cold, and wet. But it was not icy.

Not dead then. Not yet.

There was still a chance of saving this poor benighted soul. Jon swept aside some of the leaves to make a secure stand for his lamp. He needed both hands free for this. And he needed the light.

On both knees now, he pushed himself further under the bush and reached in to take the body by the shoulders, pushing all its hair back from the face. Good God! It was a woman. How could she—?

In the gloom, he could not make out her features, but her cheek was pillowed on one bare hand, with long, elegant fingers protecting her skin from the dirt and leaves on which she rested. Her pitiful clothes were soaked through and clinging to her slim body. She had neither bonnet nor gloves, only a plain dark gown and a threadbare shawl. He shook his head in frustration. Time enough to consider later who she was and how she had come here. For the moment, he must get her out and take her to safety, to somewhere she could be warm and dry.

He put his hand on her free arm and shook her, gently at first, then with more force. "You must wake up. You cannot stay here. Come! Open your eyes!"

She groaned. It seemed to Jon it was a groan of pain. Was she injured? He could not tell. There was not enough light.

He laid his bare fingers on her cheek and stroked it slowly. "Come, open your eyes. You must leave this place. You will die if you stay here."

She seemed to respond to that. Her body did not move, but her eyes opened. For a second, she gazed up at him, but it was a vacant, unfocused stare. He doubted she was seeing him at all. She was very far gone indeed. Another hour or so, he judged, and she would never wake again.

"Trust me. I will see you safe," Jon said gently, moving the lamp a little further away. Then he slid his arms beneath her inert body, one under her shoulders, the other under her knees. Forcing himself to ignore her moans of pain, he shuffled awkwardly backwards until he had her clear of the overhanging branches. He pulled her against his chest for a moment, trying to give her warmth. It was not enough. He had to get her back to his curricle.

He laid her carefully on the ground so that he could strip off his driving coat and wrap her in it. It was at least a little warmer than her own sodden clothing though she fainted again as he moved her. Now he must bring her out, but he needed the lamp to see his way back to the lane. How was he to do it? He could not carry her properly with only one arm.

He raised the lamp and gazed down at her. She was much too far gone to know what he did. Discomfort and indignity were nothing compared with saving her life. "Forgive me. I need a free hand for the lamp." The apology was automatic, though he doubted she heard a word. Setting the lamp down once more, he picked up her unresisting body and slung her over his shoulder, wrapping one arm around her thighs to prevent her from slipping out of his grasp. Then he retrieved the lamp and began to pick his way through the mud, back to the lane.

12

It was a slow and careful business. She might already be injured and, if he lost his balance, she would suffer even more. Eventually, he reached the fence and the lane beyond it. He pulled her from his shoulder and set her gently on the ground, pillowing her head with the capes of his coat. She moaned a little, but her eyes did not open. Freed of his burden, he ducked under the rail and pulled her out to him. Could he carry her properly now?

He glanced down the lane to where he had left his horses. He could make out nothing at all, not even the remaining lamp on his curricle, for the sleet had given way to lashing rain. He would still need his own lamp to light the way. The lane was muddy enough to be dangerous.

"Poor girl," he said aloud, wrapping his coat a little more closely round her. "But it will not be long now. Trust me." He gathered her into his arms.

A thready whisper came from her colourless lips. "Not long now. Trust you." It was very faint. But it was an educated voice. A *lady*?

"You *can* hear me. I do not know who you are, ma'am, but—trust me—I will take you out of this, and see you safe. I promise you."

There was no further reaction. She was gone again.

With a silent curse, Jon hefted her over his shoulder once more, lifted his lamp and started down the lane to his curricle.

• • • •

She seemed to be dreaming his voice. Words. Questions. Sometimes soothing, sometimes sharp. But never strong enough to pull her back from the cocoon of warmth that now surrounded her and held her safe. She felt she was floating away all over again, this time for ever.

And then her cocoon was gone.

She was alone with her suffering. She forced her eyes open. She was propped up in a curricle. By the dim light of its lamps, she saw that the horses were hitched to a fence. Was there a house beyond?

"You are come back to us, ma'am." His tall figure reappeared from the darkness. He had not deserted her.

13

Perhaps she could trust him, after all? "Come, let me carry you in."

He was gentle, mindful of her hurts, lifting her carefully into his arms and cradling her close to his body. She let herself relax into his reassuring strength. The scent of man and horse and leather surrounded her. For a moment, he stood still, gazing down at her. Then his jaw clenched and he started towards the house.

She saw a winding path through dark, dripping shrubs. Then an open doorway filled with light and warmth and welcome. And a small round man in clerical garb, hovering anxiously.

As her rescuer hurried towards the doorstep, a little old lady in a lace cap appeared from the depths of the hallway, followed by an even smaller maidservant.

"Mrs Aubrey. Thank goodness." He shouldered his way past the old man and into the hall. "I need your help for this poor creature. I have never seen her before, but I believe she may be a lady. I rescued her from the woods by the old oak. She is hurt. And almost frozen to death."

The old man gasped. "Dear God. Poor child. And at Christmas, too."

His wife stepped forward in order to smooth back the wet hair and peer into the new arrival's face. "What is your name, my dear?"

That came like a blow, worse than all the pain that had gone before. It was a terrible, terrifying realisation. "I–I do not know."

Chapter Three

JON LEANED BACK AND stretched his boots towards the library fire. In truth, he did not have time to relax at the rectory, or anywhere else, but it would have been the height of bad manners to rush off to Fratcombe Manor after imposing an invalid on the Aubreys. He was relieved to have given her into Mrs Aubrey's care. The old lady had tended to many cuts and sprains when Jon and his older brother had played in those woods as boys. On one occasion, indeed, she had dealt most competently with a broken arm until it could be set by the local surgeon.

"Brandy, Master Jonathan?" The Reverend Aubrey reappeared with a decanter and two glasses. He motioned to Jon to remain where he was. There was no need for ceremony between two such old friends.

"That would be most welcome, sir." Jon took the glass and cradled it in his fingers to warm the golden liquid.

The rector glanced down at Jon's outstretched legs. "I doubt any valet will be able to make those breeches wearable again." He grimaced. "Or the boots."

Jon shrugged and smiled across at the rector who had settled himself in the chair opposite, and was leaning forward to stir the fire. "You always taught me, sir, that a human life is worth more than mere fripperies. It seems your sermon on the Good Samaritan made a lasting impression on that unruly boy kicking at his pew."

The old man reddened a little and cleared his throat. "It is the Lord's word, my boy, not mine. But you have done a very good deed this day."

Jon said nothing. He had done very little.

"I noticed that you brought no baggage with the young woman. Should I send the boy back to search for it, do you think?"

Jon considered for a moment. "I saw nothing at all with her—no bonnet, no gloves, no reticule, nothing. But it was very dark. I suppose she might have dropped them on the path. Perhaps it would be worthwhile sending someone to search. Just in case."

The rector made to rise.

"But not tonight, Rector, please. I shall send out in the morning. It's impossible to see more than a yard or two in the dark. And anything she may have dropped will have been ruined long ago by the wet. Waiting until the morning will do no harm."

Mr Aubrey sank back into his chair and took a sip of his brandy. "Aye, you are right. But I was hoping that there might perhaps be some clue to her identity. She must surely have family, friends, someone who is anxious to know of her fate? I would spare them, if I could."

Jon nodded. The rector was a truly good man. He cared about the misfortunes of others and tried his best to remedy them.

For several minutes, they both sat staring at the leaping flames.

"Forgive me, my boy," the rector said suddenly. "My manners are sadly lacking. Old age, I fear. First and foremost, I must repeat our sincere condolences on the death of your wife. Caro and I—"

"Thank you, sir." It was bad manners to interrupt the rector, but Jon found he could not bear such consoling words from this gentle man. The rector would have supposed that Jon's marriage had been a happy one. It felt like lying to accept his sympathy. "Your kind letter reached me in Spain and was much appreciated. I have done my best to deal with the loss of my wife and—if you will forgive me—I should prefer not to discuss it any further." He set his mouth in a hard line. He wanted the message to be very clear.

"Of course, of course. I quite understand." The rector was shaking his head sadly, but he said nothing more. He busied himself with stirring the fire again, even though it was already burning nicely.

Eventually the rector broke the strained silence, asking brightly, "To what do we owe this visit after such a long absence? I see you are not wearing regimentals. Have you sold out? May we hope you will remain at Fratcombe for Christmas?"

Smiling gratefully back at the old man, Jon shook his head. "No, sir. On both counts, I am afraid. It is a business visit, for a few days only. There has been some, er, mismanagement at Fratcombe." He swallowed. Even to an old friend like the rector, Jon would not speak ill of his younger brother. "I have come to set matters to rights and to give new instructions to my steward before I—"

At that moment, the door burst open and Mrs Aubrey bustled in. She looked agitated.

The two men rose immediately, setting down their glasses. "What is the matter, ma'am?" Jon found himself fearing the worst. That poor woman had been so near death when he brought her in.

The rector walked calmly to the door and closed it behind his wife. Then he ushered her across to the fire and pushed her gently into Jon's vacant chair. "I can see that you have concerns about our invalid, my dear. Pray, tell us. Perhaps we can help."

Mrs Aubrey began to twist her fingers together in her lap. She looked up into Jon's face, gauging his expression. "No, my lord, she is not dead. She is recovering. We put her into a hot bath and then a warm bed. Hetty even managed to spoon some broth into her."

"Ah." Jon felt his shoulders relaxing again. "Bless you, ma'am. You are definitely on the side of the angels."

"But has she remembered who she is?" the rector asked.

"I fear that remains the problem, James. She seemed to be on the point of telling me. But then her expression became anguished. And fearful. She does not know who she is. Nor anything about her past. And she still cannot remember her name."

"The Lord preserve us. The poor child."

Jon knew he had to intervene. "Forgive me, ma'am, but I must ask. Did you believe her?" Jon had heard of cases where unscrupulous people had preyed on their benefactors by pretending to have lost their memory. Given the circumstances in which he had found the woman, he doubted that it was the case here, but he had to ask.

Mrs Aubrey shook her head impatiently. "You carried her in, my lord. Did you not see her face, when I asked her before? Did you not see the fear in her eyes? Upstairs, it was worse, if anything. If you had seen her reactions, you would not be doubting her word. She has no recollection of who she is or where she comes from. And it terrifies her."

In the silence that followed, the rector quietly fetched another glass and poured a small brandy for his wife. "Drink this, Caro, my dear. You have had a shock. It will do you good."

Mrs Aubrey frowned, but then she took a swallow. She choked and began to cough. "Goodness, I had forgotten how much brandy burns. It does warm, however, and I am grateful for it." She pressed the glass back into her husband's hand. "One mouthful is enough, I think, for an old lady. I cannot afford to be foxed when I have an invalid to care for."

Jon was glad to see that her normal twinkling good humour had returned. "I take it there was no clue to her identity among her clothing?"

"Goodness, I clean forgot. It must be the effects of the brandy that you are plying me with, husband. Shame on you."

The rector grinned sheepishly.

Mrs Aubrey produced a piece of soggy paper. "I found this in the pocket under her gown. It is utterly sodden and illegible. Almost all the ink has run. But I managed to make out two words. I think they are 'Dear Beth', but I am not absolutely sure."

The rector took the paper and frowned down at it. "The name certainly begins with B. And I think...I think the last letter is H. Yes, I'm sure you are right, my dear. The name is Beth. For what other short name begins with B and ends in H?"

"Beth. Elizabeth?" Jon wondered aloud.

"Almost certainly." The rector nodded, clearly pleased at the discovery. "Beth is quite a common pet-name for girls christened Elizabeth. And what else could it be? Her name must be Elizabeth."

"Excellent," Jon said. "We are making progress. We may tell our invalid so. It may even strike a chord in her memory, so that she will remember more. It can do no harm to try, surely?" Jon smiled at Mrs Aubrey.

The rector's wife managed only a half-smile in return. "I only wish we had more than one soggy letter to show her."

"Do not be so concerned, ma'am. Tomorrow morning, as soon as it is light, I will send the servants out to scour the woods. If our Elizabeth had any baggage with her, or anything else, you may be sure that they will find it. Besides that, I will have enquiries made of the coaching services, and the other carriers. One of them may remember having brought her to Fratcombe. If all else fails, we can advertise in the newspapers for anyone who has a missing friend or relative by the name of Elizabeth. Do not worry, ma'am. I am sure we will find a way of helping her."

Mrs Aubrey rose and put out her hands to clasp Jon's. "Thank you. I suppose you will wish to take her to the Manor to be cared for?"

"Ah." Jon shook his head slowly. "That would be, um, unwise, I think. There would be only servants to chaperon her in my house. She may be an invalid, but that would not prevent the gossip from starting. She is a lady, with a lady's reputation to lose. Do you not agree, ma'am?"

Mrs Aubrey nodded. "Her clothing is old and worn, but her hands are soft and well cared for. She has not been used to menial work, that is certain. At a guess, I would say she is a poor relation, a companion, a governess, or something of the sort. And not from a household where such people are valued."

"Poor child," said the rector.

"Well then, she must stay here at the rectory, as our guest. You do not object, James, do you?" Mrs Aubrey glanced up at her husband. Considering how small and demure she was, the sudden light of steely determination in her eyes seemed out of place. Jon marvelled at the change in her, though he had detected it once or twice before. When she was intent on helping others, there was no one, not even the rector, who could deflect her from her chosen path.

The rector clearly knew it. His brow cleared. He gazed down at his wife with a slightly lopsided smile and said quietly, "You are always the best judge in such matters, my dear. Do as you will."

Mrs Aubrey allowed herself a small, decided nod and turned for the door. Jon hurried to open it for her, but before he could reach it, the door flew open and crashed into the wall. The little maid, Hetty, was standing on the threshold, her eyes full of alarm, and her body quivering. "Oh, ma'am, she's trying to climb out of the window."

"What?" Mrs Aubrey pushed the girl aside and rushed for the stairs, with Jon barely half a pace behind her. If Elizabeth had to be physically restrained, Mrs Aubrey was much too old and frail to do it.

On the upstairs landing, the best spare bedroom door stood wide open. The fire had burned low in the hearth. By its light, he saw that the bed was empty, the covers in a tangle.

"Elizabeth," Mrs Aubrey called. "Where are you? Oh, my child, come back to where you will be warm, and safe."

Jon pushed his way past the rector's wife. He could see no one in the room. But there was a screen in front of the connecting door to the dressing room. He raced across the room and hurled it aside. Behind it, the window was wide open. The woman was sitting astride the sill. As if she were about to climb down.

Jon's heart lurched. She would injure herself even more. She must not. "No, you don't," he said, grabbing her round the waist and hauling her bodily back into the room. He felt her leg graze against the wall.

She seemed oblivious to her injury. "No," she cried. "Let me go. *Let me go.*" She tried to fight to free herself, but only her left arm seemed to have any strength.

Jon set her feet on the floor and wrapped his arms around her shoulders and back, holding her tight against his body so that she could not continue to struggle. She must not be allowed to do herself further harm. "Elizabeth. Beth. You are safe here. Trust me when I say that. Trust me."

She looked up at him. Her eyes were dark and full of fear.

"Trust me," he said again, putting all his concern and compassion into the words. "No one will harm you here, I promise you. Trust me."

Her body began to relax in his embrace. The fear melted from her eyes. "Trust you," she whispered. Her eyes closed.

For a moment, Jon thought she might have fainted, but it was not so. Her body had not gone limp. She was simply exhausted.

Her head had fallen against his shoulder. Jon realised, for the first time, that in spite of her light weight, she was quite a tall woman. In the flickering light of the fire, he could now see that her hair was the reddish-brown of the finest rosewood. Most of it was still damp, but one or two wayward curls were caressing her temples. She was incredibly pale, almost ashen, but her body was certainly warming up. He could feel that, even through his own clothing and the heavy, shapeless bedgown she wore. One of Mrs Aubrey's, he supposed. It had long sleeves tied at the cuff with ribbons, and was made high to the neck, with the merest hint of lace around the collar. Most appropriate for a rector's wife, but it was failing to protect the younger woman's slim form. He could feel her small firm breasts pressed against him. And his hands on her back were beginning to respond to a primitive impulse to stroke over her shoulder blades and down her spine, to cup her unresisting body against him.

A discreet cough at his back reminded him of where he was and doused his lustful imaginings as effectively as a pail of icy water. He sighed. He knew the cause. He had been so long without a willing woman in his bed that his body's urges were beginning to overcome his self-control. Still, once he was out of England again, there would be other things to occupy his mind. And his body, too. It could not come soon enough.

"Would you be so good as to carry Beth back to bed now? I fancy she is getting chilled all over again. Hetty, straighten the bedclothes."

Jon lifted the woman into his arms and carried her across the room, staring all the while at the hem of her bedgown. He must not allow his gaze to wander upwards over her curves. He realised suddenly that Mrs Aubrey's nightrail was very short, barely covering the poor girl's knees. She had very elegant feet. Slim and arched. The kind of feet that should be shod in the most delectable of silken slippers, while she twirled around on a dance floor in the arms of some fortunate cavalier.

Very gently, Jon laid her down and drew his arm out from under her shoulders. The curly ends of her loose hair brushed against his skin, sending a tiny shiver up his arm. He shook his head, stunned by his own reaction. Now, why should that have happened? He tried to make out her features but, in the gloom, he could see only a pale face and closed eyes. There was no reason why such an ordinary woman should have any effect on him at all. It must be because he was very tired. Once he had seen her safely bestowed, he would take his leave of the Aubreys and find his own hot bath and his own comfortable bed.

Mrs Aubrey was tucking the bedclothes carefully around the girl's shoulders. "Poor child. Whatever can have possessed her? Her feet are like blocks of ice again. I had best order another hot brick or she will never get warm."

Jon felt guilt stabbing at him. He had been so busy admiring the shape of the girl's feet that he had totally failed to notice how cold they were. It was as well that Mrs Aubrey was a good nurse, for Jon was clearly useless when it came to such things.

"I fear her right arm is very bruised, but it will mend soon enough. There is nothing broken, I am sure. I am more concerned about that blow to her head, under her hair. A fall, do you think?"

Jon nodded, though the idea of a possible assailant settled uncomfortably at the edge of his thoughts.

"I think it is safe for you to leave her now." Mrs Aubrey drew Jon away from the bed. "I shall give her a few drops of laudanum, to make sure that she sleeps." She beckoned the maid to her side. "Hetty, you will remain with her, in case anything more should happen." Mrs Aubrey paused, frowning. "But why was she trying to climb out of the window?"

"I–I don't know, ma'am." Hetty's face was pale. "She seemed to be half awake, so I was talking to her about our Christmas preparations—the Yule log, and fetching mistletoe and ivy and such. One minute she was lying peaceful like, and the next she were pushing me to the floor and trying to open the window."

"Perhaps she thought that someone wanted to do her harm? What other reason could there be?" Jon avoided mentioning a possible attacker. Mrs Aubrey was already worried enough.

"It is all very strange," Mrs Aubrey said, shaking her head so vehemently that the lace trimmings on her cap fluttered.

They were making their way to the door when Jon heard a sound from the bed. He turned swiftly and strode back. "Beth? What is it?" He bent down so that his ear was close to her lips.

"Trust you." Barely a breath. But her eyes were open.

He touched the back of his fingers to her brow. It was warm, but not hot enough for fever. "Sleep now. You are safe here. I wish you a speedy recovery. Good night, Beth."

She frowned when he spoke her name. He thought it was caused by puzzlement, rather than recognition. But as her eyes drifted closed, he saw that it was too late for questions. Another day, perhaps.

Chapter Four

THE FOLLOWING MORNING dawned bright and cold, the kind of December day when the sky was fiercely blue and the sun shone brightly, but without warmth. Jon strode out of the main door of Fratcombe Manor, sprang up into his curricle and gathered the reins in his gloved hands. His pair seemed to be none the worse for their long pull the day before.

"Stand away from their heads." The groom made to mount. "No. I shan't need you." He had travelled all the way to Fratcombe without a groom—he preferred to be without hovering servants whenever possible—and he certainly did not need one for this short journey.

He started down the long, lime-bordered avenue to the lodge gates. He had much to put right on this brief visit to Fratcombe. But, before he got down to business with his steward and his agent, he had to pay a call on the Aubreys to discover how his invalid did.

His invalid? He was taking a remarkably proprietorial interest in a young woman he barely knew. He had rescued her, certainly, but that gave him no rights over her. She was her own person, and probably her own mistress too, for she had the look of a woman in her twenties.

He kept his horses to a fast trot down the avenue. It allowed him to drive automatically and give free rein to his thoughts. Mrs Aubrey had judged that the woman, Elizabeth, was a governess, or a companion. Where could she have come from? And in such a state? Jon knew all the established gentry hereabouts, even though he had not visited Fratcombe for

24

years. He could not imagine that any of them would have treated a lady so shabbily, for his fellow landowners shared his responsible approach. Jon maintained a proper distance from his tenants, of course, but he insisted that all of them should have sound roofs over their heads and a solid income to feed their families.

Unfortunately, management of Jon's estates had become lax during his years in the Peninsula. Jon's younger brother, George, had proved disappointingly wedded to his gambling and his drinking, in spite of his promises to learn to act as a proper steward of the family lands. Jon had spent all of this leave travelling to inspect each of his estates in turn. Fratcombe was the last and the worst. Here, he had discovered that George had been helping himself to funds that should have been used to invest in the land. In Jon's absence, neither his steward nor his agent had been able to prevent it for, after the death of the countess, who but the earl's heir should take charge?

Trusting his brother too much was a mistake that Jon was planning to rectify. The Fratcombe estate managers were well paid and he could rely on their loyalty, provided they had clear instructions. He would stress to them, in person, that they were to take orders only from Jon himself from now on. Urgent matters could be referred to his mother, the dowager countess, not to his brother. George's allowance was more than ample. Henceforth, he would have to live within it.

George was extravagant where his own pleasures were concerned but penny-pinching in other ways. That was one of the aspects of his younger brother's life that worried Jon very much. George found it extremely difficult to keep servants, even in his small establishment. He treated any servant as a challenge to his ability to extract the greatest amount of labour for the smallest possible wage. It was no way to run a household and certainly no way to run a great estate. But George was not one to accept advice, especially from his older, richer brother. The last time Jon had mentioned something of the sort, they had almost come to blows.

Jon slowed his pair for the sharp turn through the gates on to the lane. He forced himself to concentrate on how he might help Elizabeth.

No. *Miss* Elizabeth. She was a lady. As a gentleman, he must treat her as such. He had sent out a posse of male servants at first light to scour the paths leading to the woods, and the woods themselves, for anything Miss Elizabeth might have dropped. They had returned with precious little—a ruined black bonnet, and one mud-filled boot. That had surprised him. How had he failed to notice that one of her boots was missing?

Because you barely looked at her. You were too intent on holding her close, so that your hands could enjoy her curves through that sodden gown.

What his conscience said was only too true. When he had carried her over his shoulder, he had been careful to put his arm only across her thighs. But he had been very conscious of her rounded bottom on his shoulder, nestled perilously close to his cheek. That memory made him heat, and curse aloud.

The offside horse's ears twitched at the sudden noise. Jon concentrated on calming the animal, resolving meanwhile that he would not permit himself to think lustful thoughts about Miss Elizabeth. She was a lady, she had been rescued, and she must be restored to her rightful place in society. He had already set the process in motion by sending a groom to enquire of the coach company. He would leave the rest of the tasks in Mr Aubrey's hands. At this point in his life, Jon had more important things to do than to focus his attention on a straying woman, even one who had lost her memory. He had learned that lesson from his disastrous marriage. If he interfered in such a business, it could only do harm. To everyone.

• • • •

The rectory door opened before Jon could raise his hand to the knocker. It was the little maid, Hetty, looking up at Jon with glowing eyes. "My mistress said as how I was to invite you to come in, my lord." She dropped him a very creditable curtsey. "If you would please to join the rector in his library? My

26

mistress will be with you directly." She made to lead him along the hallway.

"Thank you. I know my way." He gave her a slight smile as he brushed past her. She blushed. She seemed to have been dazzled. He could not imagine why. The title, perhaps? It could not be his looks. Apart from his unusual height, they were nothing out of the ordinary.

"Master Jonathan! Welcome!" The rector rose from behind his desk and came forward to shake hands.

"I have to come to enquire after Miss Elizabeth's health. I hope she is recovering?"

The rector waved Jon to a chair. "I believe so. My wife will be able to give you rather better information, I am sure."

"I suppose she has not remembered anything?"

The rector shook his head. "No, I fear not. But perhaps you—?"

Now it was Jon's turn to shake his head. He explained precisely what his servants had found, and the steps he had taken to search for any witnesses to the woman's arrival at Fratcombe. "I must return to King's Portbury in a day or two, Rector, so I shall not be able to pursue these enquiries myself. I have instructed my steward to report to you with anything he may discover, and to take further orders from you. Pray, use him as you will. I have not yet placed any advertisements in the newspapers, but I have told my man to do so if you should deem it necessary. I admit I am still hoping that we will find the information we need from one of the carriers, without having to resort to vulgar advertising. I would much prefer not to risk the lady's reputation by noising abroad that she is lost."

"Quite so. Quite so." The rector put his elbows on the desk and steepled his fingers. "How soon may we expect to see you at Fratcombe again, Master Jonathan?"

"Ah, yes, I was about to tell you last night, when we were interrupted." Jon laughed at the memory. "By a lady trying to climb out of the window, of all things."

The rector smiled encouragingly.

Jon sighed and leaned forward, putting his elbows on his knees and staring down at the worn carpet. He could not tell the rector everything, but he would explain that he now felt

27

duty-bound to return to the army to continue the vital campaign against Bonaparte. "And so I expect to be gone for a considerable time. Years, possibly, since the war goes very slowly," Jon finished. "But I have no doubt that Lord Wellington will prevail in the end," he added, with emphasis. He glanced up into the old man's sad eyes. It seemed he understood much, even though Jon had not spoken a word about his private anguish.

"Fratcombe will miss you, Jonathan," the rector responded gently. "As will I. But I promise to keep an eye on all your people here. You may rely on me."

"I know that, sir," Jon replied. "And I thank you." The rector's use of his given name was new, but oddly comforting.

"And I promise that no harm shall come to your lady foundling."

Jon's head jerked up. He stared. What on earth—?

"When you save a life, Jonathan, you owe a life. And since you will not be here to cherish it yourself, I must do it for you."

Before Jon could even begin to consider the rector's words, the door opened to admit Mrs Aubrey. "My lord, will you come upstairs? She is asking for you."

Jon rose and started for the stairs, with the old lady bustling after him, fussing with her lace cap. At the foot of the first flight, he paused for a second to smile down at her. "I would be most grateful, Mrs Aubrey, if you would forget your 'my lords'. Let it be 'Jonathan'. Or, at most, 'Master Jonathan', as it always was."

Mrs Aubrey bobbed him a very impudent curtsey and twinkled up at him. "As you say, my lord. 'Master Jonathan' it shall be."

Jon laughed back at her, but before he could reply in kind, his attention was caught by a loud and very insistent knocking at the rectory door.

• • • •

She lay back against her pillows, watching as the door closed behind Mrs Aubrey. She had a very few moments to collect her thoughts before her rescuer appeared. His name, it seemed, was Jonathan. And hers was Beth. Elizabeth. Or so they said.

She must get used to calling herself by that name, even though it seemed totally unfamiliar.

Elizabeth? Had she ever been called Elizabeth? Beth, now, that sounded better, more friendly. She would ask them to call her Beth. It was a simple, gentle name. She tried not to think about what her real name might be, or where she might be from. Why could she not remember? Surely everyone remembered what had happened to them? She was no child. She must have a past.

She knew, somehow, that there had been darkness and the sound of a storm. And then, the heat of a man's arms around her body, bringing her to safety. Had that really happened? Or was it her imagination? According to Mrs Aubrey, Beth had been found huddled in the shelter of some evergreens in a lonely wood. She had been on the point of death. Was that why she could not remember?

Perhaps her rescuer could tell her something more. She would try to be sensible and unemotional when he came and to thank him sincerely. She certainly must not allow her terrors to show. Deep inside, she had a chilling fear that she had been escaping from something wicked she had done or from someone who wished her ill. Could either be true? Even if it were, it had surely happened a long way from here. Mrs Aubrey had promised Beth that she would be safe. So had Jonathan. He had promised her, over and over, that she could trust him.

And she did.

He would be here soon. Beth put her hands to her hair which lay loose on the pillows in a wild tangle of curls. What on earth would he think of her? She must look like an utter fright. She caught up great handfuls of hair and tried to twist it into a knot at the back of her head, but it sprang free immediately. She clearly had the kind of hair that turned into a mass of unruly curls in the wet. How strange not to have known that.

She straightened the collar of her thick bedgown and pulled the bedcovers up under her arms. She would at least be as decent as possible to entertain her male visitor. It was important that he should see her, and treat her, as a lady. In spite of the wild hair.

A quiet knock and the tiny, plump figure of Mrs Aubrey appeared in the doorway. She would be present for this meeting, of course, for a lady must always have a chaperon. He must be standing behind, waiting on the landing for permission to come in.

Beth smiled as warmly as she could and gestured for her visitors to enter. "Please come in." Goodness, how weak her voice sounded.

Mrs Aubrey came in. Alone.

"I am afraid Master Jonathan—his lordship, I should say—had to leave. He asked me to give you his apologies and his best wishes for your recovery."

"H–his lordship?" Beth stuttered.

Mrs Aubrey sat on the edge of the bed and patted Beth's hand. "It's no wonder you are confused. The rector and I have always thought of him as 'Master Jonathan'. We knew him when he was just a boy, you see. He wasn't the heir then, of course. That was his older brother, Henry. But Henry died young, so Jonathan is the Earl of Portbury now. He insists that we still call him by name—and we do, when we are in private—though I fancy no one else would dare. He is a very important man. He can be kind, as you have seen for yourself, Beth, but he can also be formidable. I have seen him quell an upstart with no more than a look."

Beth let out a long breath. An *earl*. An earl had saved her from death. An earl had carried her out through the mud and dirt. It was like a fairytale.

An earl had asked her to trust him.

In spite of what Mrs Aubrey said of him, Beth had not thought him intimidating. He would perhaps have an air of...of invincibility. But her hazy memory from the night before was of warmth, and a caressing voice. Strength, of course, since he had carried her out of the woods. And gentleness when he took her up in his arms. It was a memory to treasure. If ever a woman dreamed of a knight in shining armour, she would dream of a man like Beth's earl.

"Your head and arm. Do they pain you still, my dear?"

"I— Yes, but I am mending, I think."

"Good, good. It is only bruising, I am sure. You are young. You will be fully recovered very soon. We must have you well for Christmas, you know."

"Christmas?" Beth shivered. She could not help it.

"Goodness, are you cold, child? Let me fetch you another blanket."

"No, no, ma'am. If anything, I am rather hot under all these covers. I cannot imagine why the thought of Christmas should make me quail. It is, after all, the season of goodwill to all men."

"And women," Mrs Aubrey added, with a mischievous smile. "Even those without a memory."

Beth was beginning to feel weary, as if a great weight of doubt was pressing down on her.

Mrs Aubrey patted her hand again. "You must not be discouraged, my dear. Lord Portbury told us that he had heard of such cases before, following a blow to the head, or some other accident. You probably took at least one blow, he said. You are badly bruised. And you were almost frozen to death. So your memory loss is perhaps not surprising."

"Yes, ma'am, but that is little consolation."

"His lordship said that, in such cases, people usually recover their memory quite soon. He was sure that would be the case with you."

"I do hope so. I feel s–so alone. No, isolated. As though everything around me is strange, from a different, unfamiliar world. And undeserved."

"Undeserved?" Mrs Aubrey gave her a long, assessing look. "That is not the rector's opinion. Nor mine. You are an invalid, and you must take as long as you need to recover. We have decided—and his lordship readily agreed, I may tell you—that you are to stay with us while enquiries are made."

"Oh, but I have no—"

"Do not concern yourself, child. It will be a pleasure for both of us. You shall be like the daughter we never had. It's a long time since we had young people about the place. Why, I remember patching up Master Jonathan's hurts, many and many a time. A glass of my homemade lemonade always

31

seemed to be a magic remedy for cuts and scrapes." She smiled mistily.

"Might, er, might his lordship call again another day, ma'am?"

Mrs Aubrey shook her head. "No, my dear, I am afraid not. An urgent messenger came for him. From Horse Guards. He has to return to London immediately. In fact, I expect he will be on his way there by now. He has probably been recalled to the colours in the Peninsula. I pray that he will return safely to us, but it may be years before we see him again." She clasped her hands together and sighed. "But let us look on the bright side. His lordship has asked the rector to make enquiries on his behalf to discover your history. He has even put the Manor servants at our disposal. He said that his steward would make a better fist of it than he could and that you would have no more need of him."

Oh, but I do! The words thundered through her brain like an avalanche. She bent her head to hide her blushing face and swallowed hard. "I, too, will pray for his safe return," she managed at last, in a small, quavery voice.

Mrs Aubrey rose. "I should not be keeping you talking. You need your rest." She touched a hand to Beth's brow. "Sleep now. I will return later when you are feeling stronger." She left the room, closing the door very quietly behind her.

In the silence, Beth bit down hard on her lip, trying to master the emotion that was threatening to choke her. She dug her fingernails into her palms. She would not weep. She would not. Her shining knight had gone, and would not return. But what little memory she had was full of the touch and sound of him. That, at least, would remain with her. Always.

Chapter Five

Fratcombe, summer 1812

"BETH, DEAR?"

Beth. Sometimes, it still jarred. Was that truly her name? She did not know, for the rector's discreet enquiries had yielded absolutely nothing. She was still in Fratcombe with her benefactors, and still the woman of mystery she had been on the night Jonathan rescued her.

Why could she not remember? It nagged at her constantly. Deep down, she feared that she must have run from some wicked crime. Her conscience told her that no other explanation made any sense. But what was she guilty of?

Mrs Aubrey was standing in the doorway, with her head cocked on one side like an inquisitive robin.

"Yes, ma'am?" Beth said, as brightly as she could.

"Do you think you could fetch me some ribbon from Mr Green's when you finish at the school today?"

"Yes, of course," Beth replied immediately. "What do you need?"

Mrs Aubrey brought out a length of dress fabric, and they spent a comfortable few minutes discussing colours and whether wide or narrow ribbon would most become the style the old lady planned to stitch. Both ladies now made almost all their own gowns, for Beth had proved very skilled at cutting and fitting. The money saved was used to help the poor. For Beth, it was a small attempt at atonement for the wrongs she was sure she must have committed in her previous life.

"You have chosen a delightful shade, ma'am. Not quite purple and not quite garnet red either. The only difficulty will be finding a ribbon to suit such an unusual colour. But I promise I will do my very best."

"You will have time?"

"Oh, yes. Mr Green's will be open for at least an hour after the children have gone home. If it takes me longer than that to find your ribbon, Aunt Caro, I shall be a failure indeed." She smiled down at the little old lady.

Beth had come to love Mrs Aubrey like a mother, for she was kind and generous, as well as surprisingly full of fun and mischief. Neither Mrs Aubrey nor the rector cared that Beth had no history before her arrival in the village. Her educated speech and soft white hands proved her a lady, the Aubreys said, and so, over Beth's guilty protests, they had insisted she remain with them. Indeed, the rector's wife had let it be known from the first that Beth was a distant relation, come to make a long stay in Fratcombe. Most of the village had accepted it without question. As the months passed, even Beth had come to think of herself as Miss Elizabeth Aubrey, one of the rector's family. It was a warm, comforting feeling, one she treasured. But it could not overcome the guilty fears that sometimes gave her nightmares. What had she done in the past? What could be so bad that her mind refused to let her remember?

Gathering up her basket with the snipping of dress fabric and the lesson materials she had prepared, Beth dropped a kiss on Mrs Aubrey's cheek and made her way out into the bright morning sunshine. The rectory stood next to the Saxon church at one end of the village. The school had been set up in a vacant house near the middle of Fratcombe alongside the main shops. It was an easy walk, though the day promised to be very hot later.

Beth smiled up at the clear blue sky. A Spanish sky would be a darker, deeper blue, she supposed, nearer the colour of Jonathan's eyes, as far as she could remember from that one pain-hazed night. She had never even had a chance to thank him. Although he had had to leave Fratcombe Manor in response to an urgent summons from London, he had taken the trouble to send good wishes for Beth's recovery. That thoughtfulness warmed her heart, though it saddened her that she had not seen him again. It was the life of a soldier, she supposed. Apart from that one fleeting spell of home leave, he had been in the Peninsula for years, fighting the French.

She had not thought it her place to ask questions about him. That would have been vulgar. But, by listening to others, she had learned to admire him even more. His name was Jonathan Foxe-Garway, Earl of Portbury, a man of rank and great wealth. He was the rector's patron, of course, but he was also a man the Aubreys valued for himself. They spoke of him often, telling tales of outrageous childhood escapades with his older brother, and amusing pranks when Jonathan had first gone up to Oxford. No doubt he had also done things that the rector judged unfit for a lady's ears but, if so, his sins were far outweighed by his devotion to duty and his bravery on the battlefield.

Whatever the rector might say about duty, it seemed strange to Beth that an earl should have chosen to join Lord Wellington's army, to face the hardships and dangers of campaigning. What had driven him to do it? Did he not have a greater duty to his name and his estates? He could not possibly be managing them from a windswept tent in Spain.

She would never forget her rescuer, even though his image was a blur. She had little more than a vague impression of height, and strength, coupled with penetrating blue eyes and that reassuring voice as he carried her up the rectory stairs and laid her on a warm, soft bed. Sometimes, in her dreams, she saw him clearly, but only there. He would come galloping toward her, clad in silver armour and mounted on a white charger. Then he would sweep her into his arms and carry her off to a dim and distant haven filled with happiness.

It was, she knew, quite ridiculous. She was a grown woman. She must be at least twenty-four or twenty-five. A woman of such advanced years should certainly know better than to cling to childish fantasies. Yet the sound of his voice kept haunting her dreams. She imagined it would be so until the day she died, a schoolmistress, and an old maid.

One of her pupils, a little boy called Peter, came racing up, bowling a hoop. "Miss Aubrey! Oh, Miss Aubrey, look at my hoop!" At that moment, he lost control and it toppled into a patch of nettles by the lane. Before Beth could stop him, he had dived in after it. He cried out in pain.

Poor Peter. He was only six and knew no better. Beth lifted him into her arms and wiped away his tears with a gentle finger. "You are a brave boy, Peter. Come, let me set you down and we will find something for that sting." She carefully retrieved the hoop with her gloved hand. "Hold that for me, while I look." She used the handle of her parasol to brush aside the lush greenery of high summer. "See this, Peter?" She pointed to a dock plant. "Where there are nettles, there are always docks. For nettle stings, the sovereign remedy is dock leaves. Let me show you." She picked a few, stripped off her gloves and began to rub the leaves on the reddened patches on his skin. Then she wrapped some larger leaves around his injured arm. "Hold those against the sting, Peter, while I take your hoop. It will soon stop hurting."

"Stopped hurting already, miss." He sounded much cheerier.

"Well done. You are very brave, and you will be able to teach all your friends about avoiding nettles, and curing their stings, won't you?"

He grinned cheekily, showing missing front teeth. Still, he was a clever boy, one who would make something of himself if Beth had her way, even though he was only the son of a farm labourer. In fact, his father had a cottage on the Fratcombe Manor estate.

Jonathan's estate.

Everything kept coming back to Jonathan.

This was a matter of the future of a child, she told herself sternly. If Jonathan— No, if *Lord Portbury* ever returned to Fratcombe, she would ask him to take an interest in Peter. She was sure he would not begrudge his help to a bright lad who was growing up on his own estate.

They had reached the school. Peter, mindful of the manners Beth had taught him, bowed neatly to her before racing away to show off his scars and his new hoop. The other children gathered round him, exclaiming excitedly in piping voices. There were only ten of them, six boys and four girls, but Beth was proud of what she had achieved with them in only a few short months. The village, and the rectory, had given her shelter. It was right that she should repay them with her labour, the only thing she had to offer. Besides, doing good for others helped to lessen her ever-present guilt at what might be hidden in her missing past.

It was almost the hour. She laid aside her bonnet and gloves and lifted the handbell to call the children into class.

• • • •

It took no time at all to select a ribbon from Mr Green's vast range, even though Mrs Aubrey's silk was such an unusual shade. Beth stepped out into the early afternoon heat, grateful for her parasol and straw bonnet. Mrs Aubrey would not be expecting her for at least another half hour. She had some time for herself.

She looked around a little apprehensively, wondering whether anyone from the gentry families might appear. They often drove by in the afternoons and always made a point of failing to recognise Beth. She hated that. It was humiliating.

In spite of the care the Aubreys had taken, it had been impossible to prevent some gossip. The wealthy ladies of the district had descended on the rectory to inspect the new arrival as soon as she left her bed. Unfortunately, Beth's vague answers to questions about her background and family aroused suspicion among these eagle-eyed mamas, who lost no time in issuing instructions to their sons. They might ogle pretty Beth Aubrey from a distance, but they must never ask to be introduced. One young man—haughty Sir Bertram Fitzherbert's eldest son—had approached Beth, but his only interest was in a quick grope behind a hedge. His fumbling attack had not succeeded, but it had taught her to be extremely wary of all the top-lofty young sprigs of fashion. None of them had Jonathan's honour and integrity where a poor and unprotected female was concerned. He was a shining knight; they were arrogant young puppies. Or worse.

Not surprisingly, most of the society invitations arriving at the rectory were pointedly addressed to the rector and Mrs

Aubrey alone. Mrs Aubrey had been minded, at first, to call out such "appalling rudeness". In her heart, Beth wanted to agree, for she felt the insult deeply, but she also knew the rector could not afford to confront the great families, especially when Jonathan was not in England to take his part. Besides, confrontation had always made Beth ill. Her nightmares returned, and the sick headaches that often followed. So she pleaded desperately for the insults to be ignored, and dear Mrs Aubrey, much affected by Beth's distress, was finally persuaded to agree.

Not all the families shunned her, however. In two of the grand houses—houses with no unmarried sons—Beth had actually become quite well acquainted with the younger daughters. Beth's eye for fashion was particularly valued; the girls often sought her views on the trimming of a bonnet or the important business of changing a hairstyle. Beth enjoyed it all, although she had no place at the side of young heiresses, for she knew she was nothing of the sort. Nor could she ever have been one. No heiress would have owned the dowdy, threadbare clothes that Beth had been found in.

Beth glanced up and down the village street one last time. It was safely deserted. There was no one to see which way she went.

Instead of turning right, in the direction of the church and the lodge gates, she turned left. If anyone should question her, she would say she was going to call on old Mrs Jenkinson, who lived in the last house at the far end of the village, before the sharp bend in the road. From there, it was but a step to Beth's goal.

Walking at a very brisk pace, she soon reached the woods, though she was uncomfortably hot by then. The turn in the road now concealed her from the village itself. And since it was highly unlikely that anyone would pass this way, she was at liberty to indulge herself. A very little.

She put her basket and parasol on the ground behind a fence-post and leaned on the rail, gazing round at the clearing. This was where it had all begun. This was where Jonathan had found her.

There was nothing in the least unusual about it. It was simply a clearing at the edge of a wood, surrounded by thick evergreens and with a single, venerable oak where the clearing joined the main path. She smiled up at the branches of the tree, now green and youthful where, before, they had been black, and bare. On an impulse, she ducked under the rail and started across the grass. In spite of the hot weather, it was still quite spongy underfoot. There was a stream close by, which never dried out. No wonder everywhere had been so muddy that night.

She made her way across to the overhanging shrubs and lifted the long branches to peer underneath. The heaps of leaves were still there, blown in, year after year, and too dry to rot. She was grateful for that. If she had lain down on wet leaves, soaked as she was, she would probably have died long before Jonathan could find her. His arrival had been a miracle.

She picked her way across to the path by the oak and stroked its wrinkled trunk. She had come here so many times, looking around, walking along the path, trying to retrieve some memory of what had gone before. She had never succeeded in remembering her past, and this time was no different.

"Well, well, well. Who have we here? A trespasser on my land, I do declare."

Chapter Six

THIS WAS JONATHAN'S land, but the voice was not Jonathan's. His was a voice she would never forget.

Beth spun round to face the man who had spoken.

He was young and a newcomer to Fratcombe, someone Beth had never seen before. He was dressed in the height of fashion, in a form-fitting blue coat with large silver buttons, pale pantaloons and Hessian boots. His shirt-points were so high that he could barely move his head. A rich young man, then. With an air of consequence. But why should he be claiming to own this land?

Beth stomach gave a sudden lurch. Oh God, might Jonathan be dead? Killed in battle? Could this man have inherited the estate? Beth's whole body froze at the agonising thought that her dear Jonathan might be gone for ever. Her throat tightened. She could not manage to say even a single word.

The young man was looking Beth up and down in a way that began to make her feel unclean. His smile was turning into a leer, and his eyes were gleaming with lust. Exactly like young Mr Fitzherbert. Only this time, the hedge was an oak tree.

Beth's sensible self was beginning to fight back against her fears. *Jonathan cannot be dead. The rector would have told me. Besides, if this man were Jonathan's heir, he would be in mourning, which he most certainly is not.*

She drew herself up, took a deep breath, and said coldly, "I fear we have not been introduced, sir."

"Introductions ain't necessary for =, my girl. Trespassing's a crime, you know. By rights, I should haul you before the magistrate, but I'm a generous man." He grinned nastily. "I'll settle for a few kisses instead. A gel like you won't mind sharing them, I'm sure." He reached for Beth.

She pushed him away. "I am no lightskirt to be used so, sir," she protested. "I am the Fratcombe schoolmistress. And a lady. If you were a gentleman, you would treat me as one."

"No *lady* lurks alone in the woods. Unless for an assignation? And you *are* trespassing, so a forfeit has to be paid. Come, don't argue. You will enjoy my attentions, I assure you." He pulled her into his arms. Beth realised he was stronger than he looked. And he clearly had no intention of letting her go. "Even a prim and stuffy schoolmarm can enjoy a bit of fun and frolic, you know."

"*No.*"

He ignored the protests she spat at him. He seemed to be enjoying the fact that she was resisting. His mouth descended on hers. When she tried to turn away, he seized her head with one hand to hold her steady. His mouth on hers was hot, and wet, and utterly revolting. Her stomach heaved.

He had let go of her right arm in order to grab her head. Almost without conscious thought, Beth pulled at his hair and kneed him in the groin.

With a gasp of pain, he let her go and clutched at himself, cursing ferociously between groans.

Beth fled for the railings and the lane.

It was suddenly getting very dark. In the space of only a few minutes, the sky had become almost black. There was going to be a fearsome storm. Was this clearing cursed? She was far from shelter, with no protection at all. Again.

She ran across the clearing as fast as she could, but she had forgotten the treacherous ground. When she was only yards from the railings, her ankle turned, she lost her balance and fell her length. She hauled herself up, to go on again. She must make it to the lane. And then on, to the village.

"Ouch!" The moment she put her right foot to the ground, a pain shot up her leg. For a second, she closed her eyes in frustration. Now what was she to do? She glanced back over her shoulder towards the oak tree. The man was still bent almost double, but he was starting across the soft turf towards Beth with a very nasty expression on his face.

She was out of sight of the village, she had sprained her ankle, and a storm was coming on. She was alone, and at the mercy of an angry, vengeful man.

She glanced up at the sky again. Huge black anvil clouds promised thunder and lightning, as well as rain. She *must* get away from the trees. And from *him*.

She hobbled the last few yards to the fence and leant on it to retrieve her parasol. It could act as a makeshift walking stick. It would help her to move faster, to get away. The basket did not matter.

Gritting her teeth against the pain, she ducked under the fence and started back along the lane to Fratcombe. Beyond the bend was Widow Jenkinson's house, where Beth would be able to ask for shelter. No man could molest her there.

"You won't get away from me now." His voice sounded loud and very near. Beth was almost sure she could hear his heavy breathing at her back. Refusing to turn, she hobbled awkwardly along, leaning heavily on her parasol.

The handle snapped after only a few more yards.

Her only means of escape was gone. She hurled the useless thing to the ground with a very unladylike curse.

"Only a slut uses words like that." He sounded very sure of himself now. His fingers were reaching for her arm to pull her towards him. "I was right about what you are. And now you owe me, twice over. Come here, wench. It's time you paid."

Beth closed her eyes and clenched her lips tightly against the invasion she dreaded. She would be lucky if she had only kisses to fear now.

He grabbed her but, at the same moment, the storm took hold. Huge hot drops of rain, sizzling on her bare upper arms, followed seconds later by a true cloudburst, beating down on the roadway and on the two of them. Beth was soon drenched. And so was he. He swore, at the storm, and at Beth. But at last he let her go.

"Damn you for this, woman," he raged. "Look at the state of my coat." He did not stop to say anything more. He abandoned Beth and started towards the village, and shelter, at an awkward half-limping run.

Beth was left alone on the path, with a cold, dripping skirt clinging to her legs, and the broken remnants of her parasol at her feet. She had escaped with her virtue, at the cost of a soaking. Perhaps she should be grateful to *this* storm?

"May I be of assistance, ma'am?"

She gasped. That voice had not changed. It was Jonathan's. The storm was so loud that she had not heard the sound of his horses' approach.

Beth whirled round too quickly, forgetting about her injury and putting her weight on her sprained ankle. She cried out in pain and almost fell.

"Good God, ma'am! You are hurt." Jonathan sprang out of his chaise and reached Beth as she struggled to regain her balance.

She no longer felt the pain or the wet or the cold. It was as if she had the warmth of the sun on her back and its golden glow in her heart. Her ordeal was forgotten.

It was Jonathan. He had returned. He had returned to save her, all over again.

The blue-coated figure was disappearing round the bend but, judging by the venomous glance that Jonathan threw in that direction, he must have seen the attempted assault, or enough of it to make him furious. But he said nothing of it to Beth. He was exactly the man of kindness and courtesy that she remembered.

"Let me help you into my chaise, ma'am. You must not stay out here in all this wet." He offered his arm. "Lean on me. You should not put weight on that ankle."

She accepted gladly. Even with only one good leg, she felt as if she were floating, buoyed up by his touch, but when they reached the step up into the chaise, reality intruded. She stopped, uncertain of whether she could mount.

"Allow me." With a single, swift movement he picked her up in his arms. Her mind was instantly full of the scent of him, long familiar from her dreams, but before she could relax into his embrace, he had deposited her on the soft leather seat and stepped back. She felt bereft. "Shall I fetch your parasol for you?" He pointed back to where it lay on the ground.

"If you would be so good," she said demurely, trying to avoid those penetrating eyes. She needed a few moments to collect her thoughts and regain control of her soaring emotions. This was no time for the stuff of dreams. He was bound to have questions. Her stomach lurched alarmingly at the prospect. He would want to know what she had discovered about her past. How could she ever explain that there was nothing to tell? That she had no facts to share, only guilty imaginings.

He was back in a trice, offering her the broken parasol. When she shook her head, he dropped the pieces on the floor and sprang up to take his seat beside her.

The chaise set off again at once. No doubt the postilions were keen to find shelter from the storm.

Beth tried to keep her eyes on the road, but she could not stop herself from stealing greedy sideways glances at Jonathan. This time, she would fix every detail of his image in her memory. His face was extremely brown. Too dark and leathery for a gentleman's complexion, of course, but only to be expected in a man who had served for years under the burning sun of the Peninsula. There were tiny flecks of grey in the dark hair around his temples and behind his ears. She could make out fine white lines at the corner of his eyes, too. Laughter lines, perhaps? Or simply the result of screwing up his eyes against the brilliant light? She was not at all sure that he had been laughing much. His expression seemed harsh, and there was a stern set to his jaw. He looked...he looked intimidating.

She guessed—no, she knew, by instinct—that her gallant rescuer had been changed by his years in the army, and that his experiences had not softened him. No doubt he had been involved in bloody battles. He must have suffered. He had probably lost comrades, and friends. Beth had read the lists of casualties in the rector's newspaper, always with her heart in her mouth lest the Earl of Portbury be among them. She knew his regiment had taken heavy losses, particularly at the siege of Badajoz, only months before.

44

They had almost reached the bend that led to the village. Jonathan was leaning forward, gazing out as though searching for something. Or someone. One of his gloved hands was clutching at the leather seat. He had lean, strong hands, but sensitive, too, as Beth knew from experience, both then and now. His hands had touched her skin and—

She forced herself to push the image aside and to smile politely. A real lady would never permit such wanton thoughts.

They had rounded the bend and were starting to speed up once more.

Jonathan signalled to the postilions to draw up alongside the blue-coated man. At the sound of the horses, the man slowed down and turned to face the chaise. He was frowning. As the chaise drew level, his frown cleared and his eyes widened.

"Portbury! What the devil are *you* doing here?" He had to shout to make himself heard above the rain. Then he shrugged. "No matter. Well met, wherever you've appeared from. Take me up, will you? It's dam— dashed wet out here."

Jonathan smiled tightly. It was a smile so full of fury that it sent a shiver down Beth's spine. What was between these two men? Was it more than an attempted assault on a mere schoolmistress?

"Unfortunately, George, there is no room, as you can see. So you will have to walk back to the Manor, I am afraid. I will be in the library in an hour. I will expect you there as soon as you have changed your clothes. Do not keep me waiting."

The man's jaw dropped. After a few seconds, he recovered enough to try to reply, but Jonathan had already signalled to the postilions to drive on. He did not look back, though the rain was getting even heavier.

"Are you acquainted with that gentleman, ma'am?"

"Why, no, I— He— That is, no. I had never set eyes on him before today. I was in the clearing by the great oak. He, er, he said I was trespassing on his land." It was the truth, though not all of it. But she could not bring herself to speak of the rest.

"*His* land? That, too?" He grimaced. Then, fixing his gaze on the horses' heads, he said in a hoarse voice, "I am sorry to have to tell you, ma'am, that that man—the man who tried to assault you in the lane—is my brother, George. I hope I may apologise unreservedly on his behalf."

His *brother*? Jonathan was understandably mortified. Not only was he avoiding her eyes, he was now clenching his jaw. But it was not Jonathan's fault. None of it. He was still her rescuer.

Beth hastened to reassure him that she had suffered no lasting hurt. "I am wet and grubby but that was my own fault for getting caught in the storm."

He jerked round to face her, eyebrows raised. "You seem to have a very selective memory, ma'am. And you are magnanimous. Thank you."

Beth felt herself flushing at the mention of memory. What had he meant by that? She could not begin to imagine. But he seemed to be waiting for her to speak. She swallowed and said, "I accept your apology, of course. And I would ask you to say nothing more on the subject, if you please. It is best forgotten."

He nodded and sat back in his corner to gaze out at the rain for several minutes. Then he seemed to come to himself again and turned back to Beth, with a courteous smile. "And now, ma'am, I pray you will tell me where I may set you down." He was looking at her face, his eyes widening. Was that admiration?

Her heart began to race, all over again. Was it possible that he—?

No. She was not worthy. Not of him, nor of any other true gentleman. She was a woman with a murky past that must be full of wicked secrets.

"You are a lady of remarkable courage, to smile through the pain of your injured ankle," he said, with studied politeness. "I know it is not quite the thing, but I hope you will permit me to introduce myself properly, for it is seldom that a man has the pleasure of meeting a lady of such fortitude."

Beth's smile faltered. Great waves of pain broke over her whole body.

So much for "her Jonathan". He had forgotten her completely.

• • • •

The introductions were brief and rather stilted, but Jon did not waste valuable time in enquiring what suddenly ailed his passenger. The postilions sprang their horses along the empty village street and hauled them to a stand at the rectory gate. If his lady passenger remained as wet as she was for much longer, she might well die of the ague. She must be brought into the warmth of the rectory. Polite niceties would have to wait.

Jon leapt down and hurried round to Miss Aubrey's side. "There is no time to lose, ma'am. Pray put your arm around my neck and I will carry you in." He ignored her shocked gasp and her chalk-white face. This was no time for displays of missish modesty. He slid one arm round her back and the other under her knees, hefted her into his arms and raced up the path to the rectory door.

"Would you be so good as to ply the knocker, ma'am?"

It seemed to take her a moment or two to realise what he was asking of her. Was she slow-witted? No, surely not. He was being too hard on her. Perhaps the pain in her ankle had worsened? In addition to her strange pallor, she was also biting her lip.

The door was opened by a very small maid. "Oh, miss," she cried.

"Open the door wide, that I may carry Miss Aubrey inside. Hurry." He almost pushed his way into the hall. He carried her through the first available door, into the small parlour at the front of the house. It was deserted. "Fetch the rector or Mrs Aubrey. Quickly now." The maid was still standing in the hall, open-mouthed. Jon knelt to slide Miss Aubrey on to the sofa and then rose again, frowning. He took one angry step towards the girl, who gasped in fright and took to her heels.

Jon turned back to the invalid. "Forgive me, ma'am, but I must get the horses out of this storm. If there is lightning, they might try to bolt. Perhaps you would give my regards to Mr and Mrs Aubrey? I—"

"Master Jonathan." Mrs Aubrey was standing in the doorway.

Jon spun round and sketched a quick bow. "As I was saying to Miss Aubrey, ma'am, I must get the horses to shelter before the thunder starts in earnest. Miss Aubrey, I fear, has sprained her ankle, but now that you are here, I know she will be well taken care of. I shall call again, as soon as may be." He strode to the door and smiled down at the old lady's puzzled frown. "We shall be able to talk more comfortably then." He bowed again. "My compliments to the rector." Then he hurried back to the front door.

The timid little maid was nowhere to be seen, so Jon let himself out and ran down the path to his chaise and the waiting postilions. "Right, then. Let's see what kind of speed we can make to the Manor. If this team is going to bolt, I'd much rather they did so on my own avenue than on this lane, where someone from the village might fall under their hooves."

• • • •

"You poor child, you are shivering. It must be the shock. Let me find you a shawl." Mrs Aubrey tugged hard at the bell. "Brandy. The rector always says it is the best remedy. Oh, if only he were here." She was talking as much to herself as to Beth. "Ah, Hetty. Go upstairs and fetch down Miss Beth's heaviest shawl. And then bring me the decanter of brandy from the rector's library. Quickly now. Miss Beth is injured."

The little maid bobbed a curtsey and disappeared.

Beth neither moved nor spoke. She could not. Her teeth were chattering. Her body felt as if it had been doused in freezing water. She could not feel any of her limbs, not even her injured ankle. She was totally numb. Her shining champion was nothing of the kind. She had been looking for his return for months now, while he had completely forgotten that she existed. She had been conjuring up castles in the air, like one of the tiny children in her schoolroom. She was an utter fool.

Mrs Aubrey set a chair by Beth's feet and pushed aside the grubby muslin skirts. "Oh, dear. That is very swollen." She began to ease off Beth's boots. She was trying to be gentle, but

48

pain shot up Beth's leg, pulling her sharply back to the real world. She was unable to suppress a little groan. "Aye, my dear. I know. It does look very painful." Mrs Aubrey ran her fingers very gently over Beth's foot and lower leg.

Beth gritted her teeth. She would not allow herself to make another sound. She might have behaved like a silly schoolgirl over Jonathan, but she was not such a faint heart as to scream over a turned ankle.

"I am almost certain that it is only a sprain, my dear, though once the storm has passed, I shall send the boy for the doctor. Just to check."

"Oh, ma'am—" Beth could barely find her voice.

"Hush, child. Ah, Hetty. Excellent. Here, give it to me." Mrs Aubrey helped Beth to sit up a little further and wrapped her warmly in the shawl. Then she slid extra cushions behind her, for support.

Before Beth could say a word of thanks, Hetty reappeared with the decanter and two glasses.

"Put it down there." Mrs Aubrey pointed to the small piecrust table near Beth's hand. The old lady was in her element, for she loved caring for invalids. "Now fetch me a basin of cold water, some cloths, and towels. We must put cold compresses on this ankle before it swells any more."

The little maid nodded and disappeared again.

"First, a little brandy." Mrs Aubrey poured out a small amount. She hesitated and then poured the merest film of liquid into the second glass. "I have had two shocks this afternoon. First, your sprained ankle; then Master Jonathan's unexpected return. And he has put off his regimentals again. I wonder…?" She paused, staring at nothing. Then, recollecting herself, she pressed the fuller glass into Beth's hand and raised her own. "To your speedy recovery, my dear. And poor Jonathan's also."

Chapter Seven

JON DROPPED GRATEFULLY into the huge leather chair and stretched out his legs.

His valet, Vernon, pulled off Jon's boots with gloved hands and exaggerated care. Then he padded off to the dressing room where he had already hung up Jon's wet coat.

Jon sighed as the door closed between them. There was no noise inside the bedchamber now, apart from the hiss and sputter of the newly lit fire. He let his head fall back on to the leather. For a moment, he stared vacantly at the ceiling. Then he let his eyes drift closed and forced his shoulders to relax. A few minutes of peace. At last. He had almost half an hour before he had to go down to the library for what was bound to be a most unpleasant interview. Deliberately, he put that thought aside.

It was good to be back at Fratcombe. Here he would be spared his mother's tart reminders of his duty, and he could visit his good friend, the rector, too. Jon's previous visit to Fratcombe—lasting less that twenty-four hours, all told—seemed an age ago now. It had been so short that he had barely spoken to the Aubreys. Before he could even unpack, Jon had been summoned back to the army where—

He shook his head vigorously. He did not want to think about that.

A question began to nag at the edge of his brain. He had been so busy trying to escape the storm that he had not considered it till now. Who on earth was Miss Elizabeth Aubrey? The Aubreys had no children, Jon knew. Nor had there ever been any mention of brothers on the rector's side. So, probably not a niece or great-niece either. She must be some very distant relation. But why had she never been mentioned before?

Intrigued, Jon decided that he would pay a call at the rectory first thing in the morning. A few polite questions would soon solve this little puzzle. Besides, the lady herself was quite attractive, as far as he could recall. He had been too concerned about the skittish horses to pay much attention to her—until he carried her inside. Lifting her into his chaise was one thing, but carrying her the length of the rectory path and into the little parlour was quite another. He might be unsure of the colour of her hair under her soggy straw bonnet, but he certainly remembered the feel of her curves through her wet summer muslins. A tallish lady, and slim, but rounded in exactly the right places to fill a man's hands.

It was interesting that she was unmarried, for she must be at least two- or three-and-twenty. Lack of dowry, probably. But at least she was old enough to have passed the simpering stage. He was surprised to find he was actually looking forward to becoming better acquainted with the mysterious Miss Aubrey. Perhaps he should invite all three of them to visit the Manor? Nothing at all improper in that. Yes, he would pay a call tomorrow, and if the lady proved to be amiable—as he fully expected any relation of the rector's to be—he would issue the invitation. It was too long since he had been in company with real ladies, of the kind who could converse sensibly with a man. By comparison with the insipid schoolgirls that Jon's mother favoured, Miss Aubrey might be a refreshing change. Precisely the kind of pleasant diversion he needed during this brief visit to Fratcombe Manor.

Thunder rattled the windows. The storm was now raging immediately overhead: blinding flashes of lightning, followed almost instantly by drum rolls of thunder. Between them, Mother Nature and Father Zeus were showing what they could do.

Behind the closed door of the dressing room, Jon's valet was probably still tutting over his ruined hat and coat, or muttering about the mud on his boots. Jon did not give a fig for any of that. At his mother's urging, he had finally agreed that an earl's consequence required a tonnish manservant. Vernon was certainly that, but he had little else to recommend him. Jon knew he should have chosen with more care on his return to England, but he had been too world-weary to do so.

He had of course ensured that Joseph, his army batman, was properly recompensed and given a comfortable annuity for his years of devoted service. Joseph had said he planned to set himself up in a small public house. He might even find himself a wife.

A wife?

Jon groaned. He opened his eyes and stared at the fire. It was beginning to throw out a decent amount of heat. It might be high summer, but after nearly three years in the Peninsula, Jon was finding it difficult to get warm, back here in England. Especially when it rained. The damp could get right into a fellow's bones.

He rose to put on more logs. At this moment, he really longed to see cheerful flames. One of the good and abiding memories of his years in Spain was sitting round the camp fire, sharing the local brandy with his comrades, and laughing together at the very silly tales they told each other.

The valet might be new to Jon's service, but he had at least thought to provide a decanter of brandy in the master's chamber. Jon smiled wryly and poured himself a large measure. He was minded to toss it down in a single swallow, but he did not. Once or twice in Spain, he had allowed himself to get very drunk when the pain of loss was almost unbearable. Returning to England's damp countryside did not justify seeking oblivion in drink. It would insult the friends he had left behind in baked Spanish earth.

Jon took one large mouthful, savouring the flavours. It was a much older, rounder liquor than any he had drunk in Spain. French, of course. He must make sure that it was not run. Smugglers broke the coastal blockade for more than brandy; they often traded Britain's secrets, too. It would be a breach of trust to buy the cognac they brought to England's shores.

He took another slow sip and sat down again. This brandy was too old to be run. As an adult, he had not spent much time at Fratcombe Manor, but he vaguely recalled that the house had an excellent cellar, much of it dating from his father's time. This was almost certainly part of a pre-war consignment. But he would check tomorrow, just in case.

The dressing room door opened. "Is there anything else I can do for your lordship?"

Jon shook his head and waved the man away. He was too punctilious by half. Perhaps if Joseph had not yet spent his money...? No, that would not do. Joseph was a batman, not an earl's valet. Besides, he wanted more than a business of his own. He wanted a wife, and perhaps a family. If he returned to serve Jon, what woman would have him? Let it be.

Jon sat down again and took another slow sip of his brandy.

A wife. Everything always came back to a *wife*. Particularly in his mother's eyes. Jon had barely had time to kiss her cheek before she started on the subject again. Since Jon's first wife had been dead for well over a year, the dowager maintained, he should be looking about him for another. The matter was urgent. And this time, he *must* set up his nursery.

Her ideas of duty—an earl must make a dynastic marriage and produce at least an heir and a spare—were much the same as his late father's. And as blinkered. And now, she wanted him to do it all over again, to select a bride of rank from among the simpering debutantes on the London marriage mart. It would not cross her mind that an age gap of well-nigh twenty years might be unbridgeable. He need not spend much time with a new wife, of course—except for the inescapable duty of getting an heir—and he would certainly hold himself aloof, as his rank required, but the prospect of all that empty-headed gabbling over the teacups was more than he could stomach.

Besides, how was a green girl out of the schoolroom to become a wife and companion to man of thirty-five? Or to share his bed? Good God, it was unthinkable. Such a child would be terrified of him. He could not do it.

He would not do it.

That was the kind of marriage his father had made, and his grandfather before him. But neither of them had been to war or watched friends die. War changed what a man valued in life…

• • • •

Jon had been sitting behind the mahogany desk in his library for more than ten minutes when the door opened. There had been no knock. What else had he expected? George's manners were often deplorable. And the way he had accosted Miss Aubrey in the lane had been utterly vile. Painful though it was for Jon to admit it, his brother George was no gentleman.

George pushed the door closed behind him and leant nonchalantly against it. "You summoned me, brother?" He sounded peevish, as if he had a justified grievance against Jon. How dare he, after all he had done?

Jon swallowed hard, resolving not to lose his temper, no matter how much George might goad him.

He leant forward with his elbows on the desk and steepled his fingers. "Sit down, George," he began calmly. "We have much to discuss."

George strolled across the carpet, glancing around the room. "There was a decanter of brandy here yesterday," he began airily, "but someone appears to have removed it. Pity. I could do with something to warm me after my dear brother left me to walk all the way back to the Manor in the pouring rain."

"The decanter is now in my bedchamber, I'm afraid. But I will gladly send for more brandy—" he forced a smile "—as soon as we have finished our business."

George grimaced. "Like that, is it? Oh, very well. Let's get it over with." He sat down heavily in the chair on the opposite side of Jon's desk.

Jon swallowed a sigh. He hated this, but it had to be done.

"I saw how you accosted my lady passenger on the path to the village, George. How could you *do* such a thing? You are *supposed* to be a gentleman."

"Blasted wench kneed me in the groin," George retorted.

Oh, Lord. It had clearly been even worse than Jon suspected. He managed to keep enough self-control to say, dryly, "If she was close enough to do that, she must have had cause. I take it you do not deny harassing her?"

George succeeded in looking mulish and guilty at the same time. "Didn't know she was a friend of yours," he muttered at last, sounding much younger than his twenty-five years.

"She is not. I had never met her before. I took her up because she was a lady in distress. Mostly caused by *you*. If you were a gentleman, George, you would know better than to molest a lady. Or any woman, for that matter." Jon knew he was probably wasting his breath. George frequented low-class brothels and thought nothing of attacking defenceless servant girls. Not in Jon's house, though. On the last occasion, Jon had planted George a facer. And he was beginning to wish he had done it again, now that he knew how his brother had abused Miss Aubrey.

George said nothing. There was a slight reddening, high on his cheeks.

Jon judged that his words had struck home, for once. They might even encourage George to mend his ways where women were concerned. Then again, they might be forgotten by tomorrow.

George drew himself up. "If you wish, I will call on the lady and apologise for my boorish behaviour."

That was a surprise. Jon sat back in his chair. Was George growing up, at last?

"That is a gentlemanly offer, George, but it would only embarrass her further. She has already accepted my apology on your behalf." He leant forward again. "We have other matters to discuss besides the lady. I must ask you about your dealings with the estate during my absence. I understand from the steward at Portbury Abbey that you have been taking considerably more than your allowance."

"No man could live on the paltry amount that you—"

"And that you sold several of my best hunters for ready money. Which you then spent."

"Had debts of honour to pay. It was the tits or post-obit bonds. Would you rather I'd borrowed against your death, brother?"

"I would rather you lived within your means," Jon rapped out. But there was a clear threat in George's words. He would remain the heir to the earldom unless Jon produced a son. If George had the run of the estate, no woman would be safe. Not even a lady like Beth Aubrey. And none of the tenants would be safe, either. George had no idea of duty. He believed the purpose of an estate was purely to provide money to fund the owner's pleasures. In Jon's absence the previous year, George had "persuaded" the agent at Fratcombe to advance him considerable sums against his expectations as Jon's heir. The results were disastrous, as Jon had discovered for himself during that one brief spell of home leave. He had taken steps to prevent further mismanagement at Fratcombe but, once Jon was back in Spain, George had begun the same old tricks at Portbury, Jon's principal estate. In the end, Jon had had to sell out and come back to England to prevent his brother from doing irreparable damage. He could still do so, if he remained the heir. And it would be Jon's fault, for failing to marry again.

Jon took a deep breath and said slowly, "One other thing. What, pray, are you doing here at Fratcombe? We agreed last year, did we not, that you would stay away from this estate?" Fratcombe was a special place for Jon—a haven, and a refuge. He had been determined that George would not spoil it. But he had clearly failed. He waited in silence for George's answer.

George did not meet his eyes. "Repairing lease," he muttered.

That was the obvious solution if he had been losing heavily at the tables. But it did not excuse a visit to Fratcombe in defiance of their express agreement. "You could have done that at Portbury."

"I started there, right enough, but then it became unbearable. Mama never stopped going on—"

Jon banged a fist on the desk and jumped to his feet. "That's quite enough, George. I'll thank you to remember the respect that you owe to our lady mother. You will *not* abuse her to me, or to anyone else."

"I, um, no. Sorry."

"Indeed." He sat down again and softened his tone. With George, giving orders did not work. "Look, George, I know what it's like to be a younger son. So I'm prepared to make a bargain with you. If you live within your means for the next two quarters, I'll increase your allowance. It won't be a fortune, mind, but it will be a fair bit more generous than before. How does that strike you?"

George drew himself up. "What're the conditions? With you, there are always conditions."

Jon grimaced. His brother knew him too well. And George also knew that Jon was too proud to let any member of the family face public disgrace. If George did something outrageous, Jon would always find a means of bailing him out. To keep the family name unsullied.

But Jon had to ensure his haven was not polluted even more by his brother's shameless behaviour. Perhaps this time there was a way? Even with George?

"You are right, brother. It is a condition of this bargain that you leave Fratcombe first thing tomorrow and that you never return to this estate for as long as I am earl. I'll have your solemn word on it. Else there's no bargain."

"I'll leave tomorrow."

"Your word, George."

George shrugged. "And I give you my word that I'll stay away from this miserable little hole until the day I inherit. Then Fratcombe will see what—"

Jon raised a hand to silence his brother's angry tirade. "I have every intention of depriving you of that pleasure, George. Mama is urging me to remarry. And I have decided that she is right."

George's eyebrows rose. "And who is the lady, may I ask?"

"You may ask, but I cannot tell you. I have still to make my choice." His mother would be delighted at the news and would parade hosts of simpering debutantes at the Abbey. It was a horrendous prospect. But, since the alternative was that George would inherit, Jon had no choice. He loved his brother, but he owed a higher duty to his name and his land. If George inherited, people on the estates might starve.

Jon rose again to make clear that the interview was over. "I will see you at dinner. I suggest you summon your man and get him to start packing. Don't worry, I haven't forgotten the brandy. I'll send some up to your bedchamber.

Chapter Eight

BETH FELT A BIT OF a fraud, leaning on a walking stick. It was not as if she had done any real damage. On the other hand, it was extremely painful to put her full weight on her injured ankle. So, for the moment, the walking stick would have to stay. The most difficult part of life was coping with the stairs without a strong man to help her. The rector was much too old to carry Beth. If he had offered, she would certainly have refused.

But if Jonathan had offered to take her in his arms again…

Beth's insides were melting at the mere thought of his hands on her body. She shook her head, cross with herself for allowing his image to intrude, yet again. She had been trying so hard not to think about him. Sadly, the more she tried, the more he filled her mind and confused her rioting senses.

She had spent months dreaming about a knight-like figure with Jonathan's physical appearance. Now she had learned, to her cost, that the real, living man and the shining knight were far from one and the same. Ah well. She would learn to deal with it, just as she had learned to create a life without any memory. And to bear the guilt of all those unknown sins in her past.

She stood at the top of the stairs, looking down to the hall. It seemed a very long way, but she would conquer it. With her walking stick in one hand and her other hand on the baluster rail, she started carefully down.

Hetty appeared when Beth had reached about halfway. "Oh, Miss Beth. Let me help you." She started up the stairs.

Beth paused, balanced carefully and shook her head. "Thank you, Hetty, but I am quite well enough to manage. I must learn to use my cane and, in any case, you have better things to do than to act as a crutch for me."

"Well, if you say so, miss. But you will not go out of the house, will you? I can bring you anything you need."

Beth finally reached the hallway. She was a little out of breath, but she was proud of herself. "No, Hetty, I will not go out of the house. Though I must say that I am glad that it is not a school day. The children would have worried if I had failed to turn up for their lessons."

"Mrs Aubrey said she would take over while you were poorly. She's looking forward to it, she says." Hetty grinned knowingly.

"Does she now?" Beth smiled back at the maid. It sounded as if Aunt Caro intended Beth to remain an invalid for several more days. Well, Beth would see about that. The rector's wife had responsibilities enough. She could not be expected to become the schoolmistress as well.

Beth made her way slowly into the little parlour at the front of the house so that she would be able to see the comings and goings in the street. She might even be able to see Jonathan if he drove by. "Oh, for goodness' sake."

"Did I do something wrong, Miss Beth?" Hetty sounded hurt.

Beth realised she had spoken her thoughts aloud. "I am sorry, Hetty. I was berating myself, not you." She shook her head. "This leg of mine refuses to do what I tell it." That was not the cause of her outburst, but it would do.

"Mrs Aubrey said as you was to sit on the sofa with your leg up. And I was to bring you anything you needed."

Beth gave in and subsided gratefully on to the sofa by the window. Before she could even draw breath, Hetty was lifting her bandaged leg on to the cushions. "There, miss. Now, what may I fetch you?"

"If I am to lie here, like a pampered cat basking in the sun, I had better do something useful. If you would fetch me the mending, Hetty, I will make a start on that."

Beth relaxed on to the cushions and rested her cheek on the back of the sofa. She had a good view of the road. It was empty. That was as well. She must devote her attention to practical things, not daydreaming.

When Hetty returned with the mending basket, Beth, mindful of her latest resolution, selected the most difficult piece of work she could find. That should keep her mind occupied until Aunt Caro returned from her visiting. Having time to think was too dangerous. The last thing Beth needed was one of her sick headaches on top of a sprained ankle.

She had barely completed her first neat darn when Mrs Aubrey bustled in, removing her bonnet. She handed it to the maid. "Would you fetch us some tea, Hetty? I am sure Miss Beth would enjoy a cup."

"You are very good, ma'am, though I fear I have not earned it. Look how little I have done."

"You are an invalid, child. You should be taking your ease, with nothing more than a romantic novel to amuse you. Invalids do not mend shirts."

"This one does," Beth replied pertly, but with an affectionate smile.

Mrs Aubrey chuckled and sat down opposite Beth. "I have visited Widow Jenkinson this morning. She sends her best wishes for your speedy recovery. She was sad to learn that you had not been brought to her house to escape the storm."

"It would have given her food for gossip for a month, especially if she had seen Jo—if she had seen his lordship carrying me up the path." Mrs Aubrey might have leave to use Jonathan's given name, but Beth did not.

Mrs Aubrey chuckled again. "I made a quick visit to the lodge also, as I was passing."

Beth raised her eyebrows, feigning surprise. Mrs Jenkinson and the lodge were at opposite ends of the village.

"Now *that*, young lady, is a most impudent look, I must say."

Beth raised her eyebrows even higher.

"Oh, very well. No, I was not passing, as we both know. I went there deliberately, to find out about Master Jonathan, how long he means to remain at Fratcombe, that kind of thing.

61

The least we can do is invite him to take dinner with us. Once you are well enough, of course."

The thought of seeing Jonathan again, and of the difficult exchanges that might ensue, made Beth's head pound dangerously. "I had best remain upstairs, ma'am. His lordship and the rector will have much to discuss. To have me hobbling about would be an unwelcome distraction."

"Now that is a whisker, if ever I heard one." Mrs Aubrey shook a mittened finger in mock reproof, but her eyes were twinkling. "I shall pretend that I did not hear it at all."

Hetty appeared with the tea tray and placed it carefully on the table in front of Mrs Aubrey. At that moment, someone plied the knocker, with considerable force.

Mrs Aubrey started. "Goodness, who can that be, so early in the day? Hetty, go and open the door. Slowly." Mrs Aubrey grabbed the mending out of Beth's fingers, bundled it into the basket and pushed the basket under a chair in the darkest corner of the room. Then she scurried back to resume her seat, clasping her hands demurely in her lap.

Beth was hard put to keep her face straight.

"The Earl of Portbury," Hetty announced, bobbing a curtsey.

He seemed much too large for the small family parlour.

Mrs Aubrey rose and dropped a tiny curtsey in response to her visitor's elegant bow. "Master Jonathan. How kind of you to call. Will you take tea with us?" He nodded. "Hetty, fetch another cup, if you please."

He took a couple of paces into the room and bowed, separately, to Beth. She was suddenly so weak she could not even start to rise. Her body was remembering the feel of his arms around her, and softening, as if in anticipation. "Forgive me, my lord, I cannot—"

"Pray do not attempt to move, Miss Aubrey. I am sure it took quite enough exertion for you to make your way downstairs this morning." He paused, frowning suddenly. Then, turning back to Mrs Aubrey, "Would you permit me to send over one of my footmen to help while Miss Aubrey is recovering? He could carry her up and down the stairs. And you could use him for any other convenient chores."

"Master Jonathan, I should not dream—"

He waved a dismissive hand. "You would be doing me a favour, ma'am. There are far too many servants at the Manor and, with only myself in residence now, they do not have nearly enough to do. I cannot abide idleness."

"Well…"

"Am I not to be consulted in this project of yours, my lord?" Beth's voice sounded sharp in her own ears, for she was deliberately stoking her anger against him. He was treating her like a parcel. She would not allow that.

He turned to look down at her. The very faintest tinge of redness had appeared on his cheeks. "I beg your pardon." His voice grew quieter. "It was not my intention to impose on you."

She softened again, instantly. He had sounded arrogant, but he surely meant well. She had no right to let her inner turmoil betray itself in bad temper. "Your offer is most generous, my lord, but it is not necessary. My ankle is mending extremely well and the more I exercise it, the sooner I shall be fully recovered."

"Very well, ma'am." He made to sit down beside Mrs Aubrey.

"And I would suggest," Beth continued, feeling increasingly in control of this unequal encounter, "that if your servants are underemployed, you should put them to work in the village. I am sure Mrs Aubrey can provide you with a long list of chores and repairs which need to be done."

"Beth. You go too far."

"No, ma'am. Miss Aubrey is quite right. I noticed yesterday, in spite of the storm, that some of the houses need urgent work. My agent has been most remiss in allowing such dilapidation. The repairs will be put in hand today." He took a cup of tea from Mrs Aubrey and rose politely to carry it across to Beth. "However, I fear I must disappoint Miss Aubrey. I doubt that my footmen have the inclination, or the skills, to carry them out." He was trying not to smile.

Beth took her tea with a demure nod and pursed lips. Was he roasting her? She hoped so. Strangers did not tease. But he had kept a totally straight face so she could not be sure. Until she was, she certainly must not laugh.

"Do you remain at Fratcombe long, Master Jonathan?" Mrs Aubrey poured his tea and handed it to him.

"Not on this occasion, ma'am, though I expect to return again quite soon. It is a huge change, from the army in Spain to the English countryside, I may tell you. There, our duty was simple—to fight the enemy. Since my return, I have been reminded of my other duties. To my various estates, for example, and to my position in society." His voice grated, as if he was finding duty a hard taskmaster. Then, quite suddenly, he smiled warmly at the old lady in a way that transformed him. His face was softer, younger, and his eyes were dancing. "Here, at the rectory, I know that I am welcomed as simply an unruly lad who happens to have grown up. A little."

Mrs Aubrey nodded, trying not to return his smile, but she could not conceal her fondness for Jonathan.

Beth swallowed. A knot of anxiety formed in her stomach. He had had the run of the rectory when he was a boy. Did he intend to visit often, to renew his intimacy with the Aubreys? Oh dear. When he was relaxed like this, and showing that wicked sense of humour, he was much too attractive. Soon, she would be dreaming of silver-clad knights again, and she must not. She could so easily betray herself. She must find some way of avoiding his company. It was the only solution.

Mrs Aubrey cleared her throat. "Perhaps you would tell us about your time in Spain?"

A sudden shadow crossed Jonathan's face. "If you will forgive me, ma'am, I would prefer not to speak of it. Much of it was not, er, pleasant, particularly of late."

"I understand," the old lady said quietly. "We know that you were at the siege of Badajoz." They knew, too, that he had been mentioned in dispatches for his part in the final assault, but Mrs Aubrey would not embarrass him by mentioning it. "We read about the shameful outrages after the battle."

He said nothing, but his face had assumed a very stern cast. Beth could not begin to imagine what he had experienced, or what he had seen, in that terrible siege and in the sack of the town which had followed. The casualties in the assault had been enormous, and the soldiers' conduct in the town afterwards had been utterly despicable.

The awkward silence stretched between them. Jonathan did not even move to drink his tea, though his jaw and his throat were working. He was remembering terrible things, Beth was sure. She tried desperately to think of something to say, to distract him from his obvious pain.

Mrs Aubrey was before her. "So, Master Jonathan, what do you think of your lady foundling now? She has improved a good deal, would you not say, from the drowned stray you carried across our doorstep last Christmas?"

"What? *Miss Aubrey* is the lady from the clearing?"

Chapter Nine

SHOCKED, AND EMBARRASSED, Jon moved in his seat to stare directly at the injured woman. "I beg your pardon, ma'am," he began, the words tumbling out in his haste to apologise. "I had completely forgotten the incident until Mrs Aubrey mentioned it just now, because you look so—" He stopped in time and cleared his throat.

Yesterday, he had assumed Miss Aubrey was a true lady, even if only a poor relation. But she was not an Aubrey at all. The bedraggled woman he had rescued could be anything, even a woman from the gutter. He recalled thinking at the time that she *might* be a lady, but still...

She was really very attractive, now he took the time to look at her. He let his gaze travel slowly from her curly red-brown hair and perfect complexion down the slim curves of her body, finally coming to rest on her bandaged ankle. "Forgive me, but you look considerably more like a lady than you did then." It was no more than the truth. But it was too stark. He had spoken without sufficient thought. Again. What on earth was the matter with him? Coupled with his brazen scrutiny, his words were almost an insult. She had turned bright scarlet.

Recollecting his manners at last, and the wisdom of silence, he busied himself with his teacup while he tried to gather his wits.

After a long pause, he turned to Mrs Aubrey and said, in a polite but neutral voice, "So our foundling has been here with you all this time? And with the name Aubrey? You did not discover her true identity?"

"We did everything possible. We even advertised—discreetly—in the newspapers for a missing woman by the name of Elizabeth. But none of it produced any information at all. It is as though poor Beth had emerged out of nothing, like a phantom."

Jon turned back to "poor Beth". Her heightened colour had drained away completely. "I am heartily sorry that nothing could be done, ma'am. And you have had no memory at all, not the least flash of anything, in all these months?"

"No, my lord. Nothing." Her response was very swift, and very definite.

Jon could not help wondering whether he should believe her. He had heard of cases where unscrupulous people had preyed on their benefactors by pretending to have lost their memory. Might that have happened here? Was Beth Aubrey a fraud? Perhaps that was why she had turned so pale? The Aubreys were a generous couple who would never look for such duplicity. "It is very strange, I must say. Has Doctor Willoughby nothing to suggest on the matter? You have consulted him, I assume?"

"If we had consulted him about Beth's memory loss, it would have become common knowledge. Besides, what does a country doctor know of such things? So we—the rector and I—we allowed ourselves a little white lie. We gave out that Beth was a distant relation who had come to stay with us for a while, having no remaining close family of her own."

"I see. Then no one hereabouts knows how Miss Aubrey was discovered?"

"Some of the gentry families suspect that Beth is not quite what she seems. I am sorry to say that some of them forget their Christian duty, and treat her like a servant, rather than a lady born and bred." Mrs Aubrey shook her head sorrowfully. "It is not what we would have expected of them."

"Nor I, ma'am. When I stayed here as a child, I was always struck by the kindness and generosity of all the great families of the district."

"That might have had something to do with the fact that you were heir to an earldom, sir." Miss Aubrey sounded waspish. Not surprising, perhaps, especially if her plight was genuine.

Jon looked assessingly at her and was struck by the direct way she met and held his gaze. She certainly had the air of a true lady. "As it happens, ma'am, I was not the heir then. That was my elder brother. But I do agree that my being the son of an earl might have coloured their judgement a little. And I am disappointed to learn that you have not always been accorded the respect due to a lady. The rector's sponsorship should be enough for anyone, however high their status."

Yet again, he regretted his words the moment they were spoken. After all, the rector's word had not been enough for *him*. Guilt pricked Jon's conscience. He was responsible for this. He was the one who had rescued Beth; and the one who had foisted her on the Aubreys, even though he had not expected her to remain with them for long. If she was genuine, it was now Jon's duty to ensure she was restored to her rightful place, however lowly that might be. And if she was a fraud, it was his duty to expose her. She was not to be a welcome diversion after all. She was simply one more irksome duty to be discharged.

Mrs Aubrey laid a hand on his sleeve. "If *you* were seen to accept Beth, the other families would follow your lead, I am sure. As Earl of Portbury, you outrank them all."

That was true, but was he prepared to do what she asked? Was it not his duty to satisfy himself, first of all, that Beth Aubrey was worthy of his support? He was still trying to decide how to reply when the sitting room door opened.

"Lady Fitzherbert has called, ma'am, and asks if—"

The little maid was not allowed to finish. Lady Fitzherbert, resplendent in rustling purple silk and feather-trimmed bonnet, pushed the girl aside and marched into the room. She paused barely long enough to drop a disdainful curtsey to Mrs Aubrey before launching into an angry complaint. "I have come to consult the rector on a matter of urgent business, but your servant here tells me that he is not at home to callers. I must protest, ma'am. Why, I am—"

Jon had risen at the same time as Mrs Aubrey but did nothing else to draw attention to himself. He waited to see what would happen next.

"There has been some misunderstanding, I fear," Mrs Aubrey explained. "The rector cannot see you because he is not at home. However, I expect him to return within the hour. Perhaps you would like to—?"

"Why, Lord Portbury! How delightful to see you safely returned." Lady Fitzherbert abruptly turned aside from her hostess and sank into a very elegant curtsey.

Jon prepared himself for the worst kind of toadeating. Sir Bertram Fitzherbert and his detestable wife were relative newcomers to the district, but held themselves to be above everyone but the nobility. The Fitzherberts were bound to be among those who had slighted Beth Aubrey, for in their eyes she was a nobody, with no social standing at all.

In that instant, Jon decided their behaviour was an insult to him, as well as to the lady herself. Miss Aubrey was *his* foundling, after all. The rector's word *should* be good enough for such upstarts as the Fitzherberts. This harpy needed to be taken down a peg or two.

"Sir Bertram will be so pleased to learn that you are back in residence at the Manor," Lady Fitzherbert gushed. "There is so little truly genteel society hereabouts."

"Country society can be a little restricted, to be sure," Jon said, as soon as she paused to draw breath. "But you have several families within easy driving distance. And during my absence from Fratcombe, you have had the rector and Mrs Aubrey. And Miss Aubrey, also." He stepped aside so that Lady Fitzherbert would see Beth lying on the sofa behind him. "You are already acquainted, I collect?"

"I, er—" Lady Fitzherbert's nostrils flared and her lips clamped together. For several seconds, she stared down her long nose at Beth Aubrey. Then she half-turned back to Mrs Aubrey and drew herself up very straight. "Excuse me, I may not stay longer. Pray tell the rector, when he returns, that Sir Bertram is evicting that band of dirty gypsies who are trespassing on our land. Sir Bertram wished it to be understood that they should not be given shelter in the district. Not by *anyone*."

Mrs Aubrey's eyes narrowed dangerously, but her voice was soft. "I am surprised that your husband did not come himself to deliver so important an instruction."

Lady Fitzherbert tittered. "Oh, Sir Bertram would never think to *instruct* the rector. Certainly not. Just…just a word to the wise."

Jon had heard quite enough. "I am sure the rector will be properly grateful, ma'am. But as it happens, Sir Bertram's warning is a little late. The gypsy band has leave to camp on my land at Fratcombe Manor."

Lady Fitzherbert gasped and turned bright red. Then she swallowed hard. "Since the rector is not here, I shall not trouble you further, ma'am. Lord Portbury." She dipped another elegant curtsey to Jon, inclined her head a fraction to Mrs Aubrey and hurried out, without waiting for a servant to be summoned.

"Well, I declare." Mrs Aubrey let out a long breath. Then she frowned up at Jon. "Since when has Fratcombe Manor offered hospitality to gypsies?"

"It has never yet done so. I—"

"My lord, I pray you will not allow Sir Bertram Fitzherbert to run them out of Fratcombe. He will not care what damage is done to their caravans and their horses. And there are so many helpless children—"

Jon stopped Miss Aubrey with a raised hand. His foundling was bringing him yet another problem. Now, she was prepared to plead for people who were truly outcasts from society. "I have said they may use my land. For a week or two, at least. I will not go back on that."

Nor would he, unless they broke his trust. He would instruct his estate workers to keep a sharp eye out for thieving or damage. At the first sign of either, the gypsies would be turned off. He was cynical enough to expect it within days.

"Thank you, my lord. I will impress on them that there must be no mischief."

"*You?* You have dealings with the gypsies?"

70

She coloured a little but raised her chin defiantly. "I am the Fratcombe schoolmistress. I teach all the children in the district. Whoever they are."

"Master Jonathan, Beth goes to the gypsy camp when she can and gives lessons to the children. Basic lettering and stories from the Bible. Even gypsies are God's creatures."

"Yes," Jon admitted grudgingly. The rector had often preached about the Good Samaritan. Now was Jon's chance to show that he had listened. "Yes, you are right, ma'am. As long as they respect the law, they will not suffer at my hands. I do not persecute waifs and strays."

Mrs Aubrey smiled at Jon and then very warmly across at Beth. "No, you do not. Indeed, you rescue them. You brought us the daughter we never had."

It was worse than he had imagined. If Beth Aubrey was a fraud, he could not expose her without hurting Mrs Aubrey. He knew he could never do that. The old lady had been like a mother to Jon when he and his brother had been at Fratcombe as boys. She had comforted Jon when his brother died. Her support had helped him to face the grief-stricken father who thought Jon a worthless replacement for his dead heir. How much had she understood of a young boy's desperate striving to win his father's esteem? It had never been spoken of. But she and the rector understood human failings. They would have seen how hard Jon tried, and how little he succeeded.

According to Jon's father, an earl's heir had to be brought up to understand his duty from the cradle, or he would never be more than a poor second best. Not that it stopped the old man from trying to thrash Jon into the mould he sought—duty, and distance, and distrust of everyone. He had almost succeeded, but he could never undermine Jon's trust in the Aubreys. They were truly good people, probably the only ones Jon knew. And if they loved Beth…

He turned back to the sofa. "Has Lady Fitzherbert ever acknowledged you, ma'am?" he asked sharply.

She coloured and looked down at her clasped hands, shaking her head.

So that insufferable woman really was trying to usurp Jon's place in society. A set-down over the gypsies was not enough.

There must be public retribution. It would be fitting to make Beth Aubrey his instrument. He bit down on his lip, trying not to grin.

"I have a mind to hold a splendid party at the Manor, to which I shall invite all the gentry families. If you, Mrs Aubrey, would do me the honour of acting as my hostess, with your adopted daughter by your side, we shall teach all our stiff-rumped neighbours to treat Miss Aubrey with proper respect."

"Oh, but you cannot," Beth breathed.

"I can. And I will, if Mrs Aubrey agrees. Do you approve, ma'am?"

Mrs Aubrey twinkled at him. "I do, Master Jonathan. It will succeed, I am sure, for there is not one great house that would turn down an invitation from the Earl of Portbury. Even if the price is to acknowledge Miss Elizabeth Aubrey."

He took the old lady's hand and raised it to his lips. "We have a bargain, then."

The conspiracy was sealed between her benefactress and her rescuer. Beth had had no say at all. It seemed she was still to be treated like a parcel. "I may develop a most inconvenient headache on the day of this party, my lord," she said tightly.

"I pray you will do no such thing, ma'am." He rose to fetch a hard chair from the wall by the door, and set it down by the head of the sofa where Beth lay. Sitting down, he took her left hand in both of his. His clasp was gentle and reassuring. She felt calluses on his palm from his riding and fencing. This was no sprig of fashion but a man of action. "Perhaps you could think of it, not as revenge on petty coxcombs, but as a favour for Mr and Mrs Aubrey? They have sheltered you, and accepted you as if you were a member of their own family. It is an insult to *them* that some of the local gentry have cut you. By agreeing to this, by attending my party and showing your strength of character, you will be repaying something of what you owe the Aubreys. Can you not see that?"

Beth could now see precious little. Her vision was blurry, as if she were trying to see through a howling gale. The touch of his skin on hers was flooding her whole body with heat, making her heart swell and race. She was terrified by his proposal, yet at the same time she felt light-headed, as if she might float away. When she tried to speak, no words came out.

"Miss Beth? Will you not agree? For Mrs Aubrey's sake?"

She had no choice. "I will do what you ask," she said, in a rather strangled whisper.

"Thank you, Beth." He raised her hand and kissed it, exactly as he had kissed Mrs Aubrey's.

But Mrs Aubrey could not have felt the surge of heat that travelled through Beth's fingers and up her arm. It was not quite pleasure, and not quite pain, but she almost cried out in shock. She sat quite motionless, trying to recover her wits. He had kissed her hand. And he had called her by her given name. She must be back in one of her unfathomable dreams.

Jonathan, it seemed, had noticed nothing. After a second, he laid her hand back in her lap, replaced the hard chair by the door and resumed his seat by Mrs Aubrey. "Excellent. I must look to you to oversee the arrangements, ma'am, for I am promised to King's Portbury for the next few weeks. But before I leave Fratcombe, you and I shall put our heads together and decide precisely who is to be invited. Oh, I am going to enjoy this."

Mrs Aubrey was beginning to look a little prim. "They shall be punished for their lack of Christian charity, Master Jonathan, but do not forget your own, in the process. Forgiveness is a virtue, you know. You must not enjoy yourself too much. That could be a sin."

He nodded. "I will try to suppress my baser instincts. And with you as my partner in this enterprise, ma'am, I am sure that generosity and forgiveness will prevail." Laughter burst out of him like ginger beer from a shaken bottle. "They will prevail, I promise you. Eventually."

"What will?" The door had opened without a sound. The rector stood there, looking puzzled. "Do I take it that you and my lady wife have been conspiring together, Jonathan?"

Jonathan leapt to his feet to bow politely. "Your wife has most generously agreed to act as hostess for an evening party I plan to give at the Manor next month, sir. I hope you do not object?"

73

The rector's cheery countenance suddenly became bleak. "Of course not. I appreciate that entertaining must be quite awkward for you now that you no longer have a wife by your side."

Jonathan's face had turned ashen. He said nothing, staring at the floor.

Beth could barely recognise him. The mention of his dead wife had turned him grey and gaunt. It was as though he had aged on the spot, by at least ten years. He must have loved his late wife a great deal if grief could do that to him. The fact that he had been in Spain, and unable to leave his post, would have cut him to the quick. No doubt, his countess was long buried by the time the news finally reached him. Poor, poor man.

The easy companionship in the little parlour had evaporated. Jonathan bowed to Mrs Aubrey and then, very sketchily, to Beth. "If you will excuse me now, ladies, I have a great deal of business to attend to before I leave Fratcombe." He bowed again to the rector. In a trice, he was gone.

"Oh, dear," the rector said, slumping on to the sofa beside his wife. "I fear that was *quite* the wrong thing to say."

Mrs Aubrey patted his hand. "You meant well, dear. He understands that, I am sure. However, I do have plenty of news to give you about our friend, the earl. He was affronted to learn that some of the local families had refused Beth's acquaintance. The party he plans is for Beth. Everyone is to be invited. If they attend, they will have no choice but to recognise Beth, who is to be the guest of honour." She laughed wickedly.

The rector stared. Then he, too, burst out laughing. "Good heavens! He hasn't changed one bit. He was always into some kind of mischief or other, here at Fratcombe. And now that he is grown, he is worse than ever. Bless the boy! He has a truly good heart."

• • • •

Beth flung herself out of bed and managed to reach the basin in time. It was months since she had suffered one of her sick headaches, but yesterday's encounter with Jonathan had brought back all her guilty fears. She had been tossing and turning all night. Now she had a pounding head, and sickness, as well.

She felt for her towel, dipped it in the cold water in the ewer, and wiped her face. Then she crawled back to bed, and lay there, panting. No point in trying to light her candle. At this stage in her headache, she would barely be able to see. It would be like standing in a dark, narrow tunnel, with occasional pulses of painfully bright light striking into her eyes like arrows.

She tried to push aside her fears, to blank her mind, but the ideas kept on drumming like a nasty refrain. She had agreed to take the place of honour at a Fratcombe Manor dinner. She would have to suffer all those pointing fingers, all those whispered insults. She deserved them, for she was a nobody, perhaps even a fugitive. But she had agreed. She could not escape.

The nausea gripped her again and she raced for the basin. This time she carried it back to the bed and laid it carefully on the floor. This was going to be very bad. Usually, her headaches lasted only an hour or two, at most. Usually, she managed to conceal her pain from the Aubreys and even from Hetty. But usually there was no sickness. Sickness was impossible to hide.

For a long time, she lay on her back, eyes closed, trying to control her body. She was shivering as if it were winter rather than high summer. She tried to breathe deeply, to think of innocent, beautiful things, like summer flowers and laughing children. Eventually, the shaking stopped and she dozed a little.

She was in a grand dining room. It must be Christmas, for the room was decked with holly and ivy. One moment she was sitting at table in the place of honour, the next, all the guests were attacking her, pointing fingers, screaming abuse, throwing branches of greenery into her face. She put up her hands to ward them off and was smeared with the waxy film of mistletoe berries. There was no one to defend her, not even the Aubreys. She shrank from her attackers. In her dream, she knew them all. In her dream, she knew that she was to be cast

75

out. She struggled against the hands that were trying to grab her—

"Miss Beth. Miss Beth, wake up."

She screamed.

"Miss Beth, wake up." A cold cloth was put to her brow and held firmly.

She groaned and tried to open her eyes. Hetty was hovering anxiously, mopping Beth's face. It was after dawn. There was light coming through the shutters, blessed light that Beth could see. The tunnel had gone.

"You have one of your sick headaches," Hetty said flatly. "I will tell Mrs Aubrey and then I will make your peppermint tea."

"Hetty, don't tell Mrs—"

Hetty straightened and shook her head. "I have to, Miss Beth. You can't possibly teach the children when you are in such a state." She nodded towards the basin on the floor. "I know you sometimes hide it when it's only the headache, but you can't hide this. Mrs Aubrey will want you to stay in bed until the sickness has gone. And you know it's for the best."

Beth tried to protest. She began to push herself up, but it was more than she could manage. The nausea threatened to overcome her again. She sank back on to her pillows and willed her stomach to behave.

"Lie still and breathe deeply," Hetty said gently. "I'll be back with the tisane in two shakes of a lamb's tail." She tried to smile encouragingly and then whipped out of the bedchamber.

Chastened, Beth did as she was told. She had no choice. Until this attack subsided, she was not going to be able to do anything. Except think.

She had promised Jonathan she would do it. *For the Aubreys*, he had said. But when he was holding her hand, when they were touching, skin to skin, she would have agreed to anything he asked. She was being a fool, all over again. She had berated herself before, for thinking of him as her silver knight. Now she was thinking of him as a man—a living, breathing, desirable man—which was even more idiotic. He could be nothing to her. He was a great nobleman. She was a foundling with no past, not even a name of her own. If the terrors of her dreams were even half true, she had done something wicked in her past life, and her present sufferings were probably a just punishment.

Perhaps the dinner at Fratcombe Manor was part of that punishment, an ordeal she had to undergo in order to be cleansed? That thought was oddly calming. The pounding in her head was even beginning to recede. It was a sign.

She was going to have to find a way of meeting, and enduring, the trial to come. It was her only hope of overcoming the demons that haunted her.

Chapter Ten

IT WAS LATE AFTERNOON when Jon strolled into his mother's sitting room in the east wing of Portbury Abbey, on his principal estate. She always sat here in the afternoons, to avoid the sun, she said, which was ruinous to a lady's complexion. Since Jon had returned from Spain as brown as a nut, she had stopped adding that the sun was ruinous to a gentleman's complexion, too.

"Jonathan. At last! I had almost given you up."

He came forward to kiss her hand. "Good afternoon, Mama. I hope I see you well?"

"Tolerably so, my dear." She patted the place by her side, but before he could sit down, she said, "Have you ordered tea? No, of course you have not. Ring the bell, would you, dear?"

Nothing had changed. His mother was well-intentioned, but she did have a lamentable tendency to treat her sons as though they were still in short coats.

He crossed to the empty fireplace to pull the bell. How long would it be before she drove him to distraction, all over again? He had told her he planned to remain at the Abbey for three weeks, to deal with estate business, but he had barely set foot in the place before he was wondering whether he might need to create an urgent summons back to the peaceful haven at Fratcombe. It was yet another reminder of the duty he had been trying to ignore. If he wanted to reorder this house according to his own lights, rather than his mother's, he had to find himself a wife. This time, however, he was determined that the wife would be a lady of his own careful choosing. He

78

planned to take his time. Eventually, he would install a new countess at the Abbey, and his mother would move back to the Dower House. Eventually, he would have peace.

The door opened. Jon ignored it. It was his mother's role to give instructions to the servants.

"Oh, forgive me." It was a young and educated voice, not a servant's.

Jon spun round. Standing in the doorway was possibly the loveliest young woman he had ever seen, with guinea-gold curls framing a heart-shaped face and eyes the colour of bluebells. Confound it, his mother was matchmaking again. How many beauties had she installed here to tempt him? Had she turned his working visit into a house party on the sly?

The young lady dropped Jon a very elegant curtsey and then came into the room. "Forgive me, ma'am," she said again. "Had I known you had company, I should not have intruded."

"This is not company, this is my son, Jonathan, home to do his duty as host. And about time, too." His mother rose. "You will permit me to present him to you?"

The girl blushed the colour of overripe strawberries.

"Lady Cissy, I should like to introduce my son, the Earl of Portbury, lately a major with the army in Spain. Jonathan, make your bow to Lady Cissy Middleton, second daughter of the Duke of Sherford."

Jonathan swallowed his ire and bowed courteously. It was not the child's fault, after all, that his mother was overstepping the mark yet again. As a dutiful son, he could not possibly respond in kind. Had he not berated his brother for voicing such complaints?

Lady Cissy sank into a deep curtsey. When she rose, she offered him her hand with practised elegance. "I am delighted to meet you at last, my lord," she said, looking up at him through thick golden lashes and then opening her eyes very wide, as if she were beholding something amazing.

Practised was definitely the word, Jon decided, with an inward groan. Why did his mother always choose rank and artifice over principles and honesty? He found himself remembering Beth Aubrey's sharp retorts with more admiration than he had felt at the time. She told the truth. She defended the weak. And she did not flirt. Unlike Lady Cissy.

He helped the girl to a seat beside his mother. He had a feeling this was going to be a very tedious afternoon.

Three sentences from the lady's lips confirmed his worst fears. She was as empty-headed as most of her ilk. Worse, she had a high-pitched giggle that would drive any sane man to drink.

• • • •

Jon ignored his brother and ate his breakfast in silence. His house party ordeal was almost over. Three interminable weeks, precisely as he had feared. Escape had been impossible, of course, for what reason could he have given for deserting a houseful of Portbury guests? He had been trapped by his own good manners. At least, none of the resident beauties had trapped Jon into proposing, in spite of the underhand tricks that one or two of them had tried. The rest were either so shy that they were struck dumb in his presence, or so empty-headed that their conversation bored him to death. They all had rank and beauty, to be sure, but that was no compensation. It was a relief that they would all be gone on the morrow. There was not one restful woman among them.

The door opened to admit an unexpected visitor.

"Miss Mountjoy. How splendid." George sprang up and stepped forward to bow over the lady's hand. Then he waved the butler away and pulled out a chair for her.

Jon also rose and bowed, distantly. From their very first meeting, a week before his wedding to Alicia, he had instinctively distrusted Louisa Mountjoy, who was Alicia's long-time companion and bosom bow. He had discovered soon enough that his instincts were right.

In the early weeks of their marriage, Alicia had played the loving, doting wife, in public and in private. For Jon, it was a glorious liberation from his father's emotional tyranny. He dared to have feelings again, and even to show them. Until the day of his twenty-first birthday, when he came upon Alicia cavorting naked with her lover—Louisa Mountjoy.

Alicia seemed to glory in being discovered. She immediately announced, with a sneering laugh, that she had paid her dues in the marriage bed and would never enter it again. Jon's touch had always repelled her and he was a gullible fool ever to have believed otherwise.

Jon was devastated. He certainly felt like a fool. Her betrayal had shattered all his hopeful dreams of kindness and companionship in their life together. Realising that he was tied, for life, to a wife he could not even respect, he vowed then that no one—and especially no woman—would ever have the power to humiliate him again. Feelings made a man vulnerable. Only a fool trusted anyone but himself.

Now, all these years later, Jon was free of Alicia at last. He was not free of Louisa Mountjoy, however. Under the terms of Alicia's will, he had been required to provide an annuity for the Mountjoy woman so that she might enjoy financial independence for life. Jon had been sure she would be gone from King's Portbury when he returned from Spain. Unfortunately, she had leased one of the estate cottages in the village and was a frequent visitor to the Dower House instead. It was much too late now for Jon to tell his mother the real truth.

George was talking animatedly to their visitor. Judging from his expression, George thought at least as highly of Miss Mountjoy as his mother did which was surprising, given George's usual tastes in women.

"To what do we owe the pleasure of this visit, ma'am?" Jon asked, silkily. It was a peculiar time for her to pay a call. Most of the lady guests were still asleep; any that were awake would be breakfasting in bed.

"Oh, nothing of importance by contrast with the great affairs of running an estate. Merely a receipt that I promised to your lady mother."

A receipt? The dowager had never in her life concerned herself with receipts. Cooking was to be left to cooks. Jon bit the inside of his lip to stop himself from laughing aloud at Miss Mountjoy's ridiculous attempts at deception. In his experience, this woman had a calculated motive for everything she did.

"I'm afraid my mother is still in her bedchamber," George put in quickly, "though I imagine she will be down quite soon.

Perhaps you would take some coffee while you are waiting? Or chocolate?"

Miss Mountjoy shot an assessing glance at Jon's stony expression before she replied. "Thank you, sir, but I have errands that cannot wait. I shall walk back to the village." She stood up and reached for her gloves.

The two men rose. Jon held out his hand, palm up. "If you care to give me your receipt, ma'am, I will ensure it is delivered to my mother."

"I— No, I— Thank you, my lord, but I should prefer to deliver it myself. There is no urgency and it requires, er, a little explanation. I—"

George intervened before Miss Mountjoy could tie herself in even more knots. "No need for you to involve yourself, Portbury. I will mention it to mama. I am taking her driving later this morning."

"I am sure that dear Lady Portbury will find that quite delightful, sir. You are such an excellent whip."

George preened a little. "As it happens, ma'am, I was about to take my pair for an airing, to take the edge off them before I drive out with my mother. She prefers placid horses, you know. Perhaps I could drive you to the village?"

"Why, Mr Foxe-Garway, that would be such a treat."

Jon kept his face impassive. He bowed and watched as the pair walked out into the hall, arm in arm. He could have sworn that the woman whispered something in George's ear as soon as they were beyond the doorway. Was something going on between them? No, impossible. Mountjoy had no interest in men. Yet that encounter had been much too neat. Might they be conspiring together to drain money from the estate?

Jon would need to be even more on his guard. Against his own brother. He stared into space, his coffee cup half-way to his lips. There was no point in agonising over George's failings. He had become totally set in his selfish, spendthrift ways. He would do almost anything for money. Even the dowager had stopped making excuses for him.

"Good morning, Jon."

Startled, Jon put his cup down with a clatter and sprang to his feet. "Good morning, Mama." As Jon helped her to the seat

82

next to him, the butler disappeared to fetch her usual pot of chocolate. "May I ask what brings you down so early?"

"As hostess, it is my duty to see to the welfare of our guests. Besides, George is to take me out driving this morning. Is he down yet?"

"Ages ago, Mama. He's just, er, driven out to take the edge off his horses. He knows you are a nervous passenger."

"Nothing of the sort. But I do like to drive behind well-schooled horses. George persists in driving the most unruly beasts in your stable. 'High-couraged', he calls them." She snorted in disgust. They both knew that George drove horses he could barely handle because he fancied himself to be as good a whip as Jon. It rankled with him that he was not.

The butler returned with the dowager's chocolate. She dismissed him with a nod. "I will ring if I need anything more." The man bowed and left the room, closing the door silently behind him.

Jon looked up from his plate. Her face was set. He resigned himself to what was to come.

"Jon, I need to talk to you. Ab–about things."

He reached for the coffee pot to pour himself a refill. It proved to be empty, but he did not ring for more. Instead, he sighed and leaned back in his chair. "I am listening," he said, in a flat voice.

"Jon, I have filled the house with the most eligible young ladies of the *ton*. You have played your role as host impeccably, as always, but I have not seen you—" She signed impatiently. "Does none of them take your fancy? What about Miss Danforth? Now, there's a delightful girl. And Lady Cissy, too. Even you will acknowledge that she is a glorious creature."

He stared at the ceiling for a moment. Then he picked up his cup and began to turn it in his fingers, admiring the fineness of the porcelain. "Mama, they are both pretty, beautifully behaved, and without a single interesting thought in their empty heads. After all those years in the schoolroom, you would think they would have learned something. But apparently not."

"That is because they are young, Jon. They are only just out." She laid a hand reassuringly on his arm. "A young wife can be moulded by her husband," she said stoutly. "In a few years, you can make exactly what you want of her."

"Can I?" His father had been all in favour of moulding, too. Brutally, on occasions. Jon would never follow such an example. He wanted a restful woman, but a woman of principle—her own principles, too, not a straitjacket of her husband's design. "Mama, these chits are young enough to be my daughters. I can't take a child to wife."

She was clearly shocked by his words, but she kept her tone level. "In that case, when we return to London, I shall arrange a few select evening parties at Portbury House. I can invite some of the, er, more mature single ladies. There are one or two widows also, of impeccable reputation, who might interest you if—"

He was shaking his head vehemently even before she had finished speaking. "No, Mama. I thank you, but no. When I marry, it will be to a lady of my own choosing. And in my own time. After our guests leave tomorrow, I shall return to Fratcombe."

"Fratcombe? But why? There is precious little society there."

"It is not society I need, Mama, but useful occupation. George drained that estate of funds in my absence last year and it needs— Oh, pray do not look so distressed. You could not have known what he was about."

She could not meet his gaze.

"It will require several months of work to restore Fratcombe. I find I relish the challenge there. I cannot be doing nothing, Mama, as I do here."

"But you are not doing nothing. You have guests, you—"

"I am doing nothing useful, ma'am," he snapped. He had never used such a tone with her before. "Engaging in frivolous entertainment with house guests is not what I have been used to, these last few years," he explained, rather more gently.

"I knew the army would be the ruination of you," she muttered.

He lifted her hand to his lips in an uncharacteristically gallant gesture, in apology for his bad temper. "Poor Mama. I must be a sad trial to you. I know that you mean well. But, sadly, we do not see eye to eye on what I need out of life."

"You need a wife and a son," she retorted. "Surely we are agreed on that?"

He started back and began to breathe deeply, holding himself in check. With anyone else, he would have lost his temper at such gall, but a gentleman could never do such a thing with his mother, no matter what she did.

She hastened to apologise. "I promise I will stop meddling," she finished, trying to smile. "But if there is anything you wish me to do, you have only to ask. Will you be content with that?"

"More than content. Thank you, Mama." He leaned forward to kiss her cheek.

The dowager was surprised into a blush. And rendered speechless.

The door opened. "Why, Mama, good morning. I must say you are down in excellent time, and looking quite splendid for our outing. Is that a new walking dress? Very dashing." George strolled forward and bent to kiss her cheek, exactly as he did every morning. It was an empty gesture.

Now that George had arrived to keep her company, Jon rose. "If you will excuse me, Mama, I must attend to some estate business this morning, but I will be free later to hear all about your expedition. Take care George does not overturn you," he added mischievously. "It would not do to get mud on that delicate fabric." He touched a finger to the Prussian blue silk of her sleeve. "You look as fine as fivepence. There is a matching hat, I presume?" He grinned suddenly, and she made to reach out to him. Then she let her hand drop. Jon was relieved to see that she had not forgotten how much he detested public displays of affection.

• • • •

Jon pulled Saracen to a halt at the top of the hill. They were both blowing hard after the climb but, from here, he could see the whole Portbury estate and miles beyond. It was a good place to be alone to think.

85

He dismounted, leaving the reins loose on the big bay's neck. The horse was too well trained to wander far.

Jon strolled across to lean his back against an aged hawthorn, bent sideways by the prevailing wind that scoured this ridge in winter. Fratcombe. He knew in his bones that he had to return there, though it had come to him only as he spoke the words. He needed work to occupy him. After army life, he could not return to the wasteful ways of before. He had tenants, and workers, and dependants. As Earl of Portbury, he had a duty to them all. Surprisingly, that duty no longer felt like a burden. Was that the rector's influence? He did not know but, for some reason, he was eager to return. He would try to look after his people as he had looked after his soldiers; he would seek to make their lives a little better, educate their children. Yes, even the gypsy children that Miss Aubrey defended so stoutly.

Beth Aubrey. Unlike the gang of simpering misses his mother had gathered here at Portbury, Beth was a woman of decided character, a clear-headed, practical woman who tried to do good in the world. She had not an ounce of the guile that had surrounded him, these past few weeks at King's Portbury. He could see that clearly now. But the fundamental question remained—could he really be sure she was not a fraud?

He took a deep breath of the clean air of the hilltop. He would be arriving back at Fratcombe only a few days before the evening party at the Manor. He would visit the rectory, he decided—he had the ready-made excuse of consulting Mrs Aubrey about the party arrangements—and he would use the time to judge Beth Aubrey's character, once and for all. If his foundling was as upright as he suspected—and, he admitted, as he hoped—he would use his rank to establish her position in Fratcombe, and with it, his own. After that, no one would dare to accept a Fitzherbert's judgement over the Earl of Portbury's.

Chapter Eleven

MRS AUBREY'S LITTLE MAID answered Jon's knock, as usual. At the sight of him, her eyes grew as round as saucers. She stood rooted to the spot, making no move to admit him. Impudent wench. It was not for a mere servant to have opinions on how often Jon chose to call.

"Is Mrs Aubrey at home?" he asked sharply.

She nodded and showed him directly to the parlour, without first seeking leave from her mistress. Almost as if he were one of the family.

"Why, Jonathan. Three visits in three days. We are honoured." Jon did not miss the hint of laughter in Mrs Aubrey's voice as she rose from her work table and dropped him a tiny curtsey. It was only yesterday that he had finally persuaded the old lady to return to using his given name, as her husband always did. It felt right. He was truly glad of it.

Beth—Miss Aubrey—would do nothing so intimate. She too had risen from her place, laying aside her pen. Her curtsey was a model of decorum. It showed off her slim figure and upright carriage, too. Somewhere she had been well schooled. "Good afternoon, Lord Portbury." Her voice was low, almost husky. He persuaded himself it sounded a little strained. Could she be worrying about tomorrow's party?

He smiled down at her. "You have been working too hard again, ma'am. You have ink on your fingers, I fear." He was hoping to make her laugh as readily as on the previous afternoons.

87

Instead, she looked horrified. She lifted her fingers to stare at the dark stain as if some monster had settled on her skin. "Oh, dear. I shall never get it clean in time. What shall I—?"

Mrs Aubrey stepped forward and clasped her wrinkled old hands over Beth's smooth ones. "Stop worrying, my dear. I have a remedy for that, I promise. You shall be as white as snow when you don your new evening gown."

Beth resumed her seat, but her eyes were still wide and apprehensive, Jon saw. It had not occurred to him until now that she might worry about appearing at his party. She seemed so confident in everything else she did, in the school, with the villagers, with servants, even with him. She was a lady, but she was still a nobody, and about to be foisted on to a group of haughty gentlefolk who most definitely did not wish to accept her as an equal. Of course it would be an ordeal. Why had he not seen that? In the long run, it would make her life easier, he was sure, but that was little consolation today. Even a true lady could be afraid of confrontation.

He hastened to reassure her. "In any case, you will be wearing evening gloves, and—"

"Jonathan," Mrs Aubrey interrupted sharply, adding a warning shake of her head, "will you take tea with us?"

Now, why...? Oh, yes, of course. The ladies would remove their gloves at the dinner table. Stupid of him. His wits had gone a-begging. He was not helping Beth at all. He smiled his agreement to the old lady and set about restoring poor Beth's peace of mind.

He joined her on the sofa. "You seem incredibly busy, ma'am." He gestured towards the pieces of card spread across the table. "Is this for my party, too?" He picked one up. The name "Sir Bertram Fitzherbert" was written in a very elegant hand.

"Place cards for your dinner table, my lord. We remembered them only this morning."

"Ah, yes. Yet another of the hostess's duties. I had not realised quite how many burdens I was putting on Mrs Aubrey's shoulders when I asked her to take this on." He glanced across at the old lady who was standing in the open doorway, giving instructions to her maid. "It must be much more difficult for a hostess who does not actually live in the house."

She shook her head. "It could be, but your butler is extremely competent. And we had weeks to prepare while you were away." Her voice tailed off. She threw him an enigmatic sideways glance and then quickly looked away.

Was that an accusation? That he had decreed this grand party and then fled the field? If only she knew. Those three weeks at King's Portbury had been more dangerous than any battlefield. If he had not been awake to the matchmakers' scheming, he might have found himself forcibly leg-shackled to a chit he could not abide. Fratcombe was a peaceful refuge by comparison. Here he could relax and be himself. Here, no one was scheming.

Except himself, of course.

He laughed aloud at that subversive thought.

"My lord?" She sounded hurt. She still did not know him well enough to realise he would never laugh at her.

"Forgive me, ma'am." On impulse, he reached out to cover her ink-stained fingers with his own and patted her hand reassuringly. She froze instantly. Good God, what was he doing? He drew in a quick, horrified breath, but forced himself to give her one last friendly pat before nonchalantly dropping his hand back into his lap, as if he had done nothing in the least improper. "I was laughing at the picture you painted. Of myself." He grinned down at her. "Far too top-lofty to involve myself in anything as mundane as *work*. And absconding from the scene to ensure I could not be called to account. Very remiss, I agree."

"Oh, no." She was blushing now. The tints of rose on her cheeks merely served to highlight her perfect complexion. There was colour on her neck, too, though it was partly hidden behind her high collar. Under her muslins, he had no doubt that even her bosom was delicately pink and—

She pulled another card towards her and busied herself with carefully writing the name. Just as well that she was not looking at Jon. She might be a single lady, but she was almost certainly old enough to recognise sensual awareness in a man's face. He had no right to allow himself to stray into such

89

thoughts. She was a nobody, a protégée at most. It was beneath his dignity to dally with her.

"Oh, bl—!" Her nib had broken and blotted the card. "Bother," she corrected herself quickly. When he did not react, she threw him a mischievous look. Unlike the simpering debutantes, she was sensible enough to realise that his touch had been a mistake. And to be forgotten at once. Yes, sensible, but delightful company, too, as he had learned since his return. Her eyes were now dancing with mischief. "You will permit me to observe, my lord, that your *supervision* of my work is not helping."

Excellent. She was back to her normal quick-witted self. Easy with him, and more than ready to take him to task. He much preferred her that way.

He allowed himself a sheepish grin. "I will take myself further off at once, ma'am." He rose and crossed the room to Mrs Aubrey's side. "It is clear that Miss Aubrey finds my presence a burden this afternoon. However, my intentions were of the best, I assure you. I knew there were bound to be last-minute chores and, since it is *my* party, I thought I should offer my services. Is there any way in which I can help?"

Mrs Aubrey smiled, shaking her head. "No. Apart from the place cards, everything is done. Unless you wish to help with those?"

He snorted with laughter. "If you had seen my handwriting, ma'am, you would not ask."

She laughed, too. "I thought as much. It tends to be the way with gentlemen. No, you may sit and converse with me over the teacups, so that Beth is left in peace to finish her task. We are treating you as a friend of the family, you understand, rather than an exalted visitor who must become the centre of everyone's attention." She paused. Jon thought he saw a fleeting shadow cross her face. "After all these daily visits, it could hardly be otherwise."

Was that a warning? Had he overstepped the mark?

"But we do appreciate your help and advice," the old lady went on quickly. "However, I warn you that you must not call tomorrow, Jonathan. Both Beth and I shall be fully engaged with gowns and curling tongs. Male company will definitely *not* be welcome."

He nodded an acknowledgement, trying to keep his face straight. "I shall wait with, er, interest to see the results of so much female industry. I dare say I shall not recognise my hostess and my guest of honour when they cross my threshold."

Mrs Aubrey's eyes were sparkling wickedly now. That was too much for Jon, who laughed aloud. In a moment, Mrs Aubrey was laughing, too.

For some reason, Beth did not respond at all. Clearly she was too absorbed in her work to have heard another word he said.

• • • •

Beth touched slightly shaky fingers to her lips and then, even more tentatively, to her hair. It was a splendid confection, but much too elaborate for a woman with no name. Could she go through with this? She closed her eyes. She really did not want to look at the woman in the mirror. That was not Beth. That was some other person, a fine lady, the kind of lady who could go into society and hold her head high.

She swallowed hard. She had promised Jonathan that she would do this. She had repeated the promise only two days ago. But he did not know who Beth was or where she came from, any more than she herself did. When she was with him, talking and laughing as they had been doing over these last three days, she had begun to feel calm, almost serene. He treated Beth exactly as he treated Mrs Aubrey. Like a lady. But was she a lady?

It was true that she had not been a menial. Her soft hands proved that. But she could equally as well have been a lowly companion, or in some other inferior position in a household. The fact that she enjoyed her duties as the village schoolmistress, and that she was apparently so good at it, suggested she might have been some kind of teacher, or governess. That would make her a lady—of sorts—but not one whose position in society allowed her to sit at the right hand of an earl.

Her eyes flew open in horror. She stared at her reflection. She had turned stark white at the thought of sitting in the place of honour at Jonathan's table. He was going to insist upon it. He had said so, and Mrs Aubrey had readily agreed. According to the printed invitations, the select dinner, followed by a larger evening party, was "to introduce Miss Aubrey". Therefore, she would have to take the place of honour on the host's right, no matter how high the station of any other of the lady guests.

Beth cringed inwardly. How could she possibly do this? Meeting all those haughty people who despised her? She had promised not to develop a convenient headache. Unfortunately, at the prospect of such a confrontation, she was beginning to develop a real one.

She rose and began to pace up and down her bedchamber. The skirts of the beautiful new evening gown floated about her caressingly. Oh dear. Mrs Aubrey had gone to so much trouble, and so much expense, for this. The gown was a very elegant affair of delicate white gauze over pomona-green silk. It had a low square neckline and vandyking on the sleeves and hemline, to show off the gleaming colour beneath. Much too fine for a foundling.

The bedroom door opened. Hetty was back. Her excited chatter would begin all over again. Beth was not sure she could bear it.

"Mrs Aubrey sent these." The maid opened a flat leather case with exaggerated care.

Beth stopped and gazed. "Oh," she breathed. The jewel case contained a single strand of exceedingly good pearls, with matching ear drops. Perfect.

"Sit down, Miss Beth, and I will put the necklace on for you."

What choice did she have? The whole household was determined that, like Cinderella, she should go to the ball. But, unlike Cinderella, Beth could never be worthy of this prince.

Hetty quickly clasped the pearls around Beth's neck and helped her to hook the earrings in place. Beth straightened her shoulders. There was no going back now. She had promised them all, and so she must do everything in her power to play her part in this charade. She pinched her cheeks and bit her lips a little. That was better. There was colour now, in both. She rose again and shook out her skirts. She could do this. She would.

She forced herself to smile as she drew on her long gloves and took up her matching fan and reticule. "Thank you, Hetty, for the hairstyle." On an impulse, she put her gloved hands on the girl's shoulders and dropped a kiss on her cheek. "You are a wonder."

Hetty blushed to the roots of her hair. And then she dropped a curtsey. "Miss Beth, I— Oh, ma'am, thank you."

Beth could not tell which of them was more overcome. Not wishing to embarrass Hetty further, she patted the girl's shoulder and left the room.

At the foot of the stairs, the rector and Mrs Aubrey were waiting. Mrs Aubrey had fashioned that wonderfully unusual red-purple silk into a most flattering evening gown. She had garnet drops in her ears, and a matching aigrette in her hair.

"Oh, ma'am!" Beth stopped halfway down the stairs. "How fine you look. His lordship could not have a more splendid hostess at his side."

Mrs Aubrey preened a little and touched her grey curls. She too had had the benefit of Hetty's clever fingers. "Thank you, child."

"May I say," the rector intervened, "that both my ladies look extremely fine." When Beth reached the hallway, he shook out her evening cloak and placed it gently on her shoulders.

Mrs Aubrey leant forward to tie it for her, straightening the folds so that the deep green velvet would hang beautifully. "You look radiant, Beth. Exactly how a guest of honour should be. Come now. Since his lordship has kindly sent his carriage to fetch us, we must not keep his horses standing any longer. What time do you have, James, my dear?"

The rector checked his silver pocket watch. "If we leave now, we will have at least a quarter of an hour before any of the other guests arrive."

Unless they are truly bad-mannered. What if they arrive early, in order to ogle Cinderella before she has learned how to walk in her glass slippers?

Beth could not silence that unruly voice in her head. There were certainly some of the guests who were capable of such rudeness. Beth could imagine Sir Bertram and Lady Fitzherbert doing so. Lady Fitzherbert would give that tinkling, tittering laugh of hers, place her beautifully manicured fingers on Jonathan's sleeve, and gush that she "must have mistaken the time".

I will not let them embarrass me. They shall not look down on me. Whoever I was, I am now Miss Aubrey. If the rector and Mrs Aubrey are prepared to treat me as a lady, everyone else shall do so too. Jonathan believes in me. Surely that is enough?

Chapter Twelve

JON PACED UP AND DOWN in his library, waiting for the butler to appear, to warn him that the carriage was coming up the drive. For some reason, he was a little nervous. He could not understand why. He was only preparing for an evening party, not an assault with bayonets fixed and guns blazing.

The butler entered silently and bowed. "Your lordship's carriage will be at the door in a few moments. Shall I show the guests into the crimson saloon?"

"No, Sutton. Mrs Aubrey is my hostess, and Miss Aubrey is the guest of honour. I shall meet them at the door myself." He strode out into the hallway, past the thin-lipped butler. The man clearly did not approve of such condescension to a mere rector and his family.

The footman had already thrown the great door wide. Mrs Aubrey led the way into the house, followed by the rector, with Miss Beth on his arm. Mrs Aubrey let her cloak slip from her shoulders into the footman's waiting hands. Then she curtseyed in response to Jon's deep bow. "Good evening, Jonathan."

Jon smiled broadly and returned her greeting. It still gave him a warm feeling to hear her use his given name.

He turned to greet the rector. "Good evening, sir, and welcome."

The rector was too busy removing Miss Beth's cloak to reply immediately. He took Beth's hand and led her forward. "Good evening, Jonathan." He bowed briefly. "May I present your guest of honour, Miss Aubrey?"

There was only time for a single glance before she sank into a deep curtsey, a curtsey fit for a queen, not a mere earl. When she did not rise immediately, Jon stepped forward and took her hand to raise her himself. His eyes had not deceived him. She looked utterly radiant, as beautiful as the dawn. His breath caught. For a second, he could not find any words. How did you tell a woman that she had been transformed into a vision out of a fairytale?

Mrs Aubrey was gazing at Beth with pride in her eyes and a slight smile on her lips. But it was the rector who broke the silence. "Fit to grace any man's table, I'd say. Wouldn't you agree, my boy?"

Jon found his voice at last. "Rector, I have no doubt that your ladies—both your ladies—will outshine any in the county."

. . . .

By the time the guests were seated at the dinner table, Jon had more or less recovered from the revelation of Beth's astonishing beauty. How had he failed to see it before? Had he stopped using his eyes once he decided she was a foundling in need of rescue?

It was possible. After the siege of Badajoz, when drunken British soldiers began attacking the townspeople, Jon and his fellow officers had been unable to save the women from molestation, and worse. Terrible things had been done. That failure still haunted Jon; he had sworn then that he would always defend a lone woman in distress. So he had helped the Aubreys to support Beth. But it had suited his other purposes, too, for he was intent on securing his own place in Fratcombe society. Was that why he had failed to understand that she was not merely a cause, but also a living, breathing woman?

He knew it now. The living, breathing body beneath that filmy gown was the stuff of a man's dreams.

His heart was still beating faster than normal, but he fancied he had hidden his physical reactions pretty well. He had even succeeded in escorting her to the dining room without betraying himself. She had rested her hand so lightly on the sleeve of his dress coat that he had had to check it was actually there. Was she as aware of his body as he was of

96

hers? He could not tell. But he must not allow himself to lust after her. She was far beneath him, but she *was* a lady. It was his duty to treat her as one.

The dinner was for a very select group—the Aubreys, Beth, Jonathan and the other couples who had done most to turn Beth's stay in the district into a severe trial. Worst among them were the Fitzherberts, of course. Rank dictated that, while Jon had the pleasure of seeing the beautiful Miss Beth on his right hand, he had to suffer the trial of listening to the gushing Lady Fitzherbert from his left.

The dinner progressed relatively smoothly. Knowing that Lady Fitzherbert was listening to every word, Jon began the first course by trying to draw Beth out on innocuous subjects such as books and music. Her responses were polite but unforthcoming. He could not blame her. What lady would want to offer up her opinions to Lady Fitzherbert's vinegar-soaked tongue?

After Beth's third murmured monosyllable, Jon began to feel thoroughly frustrated. What had happened to the girl who had even dared to sharpen her wits on him? He was beginning to think he preferred the rather dowdy poor relation, if the price of her physical transformation was to be the cowing of her spirit. Beauty, as he had discovered to his cost with his late and unlamented wife, was no guarantee of character.

"Mrs Aubrey tells me you have made excellent progress at the village school. Perhaps I may pay a visit and see your teaching for myself?" When that produced no response other than a rather startled glance, he continued calmly, "Do you have many pupils this year?"

It was like opening a sluice gate. She had hesitated to speak of herself, but the colour returned to her cheeks as she spoke more and more enthusiastically about her charges. "The most promising child is Peter. He has a bright, enquiring mind and is already reading very well for one so young. His figuring is good, too."

"So you foresee a golden future for him?"

She dropped her gaze to her plate and began to push some of the uneaten food around with her fork.

Something was troubling her about this child. After a moment's pause, Jon said, "In my experience, the cleverest children are often the naughtiest. Two of my cousins—Ned and Luke—were exactly like that, always into mischief, and leading all the others astray. Luckily for society, they are both in the army now."

"Oh no, Peter is extremely well behaved in school, and no more boisterous than the other boys outside. It is just that he—" She took a deep breath. Her lush bosom rose alluringly against her tight décolleté. Jon tried to keep his eyes from straying. He must remember his role as host.

"I must tell you, sir, that his father is only a labourer. As soon as Peter is strong enough to work on the farm, his father will take him out of school." She sighed. "It is his right, of course. The family has many mouths to feed."

They both knew it was not her place to interfere, however good her motives. It was no business of Jon's, either. He should turn the subject. To his surprise, he heard himself asking, "Where does the father work?"

Her silence was eloquent, as was the look she gave Jon. She had huge, and very beautiful eyes, the colour of rich chocolate. Eyes to drown in. One more entrancing feature of an entrancing girl.

"Ah. Do I take it that he is employed by one of my tenants?"

"Er, no." Her voice was barely audible. "He works on your home farm."

Jon almost laughed. Had the man been employed by one of Jon's tenants, it could have been awkward, even improper, to make special arrangements for the family. But for a home farm labourer, the solution was in Jon's gift. He would give the boy a future, in return for one more approving look from those beautiful eyes. "Estates need good men at all levels, Miss Aubrey. My agent will arrange it. If Peter continues to excel at his lessons, a place can eventually be found for him in my estate office. He will learn a good trade. Will that content you?"

She nodded to her plate. Then, when he said nothing more, she raised her head. Her peach-bloom complexion was glowing and the smile on her lips was beyond mere politeness. And her shining eyes were glorious. "Thank you, my lord. I had not thought that you could be so— Thank you."

Jon started to reach for her hand. He wanted to show her that he truly approved of her motives. At that very moment, the butler ordered the footmen forward, to clear the first course. Jon's hand dropped back to the table.

Just as well. What on earth had possessed him to do such a thing? And with Lady Fitzherbert watching, too? He must keep himself under tighter control. He must not allow himself to be beguiled by a pair of fine eyes.

Beth had begun conversing with the gentleman on her right, while Jon would now have to endure Lady Fitzherbert's incessant chatter. He consoled himself that his penance could not last too much longer. Eventually, the cloth would be removed and he could turn back to Beth. With rather more care, this time.

The conversation round the table got louder and louder during the second course. No doubt, Jon's excellent cellar was lubricating the guests' throats, particularly those of the gentlemen. He listened with half an ear to Lady Fitzherbert's boasting of her eldest son's prowess on the hunting field. One lesson had not been enough to keep the confounded woman in her place, it seemed.

"Very commendable," he said with a nod and a half-smile. Then he raised his voice a little, to be sure most of the other guests could hear, and asked casually, "I fancy Fitzherbert is not a common name. Are you, by any chance, related to Mrs Fitzherbert, ma'am? The Prince Regent's former, um, *friend*?"

One or two of the guests gasped aloud. Lady Fitzherbert's eyes goggled. She became so still she might have been stuffed. Eventually her mouth worked as she tried to speak, but no words came out.

Beth Aubrey's clear voice broke the strained silence. "Is it possible your years in Spain have led you into error, my lord? Perhaps you were not aware that Mrs Fitzherbert is a Roman Catholic?" She turned to fix big, innocent eyes on Jon, though there was nothing innocent in her neat defence of Lady

Fitzherbert. Why on earth should Beth do such a thing for a woman who had wronged her?

Because, unlike Jon, she was kind and forgiving, even to her enemies. Beth had absorbed the Aubreys' goodness in a way that Jon, to his shame, had not. He suspected he must be looking a little embarrassed now. In an effort to recover, he said quickly, "You are right, of course, Miss Aubrey. My mistake. The Fitzherberts of Fratcombe are pillars of the established church."

When he turned back to Lady Fitzherbert, he found she was glowering across the table at Beth, as if the insult were Beth's doing rather than Jon's. No sign of Christian charity there. But it was his duty to show that he had a little, at least. "I ask your pardon, ma'am, if my thoughtless remark has disturbed you in any way." He raised his eyebrows, waiting for her acceptance.

Lady Fitzherbert simpered and inclined her head, before pointedly changing the subject back to her children's achievements. Their little spat was over. Unfortunately, her ladyship looked to be even more set against Beth than before. Was that because Beth was an easy target, while Jon himself was not? In the early part of the meal, Lady Fitzherbert had been watching Beth like a cat eying a captive mouse, but Beth's behaviour had been impeccable. Jon suspected that perfect manners had been bred in her from a very early age. Everything was done correctly and without a moment's hesitation. There was nothing in the least ill bred about the delicious Miss Aubrey, however much the sight of her might stir a man's blood.

Beth was a lady. He had absolutely no doubt of that now. Her ravishing appearance this evening, coupled with her faultless and unselfish behaviour, was serving to prove that. No one should have cause to snub Miss Aubrey after this. And once Jon had carried out the final part of his plan, even the Fitzherberts would have to toe the line he had drawn.

The servants were waiting to remove the cloth. Soon the ladies would leave for the drawing room.

The moment was now. He nodded to the butler to refill the wine glasses. Then he rose in his place.

"Ladies and gentlemen, it is my great pleasure to welcome you to the first dinner party that I have given here for many years. When I was here as a boy, I found Fratcombe to be one of the friendliest and most generous parts of England. I have always remembered it with fondness. It is to return some of that generosity that I have invited you here, for you are the first families of the district."

There was a great deal of preening around the table. Most of the guests were smiling rather smugly. Two feather head-dresses were nodding vigorously.

"My other reason for this dinner party, as you will know, is to welcome Miss Aubrey into Fratcombe society." Out of the corner of his eye, he could see that she was beginning to blush and was staring down at her tightly clasped hands. No matter. This had to be done. Honour demanded it. "Miss Aubrey is a distant relative of our good rector." Jon smiled at the old man sitting half-way down one side of the long table. "Since she came to stay at the rectory, she has done immense good for all of us, by volunteering to be schoolmistress to all the children of the district. She shows the same selfless nature as Mr and Mrs Aubrey, and I am sure you will all agree that the whole district is beholden to her."

He paused, letting his gaze travel slowly round the table, resting on each guest in turn until they nodded in agreement. Good.

"Miss Aubrey will be remaining at the rectory since, sadly, she no longer has any other family of her own. However, that is Fratcombe's gain, and we are fortunate indeed to have her here among us. I therefore propose a toast. To Miss Aubrey, a most welcome, and valued, member of Fratcombe society."

Jon raised his glass. There was a scraping of chairs as all the gentlemen rose, some more willingly than others, but with Jon's eye on them, they had no choice. The toast was repeated and drunk.

Glad that his stratagem had worked, Jon tossed the contents of his wine glass down his throat in a single swallow. Then he let out a long breath and smiled round at his guests, before resuming his seat. On his right hand, Beth had not moved a fraction. Her colour had risen, but she was still staring at her clasped hands. He knew she was embarrassed and would not wish to speak to him now. She probably would not even wish to look at him. Understandable enough, in the circumstances, for he had given her no hint of what he intended.

But he would miss those glowing eyes.

He glanced at Mrs Aubrey and gave her a tiny nod. It was now up to her how this little melodrama would play out.

Barely ten minutes after the cloth had been removed and the dessert and decanters set upon the polished mahogany, Mrs Aubrey took a last sip of her wine and rose. "Ladies?" Though it was earlier than normal, her tone was commanding. She gazed round, as if daring the ladies to object.

Lady Fitzherbert whispered something, quick and low, to the dinner partner on her left. Jon did not catch it all, but he was sure he heard the word "impostor". For a second, his hands clenched. He clamped his jaws together. He must not give any hint that he had heard. He must trust Mrs Aubrey to deal with Lady Fitzherbert's venom.

Jon and all the other gentlemen had risen to help their partners from their chairs. But Beth seemed quite unaware that the ladies were about to leave. Jon moved quickly behind her, put his hands on the back of her chair and bent forward until his lips were only an inch or so above her curls. He could smell lavender—and hot, wild hillsides. "Miss Beth," he whispered, forcing himself to ignore the subtle scent of her and the tempting pictures it conjured up in his mind. "The ladies. Courage."

She started in her place, but recovered almost instantly. She rose gracefully and turned to smile a little shakily at Jon. "Thank you, sir. And for your kind words. I shall treasure them." As she spoke, she looked directly into his face. Her eyes were wide and glistening. Not tears, surely? She had shown such self-control since the moment she arrived.

"Courage," he said again, in a lower but more meaningful voice. He took her hand and placed it firmly on his sleeve. There would be no hovering this time. He led her to the door and opened it himself, for, as guest of honour, she must leave first. "We will join you soon, Miss Beth," he murmured and reluctantly let her go.

He watched as she made her way to the stairs. She had drawn herself up very tall; her spine was ramrod straight. Even from the back she looked like a soldier preparing for battle. In the drawing room upstairs, she would face the claws of the harpies.

. . . .

Beth was halfway up the stairs, still stunned by Jonathan's immensely flattering words, when she was dragged back with considerable force. She cried out in shock, grabbing for the baluster rail. Someone had trodden, hard, on the hem of her gown.

"Oh, I am so sorry." It was, of course, Lady Fitzherbert. "Have I torn your gown, child? What a pity. It is such a pretty, girlish confection, too."

Beth did nothing to betray the fact that she knew the damage was intentional. That would be a victory which the woman did not deserve. Instead, keeping a firm grip on the wooden rail, Beth turned her shoulder enough to smile sweetly into the older woman's face. "If you would be so kind as to remove your foot, ma'am, I shall see what may be done to repair the damage."

Lady Fitzherbert whipped her foot away as swiftly as if she had stepped barefoot on to burning coals. "I do apologise. Such a silly accident. I am not usually so clumsy."

"I am sure you are not, ma'am," came Mrs Aubrey's tart voice from the hallway below. There was a tightness about her pursed lips, too. She clearly knew, as Beth did, that the incident had been deliberate. If Beth had not had the presence of mind to grab the rail, she could well have tumbled all the way to the foot of the stairs.

The other ladies were twittering helplessly. Mrs Aubrey frowned up at them. "Come, ladies. Let us settle ourselves in the drawing room for coffee. Then Beth and I will see to the repairs." Mrs Aubrey ushered the stragglers on.

"Thank you, Aunt Caro," Beth said quietly. She lifted the fragile white gauze so that the ripped portion would not trail on the stairs. She doubted that Lady Fitzherbert would try the same trick again, but it was safer to give her no opportunity for further mischief. Beth hurried up the remaining stairs and waited for Mrs Aubrey to join her. "Thank you," she said again, "but I am sure that there is no need for both of us to leave the guests. With a maid's help, the damage can be quickly repaired."

Mrs Aubrey nodded. They both knew it would be best not to leave the other ladies to their own devices in the drawing room, where they could pick over Beth's reputation like vultures. Lady Fitzherbert was quite capable of acting as the malicious ringleader, given half a chance. Under Mrs Aubrey's gimlet eye, she would not dare. Probably.

The gentlemen would join them very soon, Beth was sure. Jonathan had almost said as much. He was being so very attentive, doing so much for Beth's comfort, that this dinner party was proving rather less of a trial than she had feared. Where the other guests were concerned, at least. With Jonathan himself, it was much more difficult—conversation, and compliments, and touching.

There had been too much dangerous touching.

• • • •

It had taken Jon longer than he expected to lure the gentlemen away from the decanters. Predictably, Sir Bertram Fitzherbert had been the worst. He insisted on proposing toast after toast, on ever more ridiculous subjects, culminating with the hunter he had recently bought. That had been the final straw and too much for even the rector's good nature.

As host, Jon brought up the rear when they mounted the stairs. Sir Bertram, in the lead, was definitely swaying. With luck, he would drop into a comfortable chair and fall asleep. That was certainly better than leering at the ladies and repeating the kind of suggestive remarks he had made over his port. It was also the best that Jon dared to hope for. The Fitzherberts were truly a disgrace to their class. Jon's firm intention was never to permit them to cross his threshold again.

He dawdled on the stairs, reluctant to join the noisy, self-satisfied group above. In half an hour or so, the guests for the evening party would arrive to swell the numbers to more than

104

thirty. There would be several younger ladies and gentlemen among them, so the noise level was bound to grow even worse. That prospect irked him greatly. He had endured too much horrendous noise in the last few years.

He needed peace. And peace of mind.

Yes, of course. *That* was what he longed for. Now, he understood. He wanted the comfort of a home of his own, a place where he could build his life again. Perhaps there could even be a gentle, smiling wife who would understand and share his desire—his need—for a calm, quiet refuge? A woman of principle who would do good in his name?

He did not require love, or passion. In his experience, they did not exist. Even if they had been attainable, they were not for a man of his class. Love gave a woman power she should never be permitted to have. But a comfortable room, a glowing fire, a patient partner sitting opposite, and children playing at their feet. Was that so much to ask? Surely he could find such a restful woman, such a companion, somewhere in the Upper Ten Thousand?

His decision was made without a qualm. As if he had always known what he should do. He would remain here at Fratcombe for a little longer, restoring his strength of mind in the quiet of his park. He would be able to enjoy his own company, now that he knew what he wanted from life. It was all remarkably simple.

Soon he would begin searching the *ton* for a placid, restful bride.

He took a couple of deep breaths, relishing these moments of quiet on the deserted stairway. Now that he knew his own mind, he could endure the hubbub, however bad it became. He straightened his shoulders and continued up to the drawing room.

The relative hush surprised him. He had expected chatter and laughter, but there was neither. He was shocked to see that Mrs Aubrey was sitting at the open instrument and Beth was standing next to it, looking a little flushed. It seemed they had only just finished performing. Beth must have been singing. But how could that be? She had no memory of what had gone before. How could she possibly remember music? Or how to sing?

"Bravo, my dear." That was the rector. The guests began to clap. Even Lady Fitzherbert was applauding, though without much enthusiasm.

What on earth had Jon missed?

He tried to slide into the room without being noticed, but he did not succeed. The rector came across and clapped him on the shoulder. "A host's duties are never done, eh? Such a pity you missed Beth's song."

"Perhaps, if I asked her, Miss Aubrey would sing another?" Jon had not meant to say any such thing, but the words were out now, and sounding very particular. He cursed his unruly tongue. In that same instant, he caught an exchange of knowing glances between Lady Fitzherbert and her husband. That confounded woman would make mischief if she could. Jon fervently hoped it was not too late to recover the situation. From now on, he would be wise to ensure his relationship with Beth was a model of propriety, especially in public. After all, that was the fact of the case, was it not?

Of course it was.

He found himself waiting by the door to see what would happen next. There was a lingering stillness, an atmosphere that he could not quite account for. He felt as if he were intruding into a private realm, and was there only on sufferance, even in his own house. The rector spoke quietly to his wife, and then to Beth. At first, she looked rather embarrassed, but she nodded at last and began to confer with Mrs Aubrey in a low voice. The rector was beaming as he resumed his seat.

She would sing again. In response to Jon's too particular request.

He decided to remain where he was, detached, and as far as possible from the performers. He leaned against the door jamb and let his head fall back on to the wood so that he was gazing at the ceiling. His guests might assume he had had too much wine, but he did not care. He did not want to be near any of them while Beth sang. He did not want to have to look at their hypocritical faces, either.

At the first notes of the accompaniment, he allowed his eyes to drift closed. It was not a piece he recognised, but it was gentle, and soothing. Mrs Aubrey had chosen well for Jon's mood.

Beth had not forgotten how to sing. Perhaps one never did? She had the voice of an angel, sweet and caressing. Jon felt the music rippling through his body like a cleansing cascade, washing away his troubles and leaving him refreshed. And consoled.

Consoled?

He did not understand it, yet it was true. Through her song, he was finding a degree of peace that had been lost to him for years.

Chapter Thirteen

JON GROANED ALOUD AND forced his eyes open. He was drenched in sweat, as usual, but he was accustomed to that now. He dragged his pillows back into place and pushed himself upright. The chill night air raised gooseflesh on his naked torso as he reached for his tinder box.

By the light of his candle, he checked the time. Nearly four o'clock. Little more than an hour till dawn and blessed daylight. Anything was better than the dark, and the ghosts it brought.

He would not think about them. Nor would he sleep again. In sleep, he too often fell prey to emotions he could not control. It was laughable, really. All those years when his father had been trying to school him to be cold and calculating and distant. The old man thought he had succeeded, too. Even Jon thought he had succeeded. But he had not reckoned with the ghosts.

He must not give in to such weakness. Cross with himself, he set the bedclothes to rights and lay back, hands clasped behind his head, staring up at the silken bed canopy and forcing his mind to go over the evening's events, to focus on images he could control. He was quite proud of what he had done to the upstart baronet and his wife. The Fitzherberts would know their place in future. And they would not dare to cut Beth again, he was certain. The Aubreys might not approve of Jon's methods, but they would surely approve of the result. Jon had done it for them, because of the immense debt he owed them.

He had *not* done it for Beth Aubrey. Indeed, he had barely thought of her until a few hours ago. Not as a woman, at least. She had been a foundling, a possible fraud, and a source of irritation to his ordered life.

It was impossible to think of her in those terms any more. Her memory loss must be real; he was convinced of it. Besides, she was beautiful, and desirable, and when she sang…

He could not fathom his reaction to her singing. It had been as soothing as waves on the sea shore, gently caressing the sand. Sadly, the effect had not lasted long enough. He might have felt peace and consolation in his drawing room, but here in the darkness of his bedchamber, nothing had changed.

That reminded him, uncomfortably, of his need for a woman in his bed. He had been celibate since his return from Spain. At first, even the thought of coupling had disgusted him, but now, with the passage of time, he was becoming whole again, as his thoroughly masculine reaction to Beth's ravishing appearance had proved. Unfortunately, she was the adopted daughter of the people he admired most in the world. It was shameful to want to bed her.

He forced himself to go logically through the facts of her case. He had rescued her last Christmas, and deposited her with the Aubreys like a half-drowned kitten. She had no memory of her past life, but she was certainly a lady—last night's dinner had proved that, even by Jon's exacting standards—and almost on a par with the Aubreys for generosity of spirit. She had precious little standing in life, but she cared for those who were even worse off than she was.

He must not lust after her as if she were a lightskirt. It would be dishonourable to debauch a lady, especially one who was in the care of people who trusted him. His options were stark: keep away, or marry her.

Where on earth had *that* thought come from? The Earl of Portbury could not possibly marry a woman with no past and no family. It was unthinkable, no matter how desirable the female. Nor could she become his mistress. So she could not be anything at all.

Perhaps she could be a friend?

That subversive thought came as a shock. Friendship led to attachment, and attachment was dangerous. And yet... And yet something might be possible, provided he could behave like a gentleman. The answer to misplaced desire was to keep his distance from Beth Aubrey. If he avoided her for a while, the urge would subside. That was the answer. Perfectly logical.

He would spend a week or two alone, supervising improvements to his estate. Hard work would divert his mind and tire his body. Then he would invite the Aubreys, and Miss Beth, to spend the day at Fratcombe Manor. He would treat her as a guest and prove to himself, in the process, that his hard-earned lessons in detachment still held sway. His father had surely been right. A nobleman had to be cold and unemotional; his position required it. Feelings led to weakness that would always be exploited. Jon had buried them all, long ago.

Outside in the courtyard, a dog barked.

It sounded exactly like Caesar. Horrified, Jon screwed up his eyes against the memory. It was not buried after all. His father, the gun, the boy and his beloved dog. A gundog that was gun shy. There had to be a test, his father had said. If Caesar was gun shy, he must be shot so that he could not breed. The first barrel had proved it beyond doubt. Caesar had been shivering with fear. The second barrel had ended his life. Jon, at ten years old, had been forced to pull the trigger. And then to fetch a shovel and bury his best friend. He had never had another.

The Aubreys were friends, surely?

No. The Aubreys treated him almost like a son—and they called each other "friends"—but Jon had never granted them the intimacy of true friendship. They knew how much he had mourned for his dead brother, but they knew nothing else. Once Jon became his father's heir, he had never confided in anyone. The burdens of his childhood and his marriage were his to bear. As were the horrors of war. He would bear them alone.

• • • •

"Forgive me, Miss Aubrey, but I am curious. You have no memory of your life before you came to Lower Fratcombe and yet you do remember how to sing. Quite beautifully, too. How does that come about?"

They were in company again for the first time since his dinner party in her honour. In the intervening two weeks, they had not exchanged a single word. She had thought about him, dreamt about him constantly, but since he seemed determined to maintain a certain distance, she had complied. At church, they had merely bowed. But now, walking across his park, the first thing he did was to question her about her singing?

Beth sensed increasing suspicion. Jonathan was wondering whether her lack of memory was a fraud. Deep hurt settled in her gut, where it began to eat away at the fragile self-esteem she had worked so hard to build. He had lauded her in public, at that dinner. Now, in private, he was set on cutting her down. She had been wrong to hope he trusted her. He was not her champion at all.

He was waiting for her answer. He looked implacable. Like an inquisitor.

"I cannot explain it. I must have been taught, I suppose, at some time in my past life. L–like learning to read. Or to write. I can still do both of those, but I have no memory of how or when I learned. You do not find it strange that I can read and write. Why should singing be different? It is simply one more basic skill." When he still looked doubtful, her pent-up feelings overcame her and she rounded on him. "I see that you do not believe me, my lord. That being so, I shall relieve you of my presence."

She turned on her heel and began to march back towards the Manor and the safety of the Aubreys' company. She could see them in the distance, strolling contentedly around the flower garden by the house. She would join them. Unlike Jonathan, they did not doubt her honesty.

She had gone barely half a dozen steps when he caught her by the arm and forced her to stop. His fingers were almost biting into her flesh through her fine Norwich shawl. She froze, refusing to turn to look at him. "Please release me, sir," she hissed. How could he do such a thing? This—their very first touch since the party—was neither friendly nor gentle. This was nothing like the touch she had longed for. She needed to get away from him. In a moment, her head would start to pound.

He relaxed his grip a little, but he did not let her go until he had moved to stand directly in front of her, blocking her path. Then he dropped his hand. "I apologise, ma'am, both for my words and for my actions a moment ago. It was not my intention to insult you." He raised his hand and stood gazing down at his cupped fingers as if they belonged to someone else, as if they had chosen, of their own volition, to seize Beth so roughly. After a moment, he shrugged and dropped his arm. He seemed perplexed.

She could not begin to understand him. He had been so intent on using that party to restore her to her rightful place in society, but then he had spent two whole weeks practically ignoring her. The change dated, she realised with a start, from the moment he had heard her sing. Without a shred of evidence, he had apparently concluded, there and then, that she was a fraud. And to be shunned.

Had he invited Beth and the Aubreys to visit the Manor this afternoon so that he could question her in private? She had assumed, naively, that it was a kindness to the Aubreys, because the sun was shining for the first time in a fortnight. Was he so very devious?

"Miss Aubrey." His voice was low, almost inaudible.

Beth was staring at the lush grass beneath her boots and refusing to look at him. She dared not think about him, either, lest her body betray her yet again. She focused instead on the salutary effect of two weeks of rain on the growth of grass.

"I will escort you back to the house if that is your wish, ma'am. But may I not tempt you to walk with me as far as the lake? You must be feeling the want of exercise after so many days of rain. I admit I do myself." He paused. His voice softened even more. "May we not call a truce?"

It was a real apology this time, not mere words, Beth decided. She raised her head and looked into his face. His eyes were troubled and he was frowning. Conscience, perhaps? Well, she would show him that she was not to be cowed, no matter what he might say of her. She was not such a poor creature. "If you continue to frown so blackly at me, sir, I shall not accept your escort at all." He blinked in surprise, but his frown disappeared on the instant. That made her smile. "Much better. I accept your offer of a truce. Let us talk of nothing in the past, neither mine nor yours. Shall we agree on that?"

A fleeting shadow crossed his face. Then he, too, smiled. "I am only now coming to understand how wise you are, ma'am. Will you allow me to say that I have missed our conversations these last weeks? You have such a refreshing way of seeing the world."

Beth felt herself beginning to blush. That would not do at all. "At this precise moment, sir," she replied a little tartly, "I should like to be refreshed by walking up to your lake so that we may discuss the, er, the—" she scanned the rolling parkland, desperate to light on an innocent topic of conversation "—the rearing of sheep," she finished triumphantly.

He threw back his head and laughed heartily.

Beth found herself laughing, too. Her absurd remark had served to break the increasing tension between them.

He offered Beth his arm. He was still grinning. "Let us walk then, ma'am, and I shall do my best to enlighten you on the subject of, er, sheep." When Beth hesitated a little, wary of his touch, he took her arm—gently this time—and tucked it into his. "There. That is much better."

To her surprise, it was. For once, her insides were not churning simply because her fingers were on his arm. She refused to let herself dwell on the strength of the muscles beneath that elegant sleeve. She would concentrate solely on the scenery. Surely she had enough self-control for that?

They began to walk towards the distant lake. Beth noticed that he was matching his stride to hers. He was again the considerate companion.

He managed a couple of extremely general sentences about the size of his flock. "And of course, warm weather and rain make the grass grow strongly which is, in turn, good for the sheep. More wool and more meat."

Beth waited politely for him to continue. He did not. They walked on for another twenty yards. Still nothing. Now it was Beth's turn to burst out laughing. "Have you imparted the full extent of your knowledge of sheep, sir? That they do better when they have good grass to eat?" She could not stop laughing. "I do believe that the five year olds in my schoolroom could have told me that."

He shook his head in mock contrition. "Sadly, I spent too much of my youth dreaming about the army. I was not the heir, you see, so there was no point in my learning to manage the estates. I—"

Beth stopped him by the simple expedient of laying her free hand on his arm. "Nothing of the past," she said softly. Then, after a short pause, she began brightly, "Tell me, sir, do you have many trout in your lake?" She waved her free hand in the general direction of the water. It was much safer than leaving all her fingers in contact with his warm, tempting flesh.

It seemed she had lit on a subject he did understand. He spoke at some length about his love of fishing and of the fine specimens that had been taken from the lake over the years. "Do you fish, Miss Beth? Many ladies do."

"I–I don't know." There was no point in racking her brains over it. If there was a memory, it would refuse to show itself, as always. Perhaps, if he put a rod in her hand, she would do it automatically? Perhaps the body remembered such things all by itself, like writing or singing?

He laid his free hand over hers for a moment in a brief gesture of reassurance. "Forgive me. That was clumsy of me. And in breach of our agreement, besides. But if you would like to learn to fish, I should be more than happy to teach you. I—" He stopped dead, struck by some sudden thought. "Ah, no. Not this year. What a pity."

The shock of his words numbed her senses as surely as a cascade of icy water. He must be planning to leave again soon. She was going to lose even those brief chances to feast her eyes on him. Beth's throat was suddenly too tight for speech. Her silver-armoured knight had delivered her to safety and

114

now he was about to ride off in search of new adventures, perhaps to rescue some other lady in distress.

If there had been anguish in her face, he had not noticed it, for he continued, as though thinking aloud, "Riding, now, is a different matter. That can be enjoyed all year round. I wonder, Miss Aubrey, if you ride? No, do not tell me that you do not know. Tell me instead that you are willing to give it a try. Let me mount you on my most biddable mare and then we shall both see whether you know what you are doing in the saddle."

"I—"

"If you do, then we may ride around the park together. What say you, ma'am?"

Was he planning to leave, or was he not? The question was hammering at Beth's brain, forcing out all other notions. She shook her head, trying to clear the fog of confusion.

"Oh." His voice sounded flat. Was he disappointed? "I assure you there is nothing improper in my proposal. I would ensure we were accompanied by a groom at all times."

He had misunderstood her. No wonder, for she herself was mightily confused. "I did not mean— I beg your pardon, my lord, I was not refusing your offer, merely..." She closed her mouth firmly. This was no time for gabbling like an excited schoolchild. She took a deep breath. "I do not know whether I have ever learned to ride, and I agree that it could be, um, interesting to find out. However, I cannot accept your assurance that your proposal is not improper. Perhaps you will allow me to take Mrs Aubrey's opinion on that before I decide?"

He was having trouble concealing his smile. "Whatever else your memory may conceal from you, ma'am, your sense of propriety is very much to the fore."

Beth was not at all sure that that was a compliment. Before she could work it out, he continued, "And, if you will permit me, I shall take it upon myself to persuade Mrs Aubrey to chaperon you. I am sure she will agree that the exercise would be beneficial."

Beth had no choice. She nodded her agreement and fixed her eyes on the smooth water of the lake. Something disturbed the glassy surface. Ripples were spreading from a point about thirty yards from the bank. "Oh, is that a trout?"

"Possibly." He shrugged his shoulders.

"I am surprised at your reaction. You said you were a keen fisherman, sir. Will you not be fetching your rod in order to catch him?" He smiled down at her then. Rather indulgently, she fancied, as if he were dealing with a small and ignorant child. Temper overcame her earlier turmoil. She straightened her shoulders and glared at him. "May I ask why you are laughing at me, my lord?"

He tried to school his features into a serious expression but he failed. He *was* laughing at her. Beth wrenched her arm from his and spun round so that she was presenting Jonathan with her back. She would rather not talk to him at all if this was how she was to be treated.

"If that is a trout, ma'am, it will be a miracle. No laughing matter, in truth. In my absence, the herons have had all the fish. I need to restock."

She let out a long breath. "Oh." The light dawned. She turned round to face him again. "So that explains why you said— Um."

One day she would learn to think before she opened her mouth. She was careful and measured with everyone else. So why was it that she behaved like a fool with Jonathan? And only with him? From now on, she must keep her emotions under the strictest control.

He had stopped laughing. Perhaps he had recognised her embarrassment? He held out his hand invitingly. "Now that we are both agreed on the subject of riding and fishing—"

"And sheep," Beth put in pertly, recovering a little of her composure and determined not to let him best her again.

"—and sheep," he agreed with a smile that could only be described as slightly sheepish, "I suggest that we return to the house to consult Mrs Aubrey on the subject of propriety. Will you take my arm again, Miss Beth?"

• • • •

Jon relaxed into the hot water and closed his eyes. It had been a perfect day. He could not remember when he had last enjoyed himself so much. The simplest pleasures were certainly the best, and riding round his own park, in company with Beth Aubrey, was most definitely a pleasure.

She might not know how to fish, though until they tried it, there was no way of knowing that for certain, but she had certainly been taught to ride. Well taught, too. It had been obvious from the first moment he had thrown her up into Polly's saddle. She sat tall and secure, controlling the old mare easily with whip and heel.

She was definitely a lady. Well educated, cultured, musical, good in the saddle. So who on earth was she? And why was it that no one was searching for her? She had spent the best part of a year at the Fratcombe rectory and there had been not the slightest hint of who she was or where she came from.

A mystery. A truly baffling mystery.

He began to soap his limbs. Was Beth doing the same at this very moment? Her muscles must be aching after riding for so long. Mrs Aubrey had smiled benignly and waved them off into the park, with the obligatory groom trotting behind. It had been such a glorious, liberating day that Jon had allowed his pleasure in her company to overcome his common sense. He knew perfectly well that, if Beth rode too long, she would suffer for it. She had made no complaint, of course. She was too much the lady to do so. And he fancied that she had been enjoying Jon's company too much to call a halt.

He threw the soap into the water in disgust. What a coxcomb he was becoming. Beth Aubrey was his lady guest, nothing more. If she had been enjoying his company as they rode together, it was not to be wondered at, for she had precious little recreation time. She occasionally visited the Miss Alleyns and Miss Grantley, but apart from that, she spent her time as unpaid schoolmistress to the village and unpaid helper for all Mrs Aubrey's charity projects. Beth would maintain that she was more than content, that she was merely repaying the Aubreys' generosity, but Jon was far from convinced. She was a young woman still, and she should have at least a little time to herself to enjoy a young woman's pleasures. Such as riding.

With him?

He was suddenly glad that he was leaving Fratcombe in a few days, for Beth Aubrey was much too tempting. He could not take her riding again, much as he might wish to. That would start the worst kind of gossip. However, since he was an acknowledged friend of the Aubreys, he could make provision for Beth to ride the old mare in his absence. His grooms had little enough to do. He would instruct them to make the mare ready every day and to accompany Miss Aubrey whenever she wished to ride out. She would have free rein over the whole of his park which was the least he could do. Once her muscles were used to riding regularly, she would enjoy the exercise, he was sure. And she would have no need of Jon's company.

He realised, with a start, that he would miss her. With Beth Aubrey, he did not have to mind his tongue. Indeed, she seemed to understand what he was going to say before his words were out. They laughed together. They talked of anything and everything, without restraint. And they shared the simple joys of nature and fresh air, and a love of the land. It was a pity Beth was not a man. A man could perhaps have become a friend.

He would miss her company, but it was wise, he knew, to avoid her. He had assumed that a little distance would subdue his desire to possess her delectable body. It had not. And now, in addition to desire, there was something more, something deeper—admiration, and liking, also.

With a groan, he dug into the cooling water for the soap and began to scrub at his legs.

• • • •

"I've brought your hot water, Miss Beth." It was Hetty, carrying the large brass can across to the dressing table.

"Goodness, I have overslept. How could I have—?" Beth made to sit up and throw back the covers. "Argh!" She could hardly move. Every single muscle was shrieking with pain. With a supreme effort, she rolled on to her side and forced her legs out of the bedclothes so that she could push herself up with her hands. "Good grief. I feel as if someone has pounded me all over with a–a cricket bat."

Hetty set the can down and came across to help Beth to stand. "I did warn you, miss, but you wouldn't listen. You should have had a long hot bath and some of that embarkation rubbed into your muscles."

Beth laughed. She stopped pretty sharply though, for it hurt. "Embrocation, Hetty."

"Whatever. You shouldn't have gone riding for so long, miss, when you're not used to it. No, not even at his lordship's invitation. He should have known better, an' all." Of late, Hetty had become extremely forthright with Beth. But Beth valued the maid too much to correct her ready tongue.

"Besides, there ain't no point in you learning to ride all over again, when you'll be stopping just as quick. You can't go riding out on your own, after all, can you? You'll have had all this pain for no gain, as they say." Hetty swung Beth's wrapper over her shoulders and helped her into it.

Beth winced. She had forgotten that Jonathan would be leaving soon to go to one of his other estates. He had not said which one. He had several, he had explained, and all of them needed the master's careful supervision. That was his duty as earl.

He took his duties seriously, of course. But he had a lighter side, too, and she was glad to have discovered it. He was not like Sir Lancelot at all. Moreover, she did not want him to be. She wanted him to be a friend, the kind of person with whom she could share everyday pleasures like riding out with the sun on her back, or walking for miles across lush meadows and shady country paths. The kind of friend who would share her wit, who could tease her until she was doubled up with laughter, and who could subside into easy silence when they were both content to commune with nature and their own thoughts. One day, perhaps, they might come to be all those things together. She must not hope, or dream, of anything more.

She would miss him when he left, but friends parted. It was the way of the world.

"The groom said as he's leaving Fratcombe on Monday morning."

"Monday?" Beth choked and began to cough, in an attempt to cover up her shock. Monday? That was the day after tomorrow. Was she to see him at church and then never again?

Hetty poured a glass of water and handed it to Beth, who gulped it greedily.

"Well, Sam—that's the groom, miss—said it would definitely be Monday. Unless his lordship changes his mind again."

"Again?" Beth croaked.

"Aye. Apparently he were all set to leave last week, but decided he wanted to stay on a bit. To enjoy the fine weather and the peace, Sam said."

"That sounds rather strange. Are you sure, Hetty?"

"Oh, yes, miss. When he's at his main estate, it's just one long round of parties and entertainments, Sam says, with house guests all the time. Sam reckons it's because his lordship's mama is determined to get him married off again, so she fills the house with pretty girls. Can't see it m'self. I'd say his lordship is too much his own man to be governed by his mama, or any other lady. Don't you think so, Miss Beth?"

Beth swallowed the rest of her water and muttered something that could have been agreement. Hetty might be right about Jonathan's character, but the maid did not understand the demands of his position in society. Here at Fratcombe, he behaved like a simple country squire. He was attentive to the Aubreys and exceedingly kind to the rector's adopted daughter. But he was a man of rank. He had been a widower for a considerable time. He had no son. He would not need his mother's urging to understand that it was high time he married again and set up his nursery. No doubt he was returning to King's Portbury, to look over yet more candidates to be his new countess.

So much for friendship, and simple shared pleasures.

Chapter Fourteen

FRATCOMBE MANOR HAD BEEN a peaceful refuge but Lorrington was utter bliss. Jon had forgotten how wild and remote it was here. George had never visited, probably because the Lorrington estate was too poor to provide him with any ready money. And the place was blessedly free of women, too, for there were no gentry families for miles. Jon was spared the plaguey females that always bedevilled him at King's Portbury.

After two weeks of riding the land and speaking to all his tenants, Jon was ashamed of what he had allowed to happen here. It was his smallest estate, to be sure, but he had failed in his duty to those who depended on him. Their farms were ramshackle and their livestock was scrawny, barely surviving on the thin hill land. There was some good land, but it was not productive, for the tenant farmers had no ready cash for seed or new tools. He would change all that. Some of the surplus from King's Portbury would be invested here. Lorrington would never be rich, but his people's lives would be improved. He was determined on that.

Spain had changed him. War had changed him. Among his soldiers, there had been men from the land, good men who had taken the king's shilling because their families could not afford to feed another mouth. He had seen those men fight, and he had seen some of them die. And in the depths of the Spanish winter, he had seen what hunger could do to a man. He would not allow it to touch any of his lands. Never again.

It was a matter of honour, for those who had died. And a matter of duty.

He would discharge his duty here at Lorrington and then he would take a wife. He had delayed for long enough now. There must be no more excuses. Surely there was one lady of rank, somewhere, who was not simply out for herself, simpering and blushing in her efforts to snare a rich husband?

If such a one existed, he had not yet set eyes on her.

He sighed and reached forward to run his gloved hand over his horse's glossy neck. As far as he could tell, debutantes were all the same. It was enough to give a man permanent indigestion. Why could none of them be like Beth Aubrey?

He swore aloud. She was intruding again. He kicked his horse into a gallop and began to race across the grass to the foot of the gorse-covered hill. He would make his way to the top for a final check of the Lorrington estate. He might see something he had missed, some out-of-the-way farmstead where the children were barefoot or unable to go to school. It was his duty—he was happy to accept that now—to ensure that all the children on his estates had a better chance in life.

That reminded him that he had promised Miss Aubrey he would do something for that young protégé of hers. Peter, was it?

Yes, Peter. Jon would speak to his agent about the child as soon as he got back to Fratcombe. He did not want to see the disappointment in Beth's fine eyes if she discovered that he had failed to live up to his promises. Why had she not challenged him on it before he left?

Because she trusted him to keep his word. She trusted him, and confided in him, as a friend.

He could not return that trust—he confided in no one apart from his cousins, Ned and Luke, both still fighting in Spain— but he could rely on her word. He knew that, without a shadow of a doubt, because of the remarkable person she was.

He would rather spend an hour with her than whole weeks among the carp and cackle of the ladies of the *ton*. Unlike them, Beth was an eminently restful woman, now he came to think about it. Had he been so taken with her luscious curves that he had failed to see that? And value it?

He hauled his horse to a stand and threw himself out of the saddle so that he could make the rest of the steep climb on foot. Beth was the only woman in England who came near to being the kind of wife he wanted, and needed. Yet she was a woman he could not have. Why was fate so determined to laugh in his face?

He plodded on. Somewhere in the back of his mind, a beautiful voice began to sing, softly at first, and then more clearly, so that the bitter fury of his thoughts was calmed. It was Beth Aubrey's voice, as if from far away. And it consoled him.

Why could he not marry her?

Because he was the Earl of Portbury and his duty required him to marry a lady of rank.

Duty. It had driven him for years, but what had it brought him, apart from hardship and heartache? Surely a man could be more than the sum of his duties? Jon was a man of rank and wealth. An earl. An earl did not need to play by the rules of lesser mortals. Nor did he have to pay heed to anyone else's opinion. Not even his dead father's. Not any more. An earl could decide for himself where his duty—and his own best interests—lay.

Jon's decision was made. He would call at the rectory as soon as he was back at Fratcombe Manor.

• • • •

Beth was glad when her solo ended and she could resume her place in the rectory pew. Glad, too, that Jonathan had not returned, to hear her sing and to wonder yet again if her memory loss was some kind of fraud.

If only it were. Then she might have some certainty about who she was. There were those dreams—nightmares, sometimes—in which she saw bits and pieces of memories, of places, even of people, but none of it made any sense at all when she woke up.

But last night's dream had not been like that. It had been full of colour and scent, almost more vivid than life itself. Because of him. Because of Jonathan. She had been dreaming about Jonathan.

"Let us pray." The rector's voice recalled Beth to her devotions. She knelt and began to pray, fervently, for deliverance from the man who was haunting her. The man she had not dared even to address as her *friend*.

The service passed more quickly than usual. Beth knew she had made all the responses, though she could remember none of it. But it was over. The rector was standing in his normal place outside the door, exchanging kind words with everyone, asking after missing parishioners, the sick and the old. From inside the church, he was only a dark silhouette. Beth watched from the far end of the aisle, waiting for her turn to leave. He was such a good man. No wonder the whole district loved him.

"I think we may go now, Beth, dear," Mrs Aubrey said at last, nodding towards the empty doorway. "I wonder if the rector has invited any guests?" she added, as an afterthought. After divine service, he made a habit of inviting needy souls to eat in the rectory kitchen. It was part of God's charitable purpose, he always said, and his wife did not disagree.

For once, there seemed to be no unexpected guests waiting around when the two ladies emerged, though it was difficult to see clearly. Beth blinked and screwed up her eyes against the sudden dazzle. It had been overcast when they went into church, but now the sky was a bright, clear blue and the slight breeze was warm from the early autumn sunshine, contrasting with the cool airiness from which they had come. Beth let her shawl drop down her back, closed her eyes and turned her face up into the warmth.

"Beautiful, is it not?"

That was not the rector's voice. Jonathan had returned.

Beth stepped back so quickly that she almost tripped over her skirts.

A strong arm held her up. "You must take more care, Miss Aubrey, or you will fall. Wait until your eyes are accustomed to the light before you start prancing about."

He was still holding her arm. She could feel the strength of his fingers through her muslin sleeve. And the warmth of his body—

"Miss Aubrey? Is anything amiss?"

124

She forced herself to turn to look at him. Jonathan. The face from her dreams. This time, he was not surrounded by vibrant colour but starkly outlined against the venerable grey stones of the church. And still he was beautiful.

"Lord Portbury," she said softly, trying to withdraw her arm from his clasp without seeming to struggle. "We did not look to see you in Fratcombe again so soon." That sounded suitably polite. And distant, too.

"I'm afraid I arrived too late to attend divine service this morning. I was apologising to the rector, but he will have none of it."

"Do you tell me, Jonathan, that you have been travelling on the Sabbath?" Mrs Aubrey wagged a finger at him. "Fie on you, sir. I hope the rector has reproved you soundly."

"Unfortunately not, ma'am." He was grinning like a naughty schoolboy.

"No, indeed," the rector put in, "for what good would it do? But you may take him to task yourself, Caro. I have invited him home to dine with us."

• • • •

It was almost over. He must go soon, surely? He seemed to be taking an inordinate length of time to drink a single cup of coffee.

Beth concentrated on listening to the rector's words. And trying to avoid Jonathan's eyes.

At last, he rose from his place by the rector and crossed to the table where Beth sat over the tea and coffee pots. He was simply doing her the courtesy of returning his empty cup. Now, he must certainly go.

He seemed a little hesitant. He stood over Beth, but made no move to put down his cup. He half-turned to glance at Mrs Aubrey, and then back to Beth. His behaviour was most disconcerting, and it was making Beth's inner turmoil even worse. She had known and admired him as a decisive man. What had happened to him during his absence from Fratcombe?

The thought settled around her like a shroud. He was going to announce that he was about to marry again. Yes, that must be it. It was common knowledge in Fratcombe that his mother

125

had been inviting all the most eligible young ladies of the *ton* to visit King's Portbury. Even a duke's daughter, according to the lodge-keeper. Beth told herself it was only what he deserved. He had an ancient title and needed a wife of suitable rank. A duke's daughter would suit admirably.

Beth tensed her muscles, held her breath and waited for the words she was dreading. She was resolved that she would not betray, by the slightest blush or blink, that his news was a disappointment. For who was she, the supposed Elizabeth Aubrey, to believe she had any claim on such a man? She was, as he said, a foundling. A nobody. Not even high enough to be a friend.

"Mrs Aubrey, you and the rector have given me the friendliest possible welcome on my return, by inviting me to your table. I am truly grateful. But I wonder if I might impose on you even more? I should very much like to take a turn round your garden before I go back to the Manor."

What on earth is he talking about? Walking round the garden? At the beginning of October?

"I could not help but notice that some of your trees are looking very fine in their early autumn colours. Especially in the late afternoon light."

"I did not have you down as a garden lover, Jonathan," the rector said with a hint of laughter in his gentle voice. "But even if it be a recent conversion, I will not deny you." He made to rise. "My dear, would you—?"

Mrs Aubrey shook her head, settling herself more comfortably.

Jonathan quickly raised his hand. "Forgive me, sir, Mrs Aubrey, I did not mean to impose my whims on you. Pray do not disturb yourselves on my account."

The rector nodded and sank back gratefully into his seat. "I am sure Beth would welcome a chance to take a stroll, after sitting for so long listening to an old man prosing on." When Beth immediately began to protest, he shook his head firmly. "Come, come, my child, we cannot let our guest wander our shrubberies without escort. Spare my old bones, if you would be so good."

Beth knew she was about to lose. She threw one pleading glance at Mrs Aubrey, in hopes that the old lady would change her mind and accompany them, but Mrs Aubrey was gazing at the rector with concern.

"I am a little tired, Caro, that is all. Sunday is not a day of rest for the clergy, you know." He chuckled. "I am saving my strength for evensong."

Mrs Aubrey seemed to be reassured, for her features softened. She turned to Beth instead. "Do make sure you take a wrap with you, my dear. The afternoons soon grow chilly at this time of year."

Beth nodded and looked around for her shawl. She had had it earlier, but in the confusion of the moment, she could not remember where she had laid it down. Before she could move an inch, Jonathan came forward with it in his hands and stroked it round her shoulders without even asking leave. His touch was so caressing that her skin began to burn. Her mouth was suddenly too dry to say a word, even though she knew she ought to upbraid him for taking such a liberty.

He was smiling down at her. "Shall we, ma'am? Before the sun goes down and we lose the last of the warmth?"

She gave a tiny nod. It was the most she could manage. Together they strolled out through the French windows and into the garden.

They had gone the length of the shrubbery path before Beth forced herself to break the silence. "For a garden lover, sir, you are paying remarkably little attention to the turning trees." She had not meant it to sound like an accusation of bad faith, but it did. She could not help herself. She was barely in control.

His voice, when it came, was strained. "Miss Aubrey. Miss Beth. I was hoping for a moment's private conversation with you. My excuse was clumsy, I am afraid." He stopped dead. Beth had no choice but to do the same. He took a sideways step so that he was standing in front of her. The movement released her hand which she let fall, heavy and limp, to her side. "There are, er, things I need to say to you."

Beth's heart began to beat very fast. He was going to do her the courtesy of confiding his plans in private. That was

127

more than she had looked for. He really was treating her like a friend. A tiny spark of warmth flickered around her heart but quickly died. This friendship would be doused as easily as an uncertain flame.

He was gazing out over Beth's head towards the trees and the graveyard beyond, but he was focused on nothing. "I, er, I have decided that I must remarry. It is essential, given my position in society. There needs to be a Countess of Portbury. And, er—" He glanced down into Beth's face at that moment. She saw the hint of embarrassment in his eyes, though he was not blushing.

Beth's emotions might be in confusion, but she was not fool enough to mistake his meaning. He needed a wife, and then a son.

"I have considered carefully. I find I do not hold with these new-fangled notions of love." He was trying to sound matter of fact and uncaring. Perhaps, when it came to marriage, he was both of those? "I do not believe in such things. A man must choose a partner who suits him in every way—a lady who will grace his table and take charge of his household, a lady who will create a comfortable, restful home, a refuge where a man can take his ease."

A *refuge*? It was clearly of huge importance to Jonathan. Beth was not quite sure why that should be. Perhaps it was to do with his time in Spain? It was strange that such a strong man could seem so vulnerable.

He took a deep breath. It would be now. He was going to tell her the name of the lady he had chosen to share his peaceful refuge. "I can tell from your face that I am making a mull of this. Forgive me. It is not often a man puts such thoughts into words. I was trying only to describe, to set out what I seek. I would not, for the world, mislead you about my motives." Abruptly, he took both her hands in his. It was a gesture of kindness, the gesture of one friend to another. But now he was silent, waiting for her to speak.

Beth gulped. "I–I never doubted your intentions, sir," she said. It was a rather bald reassurance, but it was the most she could manage.

128

"No, you would not. You see the best in everything, and everyone."

Beth felt the beginnings of heat on her neck. Such a simple compliment, but she was blushing. He was still holding her hands in his. She looked down at them, just as he gave her fingers a tiny squeeze. That was a shock. Beth jerked her gaze up from their clasped hands to his face.

"Beth, will you do me the honour of becoming my wife?"

Her mouth fell open, but no words came out. Her head began to spin. Soon she was swaying on her feet. *I am going to faint. But I never faint.*

• • • •

Jon caught her by the shoulders as she staggered, and then he steered her to the bench beneath the massive beech. Its leaves were beginning to turn brown, but most of them still clung to the parent tree. He guided her onto the seat and unceremoniously pushed her head down between her knees. "I have shocked you. It was not my intention." He must give her a chance to recover.

After a few moments, she straightened. Her eyes were very wide, and very dark in her ashen face. "It is unkind of you to make a may-game of me, my lord." Her voice cracked. She looked away.

Heavens, she did not believe he meant those words, the most difficult for any man to utter. Jon had been standing over her, watching her, worrying. Now, he threw himself on to the seat beside her and seized both her hands. He was not about to let them go until he had received his answer.

"Beth, I value your good opinion far too much to do any such thing. We are friends, surely? Friends do not— Beth, I would never mock you. My proposal is utterly sincere. You are the most restful woman of my acquaintance. I know it is a rather bloodless union that I am offering you, but there must be honesty between us. I will not attempt to dupe you with false protestations of love. For you are not an empty-headed chit who takes her notions from the pages of the latest romantic novel. You are sensible, and practical. I had hoped that my offer would tempt you: a home of your own where you could be mistress; a proper station in society. It would give you certainty, Beth. You would have your rightful place. Will you have me?"

She jerked her hands out of his with a sound that could have been a strangled sob. She surged to her feet as if she were about to flee, but at the last moment, she turned back to him, holding up one small white hand to prevent him from rising. "There can be no certainty for me, my lord. I am nothing, nobody. I have no name but the one the Aubreys were kind enough to lend to me. I am no fit wife for any gentleman. And certainly *not* for the Earl of Portbury. It is wicked to suggest otherwise, but I will forgive your ill-conceived jest. Let us forget the words were ever spoken."

She had become as rigid as the beech trunk at Jon's back. He realised he had been clinging to a vision of his comfortable life with her. He had seen Beth there by the fireplace, sitting quietly opposite him, but he had never once considered that she might not share his longing for a peaceful refuge. In truth, he had not considered her at all. He scrutinised her features carefully now, for the first time in a long while. She was holding herself together by sheer force of will. She was affronted by his proposal, and deeply hurt. In a moment, she would regain enough strength to flee. Unless...

Ignoring her still outstretched hand, he stood up and put his arms around her. Since she did not believe a word he said, he had best try something other than words.

He kissed her.

It was Jon's first real kiss in a long time. He brushed his lips over hers, very lightly, unsure of how she might react. Her lips parted, and he felt the warmth of a tiny sigh on his skin, as if she had been waiting for his touch, holding her breath. And yet her response was hesitant, the response of an innocent girl. She did not have the way of kissing.

A strange feeling surged through Jon, an unfathomable mixture of pride and possession. He was almost sure that Beth Aubrey had never been kissed before. And yet she was trying to respond to him. Her head might be telling her that Jon's proposal was a wicked jest, but her warm body and her soft mouth wanted to reach for him. Jon stopped trying to analyse her reactions and gave himself up to the simple pleasure of

130

kissing her. He wrapped her even more snugly against his body and put a hand to the back of her head, holding her still so that he could explore. He feathered tiny kisses along her bottom lip. She tasted of coffee, and sweetness. He risked a bolder touch, putting the tip of his tongue to the tiny sighing gap between her lips. This time it was no sigh, but a groan he heard, from deep within her. That was too much.

He deepened the kiss. Now she truly did respond. Her hands slid up his chest and around his neck. She opened her lips to welcome him in. Desire swept through Jon's body. There could be something between them after all, more than mere companionship. They would sit restfully together by the fire, no doubt, but he fancied the getting of an heir could be pleasurable for them both.

Chapter Fifteen

IT WAS AS IF HER BODY WERE relaxing into a bath of warm, scented water, which lapped over her limbs and caressed her flesh. She was floating. Yet she had never been so alive. Her skin, all over—from her cheek to her throat to her breasts to her belly—was awake, reaching and yearning. She wanted him to touch her. Everywhere.

She drove her fingers into the thick hair at the back of his head and pushed her body closer into his embrace. She could feel the strength of him, held in check, restrained so as not to alarm her. But it was there, none the less, a warm, reassuring strength. She could feel that what had begun as a simple kiss was turning into something much more demanding. He desired her.

That sudden awareness brought her back to grim reality as surely as if he had scrubbed handfuls of snow on to her naked skin. She pulled her hands down to his chest and pushed hard, with balled fists. She tore her mouth from his. The moment her lips were free, she cried out. "No!"

The reaction was instantaneous. His hand had been in her hair, holding her steady for the exploration of his lips and tongue, but he did not try to restrain her. He dropped his hands to his sides and took a very deliberate step away from her.

Beth clasped her hands together very tightly. She refused to let them shake. "My lord, you—"

"Jonathan. My name is Jonathan." He did not move to close the space between them, but his gaze softened and the merest hint of a smile curved his lips as he looked down at Beth. "Jon," he said, in a deeper, warmer voice.

He was asking her to use his given name? She shook her head vehemently, trying to clear her thoughts. He had proposed. He *was* proposing. To her? And it seemed it was no jest, after all. She could not think straight. That kiss— Oh, heavens, that kiss had turned her bones to butter. Her body was burning hot and icy cold, all at once. She was quivering. Would she melt altogether? Or freeze?

"Beth?" He was uncertain, too. She could hear it in his voice. He raised his right hand, palm up, and offered it. "Beth, will you have me?"

She dared one look at his face, but she could not read his expression. Whatever his emotions, he was managing to conceal them. All she knew was that his proposal must be sincere. "It is impossible," she burst out. "You know it is."

He was standing as still as the statues in his park. His outstretched hand had not moved even a fraction.

"Oh, you ridiculous man." She let anger bury the hurt. "You must know it is impossible. You are the Earl of Portbury and I am nobody. I have no past, no family, not even a name. You insult me by suggesting you would take me to wife." That spurt of anger saved her. She was back in control. She was even managing to bury the delicious sensations that his kiss had brought to the surface and that had been threatening to overwhelm her. She would not think of those. She turned abruptly and began to march along the path towards the rectory. That was where her refuge lay. That was where she could be free of this torment.

He caught up to her after three paces. He did not touch her. If he had, she might have cried out, so tense were the feelings consuming her. No, he simply strode past her and planted himself like a rock on the path, as if a landslide had suddenly blocked the way. Heavy, impenetrable, dangerous. He was not smiling. He held up a hand, not an offering this time, but a command.

She stopped. She had no choice.

"You *would* have a name. My name. You would be the Countess of Portbury. My wife. Your position in society would be alongside mine. No one would dare to question that."

He was very sure. And absolutely wrong. "Of course they would," she retorted, trying to swallow the pain that was gripping her heart. "You have no idea what black deeds there may be in my past that led me to flee. Have you never thought that my memory is shuttered because of what lies hidden there? The Earl of Portbury cannot risk discovering that his wife is a fugitive. Or worse. What would society say then?"

"No one would dare to accuse my wife of *anything*," he retorted, with a dismissive wave of his hand.

His tone was so arrogant that Beth was stunned into silence. He frowned down at her for a moment, and then said, in a more thoughtful voice, "You are a truly fine woman, Beth. If you fled, it was from someone else's wickedness, not your own. I believe— No, I know that to be true. No one would dare to suggest otherwise."

"Of course they would," she said again, though less forcefully. "They would say that the Earl of Portbury had taken leave of his senses, in marrying such a woman. They would obey the outward forms, no doubt, but the gossip, the sly, sneering comments, would be made at every turn. Not only about me, but also about *you*. Can you not understand that, Jonatha—? My lord?" She winced. His stony expression had softened at the sound of his given name. The moment she retracted it, he had begun to frown again.

"I understand no such thing. What's more, I would not care a jot about society gossip. I do not seek to marry for society's sake, but for my own. I do not seek to cut a fine figure in this world of theirs. I do not give a fig for that. And I had thought that you would not, either. Beth? Beth, do you care for such things? I thought you would wish to live retired from society, as I do. Let the tabbies say what they will of us. We have no need of them, and their stiff-rumped opinions. Our life together will be peaceful, and content. As far from society as we wish to be. It is a delightful prospect, is it not?"

It was more than delightful. It would be paradise. But she could not possibly answer with the truth.

Nor could she lie. She could only stare at him.

He cleared his throat. "I can see that I have shocked you with my proposal. It is no wonder, for you are a gently-bred lady."

At that, her head came up even more. He did not know— He *could* not know anything about her upbringing. She herself did not know.

"But I beg you to understand that my proposal is sincerely meant. You would do me the utmost honour if you accepted me. Will you not at least take a little time, a day, to consider what I am offering?" He took half a step towards her. "Please, Beth. Do at least consider."

She felt an almost overpowering urge to raise her fingers to his face, to stroke away the tension that was so evident in his frown and in his narrowed eyes. She clasped her hands together once again, forbidding them to stray.

She had to stop him, to save him. She must not let her feelings overcome her principles. She fixed her gaze on the ground at her feet, knowing she dare not look at him for this. "I suggest that *you* consider, my lord. Has it not occurred to you that you are proposing to a woman who may be married already?"

• • • •

She had planted him a facer.

Jon had been boxing for too many years to give in because he had been floored once. He refused to quit, especially now that his goal had suddenly become so much more important.

"Look at me, Beth," he said, as gently as he could, reaching for her tightly clasped hands. She tensed for a moment, but then she yielded enough for Jon to take them in his. He did not attempt to prise her hands apart. He simply lifted them to his lips and dropped a featherlight kiss on her fingers. She was still staring at the ground, however. She seemed determined to resist him. Was she afraid, perhaps? "There is no need to be anxious. I know you for a strong woman who is afraid of nothing, and no one. I am your friend, Beth. Please look at me."

It seemed the word "friend" was able to reach her, where his touch had not. Without moving her hands in his, she slowly raised her head and her gaze joined with his. She was

135

as white as her tucker; her eyes were huge and dark in her pale face. She made no move to speak, but she did not need to, for her emotions were written in her brilliant eyes. His proposal had injured her. Even if she now accepted that Jon was not mocking her, she was certainly not convinced that there was any kind of a future for them as man and wife. She thought Jon was too high, and she—a woman with a shadowy past and no memory—was much too low.

"I can assure you, Beth, that you are wrong about marriage."

"I–I know I am not wrong about this one. It is impossible."

"I understand your reluctance, but I cannot agree with you. Will you allow me to explain why?" He drew her arm into his—she had stopped resisting, he was glad to see—and escorted her back to the bench under the beech tree. He had a chance now, though perhaps not for long. He was going to have to be truly silver-tongued, for she was clearly set against him.

He took his seat beside her, still holding her hand tucked into his arm, but he took care not to sit too close. "I must ask you first, Beth, if you still think I am trying to play a base trick on you with my proposal?" He needed to know that she would listen.

She coloured a little and shook her head.

"Good. That is a start." He patted her hand, with the lightest of touches. It was too intimate, it seemed, for she flinched. He felt the tightening of her muscles through the layers of clothing. He let his free arm drop back to his side. One more false move and she might run.

"You think you may already be married. I can see why you would think that. For a lady, it is a logical assumption but, as a man, I can tell you that you are certainly, er, untouched." No married woman would have responded so innocently to Jon's kisses. He was not mistaken there.

"*Untouched?*" She blushed, like a white rosebud caressed by the first rays of the early morning sun.

Jon cleared his throat. That had not been a good choice of word. There were some aspects of marriage that one did not discuss with a gently-bred, single lady. "Beth, you think you

136

are not good enough to become a countess. To become *my* countess. Will you not permit me to be the judge of that? Believe me, your lack of memory does not matter. You are a lady, bred in the bone. It is clear in every word you say, in everything you do, in every step you take. No one doubts it. My wife must be a lady, I admit that. But you fulfil the requirement admirably."

When she began to protest, he shook his head and continued without allowing her to speak. "Beth, I have had my fill of ladies of rank. My first marriage—" He swallowed hard. "Normally, I would not discuss the failure of my first marriage, but you are entitled to know. My late wife was a duke's daughter, with all the accomplishments her position entailed, but she brought me nothing. Another dynastic marriage to a chit out of the schoolroom could easily be as bad. I want— I *need* a wife who will be a companion and a friend, a woman I can esteem, not an empty-headed child whose world revolves around balls and bonnets. You, Beth, are a truly remarkable woman. You care for others. You look to do good in the world. As my wife, you would be able to use my wealth and position to achieve all that you desire. Think what you could do."

There was a small, sharp intake of breath beside him. Then silence.

"My rank would protect you. And we would be comfortable together, I am sure of it. Imagine how our life could be." Jon waited. Had he said enough to persuade her? Would she at least consider his offer?

She withdrew her hand and clasped her fingers in her lap once more. Not a good sign. Was she going to refuse him again?

"If I do not accept you, sir, what will you do?"

Another facer. "I would—" His answer began automatically, but then he stopped short, trying to collect his thoughts. He owed her a considered response on something so important.

That was when he realised that he had no answer to give her. He had not the faintest notion of what he would do if she turned him down.

The silence stretched between them. Jon found that it was surprisingly comfortable to sit in silence with Beth, even when he was trying to decide how to reply to her searching question. It was precisely as he had supposed: she was a restful woman and an estimable companion. She was exactly the wife he needed. He could not afford to lose her. He must not.

That sudden urgency had started his mind racing, as if he were back facing the enemy. He was going to have to fight—and fight harder—to convince her to accept him. His tactics so far had failed. He needed—

A new idea exploded in his rioting thoughts. Now, at last, he knew how to begin. "I have a bargain to offer you, Beth."

"A bargain?" Her voice had become hoarse. "I don't understand."

He grinned at her, feeling himself regaining control at last. "I have made you a sincere proposal of marriage. You have asked, reasonably enough, what I will do if you refuse me. I will answer you, and truthfully, but not now, not here. Tomorrow, if you agree, I shall call at the rectory to take you out driving. I will dismiss the groom as soon as we reach the park, so all our conversation will be private. Then, I promise, I will answer your question. And perhaps you, in turn, will give me your response to my proposal?"

"I–I should not— You will not take my answer now?"

He shook his head. He allowed his self-assured grin to subside into a wry smile as he looked down at her, but he could see that her resolve was weakening. If he could make her wait, make her reflect, then all hope was not lost. "If you want to hear my answer before you speak, Beth, you will have to drive with me tomorrow. Do we have a bargain?"

She sat immobile for a long time, staring vacantly across the garden. Jon waited. The longer she thought, the better his chances, he decided. He would wait until darkness fell if that would help his cause.

Beth rose quite suddenly, in a single graceful movement. A well-bred lady's movement. This time she did not try to stop him from joining her on the path. "Perhaps we should go in?" she said, in what Jon could only describe as her company voice. "It is beginning to get a little chilly out here and Aunt Caro will be wondering what has happened to us."

Without waiting to be asked, she tucked her arm into his. It was a confiding gesture, Jon thought. And hopeful?

They began to stroll towards the house. "Let us hope that the fine weather continues for a few days yet." She glanced up at the sky. "It looks to be set fair." She smiled at nothing in particular and twisted her head to look up at him. "At what time do you plan to call for me tomorrow?"

• • • •

Beth began to pace up and down in the small free space between the end of her bed and the window overlooking the shrubbery.

Untouched. The word was echoing in her head like a drumbeat in an empty hall. *Untouched.* How could he know for certain? Surely he might be mistaken?

But did it matter, provided he really wanted Beth to wife? He said he did. And it was more than wanting. It seemed that he needed her. Beth had been wrong to believe he had loved Alicia. In fact, his first marriage had been a failure. He had no son. And she sensed that he was very lonely. He wanted a companion and a friend more than he wanted a wife. He had almost said as much.

Could she really be that woman? Wife to an earl? Would it be such a sin for a woman with no past to accept him?

It would be a sin to condemn him to loneliness. And it would be worse to condemn him to another marriage like his first. Perhaps he would prefer no wife, and no heir, to marriage to a woman he could not esteem? He did esteem Beth, for all her lack of family and history. He maintained that there could be nothing truly wicked in her past, that he knew her well enough to make a judgement about her character. He was so sure of it that she had begun to believe him. But did *she* know *him*?

Yes, of course she did. He was a fine man, a man of integrity who cared for his tenants, and for all those who depended upon him. When he returned from Spain and discovered what his brother had done at Fratcombe, he had set about putting matters to rights. The repairs had been done, the workers had received fair prices for their labours, and he had paid for the children to be sent to school. Yes, he was a good man. He did need an heir, certainly. Unless he married again, and produced a son, his heir would remain his younger brother, George, the reprobate who would bleed the earldom of every penny it would yield.

It had been so simple to refuse him when he first proposed. His offer had come as a shock, and her answer had been automatic. But it was not simple any longer. Was Beth truly the only woman he could bear to think of as a wife? She would not know the answer to that until tomorrow. If he said it was Beth or no one, would she accept him? She refused to think about that. Jonathan was a man of the world. He knew he had to marry. If Beth refused him, he would find someone else, surely? He would not marry a girl out of the schoolroom. That was abundantly clear. But there must be other women, other ladies, who were older, more knowledgeable. A widow might suit him, perhaps. Yes. A widow of rank.

Beth's pacing had brought her back to the window yet again. She stopped. The sun was setting. The red-gold light was shining through the leaves of the huge beech, making them glow like amber jewels. In a few weeks, its branches would be bare. It was nearly winter. This golden autumn was a joy, but short-lived.

She pressed her palms to the panes, leant her forehead against the wood and closed her eyes. She tried to visualise Jonathan sitting in comfort by his fire, his new wife on the opposite side, calmly reading a book of sermons. The new countess's face was hidden from Beth's view. She was wearing a fine silk gown in a deep shade of red, her hair concealed by an expensive lace cap and her head bent as she concentrated on her reading. Was she reading aloud? It appeared not.

And Jonathan? What was he doing? He seemed to be leaning back, staring at the fire. His hands were resting on the carved wooden arms of his chair. He looked... He looked...

Beth could not decide. His expression was rather vacant. It was not happy, not even content. He was somewhere else entirely. And his wife, the high-ranking widow he had married, was quite oblivious of it.

"Oh, it is wishful thinking," Beth exclaimed, exasperated at her own wilful daydreaming. "You want him. That is the truth of it. You have always wanted him. And you are looking for reasons to persuade yourself that he needs you, that you should not refuse him. You are a fool, Beth Aubrey, or whatever your true name is. You are a fool."

But what if he really does need me? Just as I need him? What then? What if he might come to love me, as I love him?

Those forbidden words. She had spent so long trying to banish them from her thoughts. And now they had ambushed her. Did she really love him?

She took one last look at the glowing golden tree and sank to her knees on the floor, pillowing her head in her hands. Of course she did. She wanted him in her heart, and in her bed. She wanted more than that one spellbinding kiss. And she wanted to spend her whole life trying to make him happy, to ease the loneliness and hurt from which he was suffering. Perhaps one day, he might even confide in Beth about what had happened when he was in Spain.

He had never said a word in her hearing, but she was sure that something he had done, or something he had seen in his time there, was at the root of what troubled him. The man who had carried a shivering foundling to the refuge of the rectory was a man who needed a refuge of his own. He seemed to be sure, in his own mind, that Beth was the woman who would provide the sanctuary he was seeking. Why deny him and, in so doing, deny her own deepest longings?

Because you have no right to inflict a nameless wife upon him, no matter how much you may love him. If you really loved him, you would not do so. Who knows what there is in your past? Who knows what men you may have known? Whatever he says, Jonathan cannot know *that you are untouched.*

That was surely the cause of her recurring guilt. Somewhere in her past, she must have lost her virtue, perhaps even colluded in her own disgrace. No wonder her memory was blank. She deserved to be a nameless outcast. If she had done such a wicked thing, she was no fit wife for any man.

141

The dream had come so close, yet now it was floating away again like a soap bubble borne aloft on the tiniest breath of air. She could not do it. She must not. The Countess of Portbury must come to her husband untouched, and unsullied.

Beth could not swear to be that woman. And without that, she had no choice. She wiped the back of her hand across her eyes. It was no weakness to allow a single tear, or even two, for the man she loved—the man she would have to refuse.

Chapter Sixteen

BETH COULD NOT SLEEP. It was not surprising, for her mind was full of tomorrow, what she would say, how much he would be hurt. She rolled over yet again and punched the pillow.

She was going to look a fright when he appeared to escort her to his curricle. Perhaps that would be some consolation to him? However estimable he thought her, he would not wish to marry a woman with black circles round her eyes and quivering limbs.

She pushed the coverlet down to her waist. It was remarkably hot considering that it was already autumn. Should she open the window? A little fresh air, even night air, would do her no harm. She could shut it again before Hetty appeared to berate her for doing something so foolish.

She crossed to the window to push the curtains back a little and then eased the sash up an inch or two, working slowly and carefully to avoid any squeaks that might disturb the rest of the household. There was a sliver of moon behind the beech tree. Where earlier its leaves had been golden and glowing, they were now dark, cold shadows. There was no movement, no wind. The great tree was holding its breath, waiting for the embrace of winter, making ready to fall asleep. As Beth should sleep.

If only there were a way… If only…

From the fields beyond the glebe, the sheep were bleating. Strange, for the lambs were long gone. Was the ram back in the field to ensure next spring's crop of lambs? The ewes would be ready, for they could certainly not remain untouched. That was the way of nature.

She shook her head. What a strange pattern of thought. She yawned. Good. At last she should be able to sleep.

Beth took one final breath and pulled the curtains closed, resolving she would rise early to shut the window again. She was sure she would sleep better with the sweet night air around her. She climbed back into bed, pulled the covers up over her shoulders and closed her eyes.

The last thing she heard was the bleat of the ewes beyond the glebe.

••••

"Miss Beth, you *never* slept with the window open?"

It was Hetty with the morning hot water. So much for Beth's good intentions. She sat up with a jerk and put her hands to her hair, sensing something was amiss. Her plaits had come undone in the night. Her hair was a mass of tangles and her nightrail was all bunched up above her waist. The bedclothes, too, seemed to have tied themselves in knots. She—

Heavens, she had been dreaming about Jonathan. *Again.* This time, she had been in his arms while he covered every inch of her skin with passionate kisses. Every last inch. Her whole body had been hot and alive. And willing. It had been blissful. It was a wonder she had not torn off her nightrail along with the fastenings of her hair. In her dreams, she had been so very sure, so—

In your dreams, you were wanton. You should be ashamed.

Beth forced herself to ignore the warnings of her conscience. He would arrive soon. "Hetty, would you bring me a large jug of cool water please? I seem to have become very hot in the night. It would be best if I give myself a sponge bath before I dress."

"You've caught a fever, Miss Beth. On account of the open window."

Beth shook her head. Her fever was not of the kind Hetty meant. Hetty's fevers could be cured. "I am not ill. But I am going driving with his lordship this morning and I must be looking my best. Make haste with the water, if you please. It is going to take you an age to comb the tangles out of my hair."

Hetty paused a moment, looking mutinous, but then she obeyed.

Beth breathed a sigh of relief and jumped out of bed, allowing the rumpled nightrail to fall back to her ankles. She was decent again. Outwardly. A quick glance in the mirror showed her that her skin was still flushed, especially where the ribbon ties had come undone to expose her throat and breasts. Yes, in her dreams, he had kissed her there, too. And she had gloried in it.

In her dreams, she was not untouched.

And in her dreams, she had discovered what she must do.

• • • •

It was a beautiful morning, more like late August than early October. The sky was blue and cloudless, and the slight breeze was warm. Only the turning trees betrayed how late in the year it was. Soon their crisp leaves would be heaped in the gutters and under the hedgerows, offering winter hiding places to small animals and rich food for worms and beetles.

Beth refused to think about the dead leaves that had saved her from oblivion, long ago. Better to think about her rescuer, the man who now sat beside her in the curricle, his lean hands guiding his matched pair along the curving path through Fratcombe Manor park. She and Jonathan were easy enough together, even though he had spoken barely a word beyond the normal courtesies. She was starting to wonder if he felt as tongue-tied as she did.

He had promised to tell her what he would do if she refused him. And she—heaven help her—had promised to respond to his proposal.

She could not bring herself to ask him to begin. Once he did, she would have to speak, too. This was one confrontation she could not run from, no matter what was said. She had to trust him.

She did trust him.

He spoke at last. "I thought I would drive you to the far side of the park this morning. For once, the track is dry enough to take a carriage." His voice sounded remarkably normal. How did he do that? Could he feel none of the confusion that was threatening to overwhelm her?

"Usually the ground is too marshy for wheeled vehicles. Pray do not upbraid me, Miss Beth," he added hastily, with a hint of humour in his tone. "I do intend to drain that land as soon as I can. I am fully aware of my duties there, I promise you." He turned slightly. Beth saw that he was smiling.

She found herself smiling back. She could not help it. He was in control of this encounter and, strangely, it made her feel protected. He was deliberately teasing her into relaxing with him once more. "Have I been such a termagant, sir? It was not my intent to badger you."

"No?" He chuckled. "No, I am sure your reproofs were kindly meant. Such as when you told me to look to the repairs of my tenants' houses. And to ensure that travelling gypsy bands could camp unmolested."

"Oh." Yes, she had done both of those. "I apologise if I overstepped the mark, sir. My intentions were of the best. I was trying to—"

"You were trying to take care of others, to do God's work, as you always do, Beth, which is one of the reasons why I admire you so much. And why I want you to be my wife."

Beth's heart clutched in her breast. She could not breathe.

"But before I press you for your answer, I owe you mine. A promise is a promise, especially between friends. Do you not agree?" He waited a beat. When she said nothing, he continued, airily, "I have decided that, if you refuse me, I shall keep repeating my proposal until you accept. In other words, you might as well accept me at once." His voice dropped a little, to a deeper, more serious tone. "Will you marry me, Beth? Please?"

Beth had been screwing up her courage for this since the moment she awoke from that beckoning dream. She lifted her chin, focused on the horses' ears and launched into her prepared answer. "I will accept your proposal, sir—"

"Beth, that is wonderful—"

"—but on one condition."

"Ah. Name it."

146

She took a deep breath. "On condition that you prove to my satisfaction, and to your own, that I am still a virgin *before* you lead me to the altar."

The noise he made sounded to Beth like the growl of a furiously angry bear, beset by slavering dogs.

She swallowed. She had to finish this. It had to be said. "If I am a virgin, I cannot have been married before. And I–I would not be dishonouring you by accepting your proposal. My plan provides the only sensible solution."

"And how do you propose, sensible Miss Aubrey, that I should establish your virginity? I take it you have a plan for that, too?" His voice was very hard, very cold.

Beth shivered at the sound, but she would not give up now. She was mortified enough and already scarlet to her hairline, she knew. She had nothing more to lose. "I believe the only reliable method is th–the natural one. I–I will come to your bed and let you—"

His string of curses included mostly words that Beth did not recognise. "I beg your pardon," he said at last, recovering his control, though not his colour. He was sheet white under his tan. "You are proposing that I should deflower you in order to prove you are fit to be my wife? What kind of cold-blooded devil do you take me for?"

"If you do indeed discover that I am a virgin, then I will marry you. But if you do not, if I am already, um, *deflowered* as you call it, I will not marry you, for that could be bigamy. It seems simple enough."

"Simple?" He was having even more trouble controlling his temper now. That one word was a howl of rage. "Has it not occurred to you that, as a result of this *plan* of yours, you could end up carrying my child? Virgin or no, would you marry me then?"

"I–I—" In for a penny, in for a pound. "I am not totally ignorant of such matters, sir. I know how children are got. I do not know precisely how they are prevented, but I have heard that there are w–ways of ensuring that—" She stopped and swallowed hard. She knew she had to go on with this, no matter what. She mustered all her remaining courage and dared to meet and hold his stormy gaze. "I know you to be a man of the world. I assumed you would know the way of it. Was I wrong?"

• • • •

At that moment, Jon could have strangled Beth Aubrey, even if he had to swing for it. Luckily for her, his hands were fully occupied in controlling his horses. They had sensed his anger and were becoming extremely restive. He must calm them, or they would probably bolt.

It took more than five straining minutes to ensure that his pair—and his unruly temper—were back under control. He did not dare to speak until they were. In fact, he did not dare to speak at all. What an extraordinary proposal, from an innocent young lady. And yet...

And yet her logic could well be less flawed than Jon's. How could he truly be sure she was unspoilt on the basis of one single kiss? Beth's test was a surer touchstone than Jon's. How much courage it must have taken for her to propose such a thing. And to go further, to speak of preventing pregnancy. It was utterly outrageous.

It was one of the bravest things he had ever heard.

It appeared she was indeed willing to accept Jon, but only if there was no risk to his honour. *His* honour, not hers. As if she cared more for Jon's honour than he did himself.

He risked another quick sideways glance. Beth's shoulders had not drooped even a fraction from her normal upright carriage, and she was staring down at her gloved hands. She was implacable. He could see that in every line of her tense body. Either he accepted her offer—her extraordinary plan— or she would be lost to him. That must not happen. In the course of this summer and autumn, Beth Aubrey had become the woman he wanted. He would not part with her. He needed her beside him. And so he was going to have to accept her terms.

She would come to his bed and let him—

Poor Beth. She had been unable to say the word. Yet it had taken courage to go as far as she had. She was as brave as any comrade he had served with.

She would come to his bed—

Oh dear. He laughed aloud, his black doubts disappearing with the sound. Poor Beth, indeed. Her carefully constructed plan was going to be her undoing.

"You find my question amusing, my lord?" Her tone was frosty.

"No, Beth. Forgive me. I was not laughing at you, but at the extraordinary predicament in which we find ourselves." He slowed his horses for the sharp bend in the track. The right fork led round the back of the stable block to the furthest parts of his land. The left fork led to the lake and the tamer parkland beyond, where the folly lay hidden. "You asked me about, um, prevention. Yes, I do know how it can be done."

"Good." She nodded. "Then there is nothing to stop us from following my plan, is there?"

The die was cast, by her own hand. Jon turned his horses towards the lake.

She glanced sharply up at him, her eyes questioning, but she did not speak. Unlike most of her sex, she would be content to wait in silence.

"Your plan, ma'am. I think it needs to be, er, fleshed out a little. You said you would come to my bed. Believe me, I am honoured by your offer. Might I ask, though, how you were, um, planning to manage it?" He was having trouble keeping the laughter out of his voice. His mind was filled with the ludicrous image of his butler announcing Beth at his bedchamber door. *Miss Aubrey is here, my lord. To be deflowered.*

Beth gave a gasp of horror and began to cough, trying to cover her acute embarrassment. If he had not seen it with his own eyes, he would not have believed a lady could turn that particular shade of vermilion.

Yes, the die was cast. And the play was his.

Jon relaxed and let the horses have their heads up the gentle slope. His path was clear. Beth would have her assignation. On Jon's terms.

• • • •

"Someone is living here."

The folly consisted of a single square room. Beth would have expected it to be empty, or to contain a few chairs, at most, where guests might sit to recover after the long climb up from the house and past the lake. Instead, it looked like the cluttered living quarters of some rich young buck with an extremely idle servant. There was a fireplace, with a kettle suspended, but the fire had burned down long ago, and the ashes had spilled out over the small hearth. In front of it were comfortable chairs and a table strewn with used plates and glasses. There was at least one empty wine bottle on the floor.

Beth turned away. She had seen quite enough. The only part of the room that was not at sixes and sevens was the desk, where a neat row of books stood propped against the wall. Next to them were several leather-bound notebooks, a pile of writing paper and an inkstand. The desk was so tidy, it could have been in the rector's study. But the rest—?

"No. Not living." He gazed round, apparently trying to view the chaos as Beth had done. "I use this place from time to time for my own pleasure. It is totally private. The servants are not permitted to enter, even to clean and restock it, without special leave. And as you can see—" he waved a hand in the direction of the tumbled cushions and the dirty plates "—I have not yet given them leave today."

"You were here last night?"

"Yes, I was here. I prefer solitude when I want to think. Besides, it was a splendid night."

She frowned. A splendid night? What on earth did he mean? Glancing round again at the mess and at what, she now realised, was a kind of bed in the far corner, she decided that she did not wish to know.

He was smiling down at her. It was the kind of superior, knowing smile that made her want to slap him. He was waiting for her to ask. Well, she would not. Whatever his *splendid* nocturnal activities might be, he could keep them to himself. "Might I ask why you have brought me here, sir? It is barely minutes since you said you would drive me to the marshes. The marshes that you have promised to drain," she added, with emphasis. That wiped the superior smile from his face, she was glad to see.

From mocking to serious in an instant. "I brought you here to make plans. I understand now—forgive me, I did not

150

understand before—how strongly you feel on the subject of our, um, our possible union. I understand, too, that the condition you have laid down is absolute." He took her right hand in his, holding it lightly. "But I think you must now realise, Beth, that meeting your condition will be far from easy. I cannot simply walk into your bedchamber, nor you into mine."

Beth felt herself colouring yet again. It seemed she had done nothing else since the moment he had arrived at the rectory door. But he was right that she had been a fool. Society, especially in villages like Fratcombe, was arranged precisely to prevent such carnal assignations.

Jonathan led her across to the desk and invited her to sit. There was only one chair. Once she was seated, he let go of her hand and leaned nonchalantly against the corner of the desk. "Our meeting cannot be at the rectory, clearly. Nor at the Manor, for there are too many servants with prying eyes and long noses. Did you imagine you could come there, alone, and be admitted by my butler?"

"I...um..." Beth fixed her gaze on the tooled leather of the notebook.

"I have a better plan to propose. First, you must be conveyed from the rectory to our meeting place. You cannot be expected to go on foot, alone, in the dark. I suggest you slip out and wait behind the beech tree. At the appointed hour, I will meet you and bring you to our rendezvous. You have only to leave the rectory without being seen. And to return again before first light, of course. Do you think you can do that, Beth?"

"I–I—" This was no time for missishness. Jonathan was providing a practical plan that would allow the condition— Beth's own condition—to be met. "Yes. Yes, I can do that."

"Beth." He reached for her hand again and held it in a strong clasp. "Are you sure you want to do this? It is not necessary, believe me. I really do want to marry you, and I require no such demonstration of your virtue beforehand. What's more, I am sure you would be easier if our first lovemaking took place when we were already man and wife."

"No," she declared stoutly. "That cannot be the way of it, for the reasons I have given you. I will not risk bigamy. Nor your honour. Unless we fulfil my condition, there will be no marriage."

He shook his head. "You are a stubborn woman, Beth Aubrey. Very well, it shall be as you wish. You may leave all the arrangements to me. Apart from one thing. You must be sure to be warmly clad and sensibly shod, for I will not be able to bring a carriage for you. That would attract too much attention, even in the dark. I shall come for you on horseback."

She could see the sense in that. She nodded. "Do I need to ride, too?"

"No. Saracen is more than capable of carrying us both."

He was going to take her up before him and ride with her in his arms, close against his powerful body. The prospect sent a delicious frisson down her spine. Especially as it would be followed by...

Oh dear. A virtuous lady should not be thinking of such things, but she could not help it. She wanted him so. "Will you bring me here?" she asked quietly, trying not to dwell on the sensual images that were invading her brain. She glanced round the room. Unfortunately that added even more wanton thoughts, for the room had an air of wild abandon.

"Yes. And it will be quite private." He grinned ruefully. "I will have it set to rights before you arrive. There will be nothing to offend your delicate sensibilities, I promise you."

Nothing except what they were going to do in this private place.

Jonathan's eyes were twinkling with mischief. Her face must have given her away, yet she could not bring herself to be angry with him this time. After all, the condition was hers. And he had found a way of making a reality of it. If he was teasing her a little in the process, she would not object. Better to respond in kind. "I should hope so, indeed, sir," she said brightly, reaching out to run a gloved finger along the window sill behind the books. She examined it closely, shaking her head in mock disgust. That window had not been dusted for some time. "A lady likes to meet her— A lady likes to go to

152

an encounter with a gentleman knowing that all her needs will be met—warmth, comfort, *and* cleanliness."

He chuckled. "I promise you that all your requirements will be met." He raised her hands to his lips, kissing each in turn. "All of them. Now, if you are content, ma'am, I suggest we continue our drive."

How very matter of fact he was about such a momentous thing. Yet those kisses on her hands had not been matter of fact, or even necessary. She sensed they were his way of sealing their very special bargain.

She nodded. She would try to sound as normal as he had. "Yes. By all means. Let us view your marshes."

He tucked her hand into the crook of his arm and started for the door, stopping there for a last swift glance back at the room. "It will be transformed, I promise you, Beth. Meet me behind the beech tree at a quarter to midnight and you shall see for yourself."

Tonight? It was for tonight?

He was smiling down at her. It was not a leer, nor anything like. It was a smile of encouragement, the kind of smile Beth often used in the schoolroom when a child was facing a new and daunting task. "Courage, little one," he said softly. "A quarter to midnight."

She met his gaze bravely. "A quarter to midnight? So be it."

Chapter Seventeen

THE BIG BAY STOPPED by the entrance to the folly. The whole park was in darkness except for a single candle glowing through the slit window alongside the door. In the silence, a long shiver passed down Beth's body. Jonathan must have felt it, for he pulled her a little more closely against his body. He made no comment. He had made clear from the outset that this condition of hers did not need to be met. He had repeated it as he pulled her up before him and settled her into his arms. She had only to say the word, at any stage, and he would return her to the rectory.

She did not say the word now. And he did not hector her. He was paying her the compliment of treating her like an equal, able to make her own decisions. If she changed her mind, he was trusting her to say so.

"You are chilled," he murmured against her ear, his breath caressing her cheek. "You must go in to the warm." He dismounted and helped her down, holding her close against his side. Then he led her to the door and reached for the handle. "Go in. Make yourself comfortable. And warm. I will join you in a moment, once I have seen Saracen safely bestowed."

Beth glanced back at the horse which stood motionless, waiting patiently. "He looks as though he would stand there all night." She was trying to inject a degree of lightness into her voice.

Jonathan chuckled. "Aye, he would. But I think he deserves a net of hay, and to be rid of the weight of the saddle on his back." He opened the door for Beth and pushed her gently inside, closing it behind her.

The room was transformed. A few hours earlier, there had been chaos and abandon. Now everything had been set to rights; it was warm and welcoming. Indeed, as a venue for an illicit tryst, it seemed a little tame. A good fire was burning in the hearth and the kettle had been swung close enough to sing, though not to boil. The fire, an oil lamp on the desk and that single candle by the door provided the only illumination, although several branches of new, unlit candles had been set around the room.

Beth risked one quick glance at the bed in the far corner. It had been piled high with cushions so that it looked more like a sofa than a bed.

Almost unthreatening.

She shivered again. She must be cold. There was no other reason for it. She was not being forced. Everything that took place now would be by her own choice and her own will. Crossing to the fire, she stripped off her gloves to warm her hands. Ah, delicious. It was only then that she noticed a tea tray standing ready on a low stool by the hearth. Tea? After midnight? And at an assignation?

She began to laugh. If she had been afraid, even a very little afraid, she was so no longer. She was here, tonight, to be in the arms of the man she loved. It was a time for anticipation, not for fear.

In that moment she knew that, whatever the outcome of this encounter, she wanted it. More than anything. Even if they parted after this one night, she would cherish every second of it, for the rest of her life.

• • • •

Jon gave Saracen one last pat and left him contentedly munching hay in the lean-to behind the folly. The big horse was well used to being left there at night, while Jon enjoyed the peace and isolation of the place.

Jon slowly made his way round to the front. He could see through the small window that Beth had not lit any of the candles inside. What was she doing? Would she now finally realise what a momentous step she had chosen to take and change her mind? He hoped so.

And yet he hoped not. The thought of making love to Beth Aubrey—the woman he fully intended to marry—was an arousing one. She was everything a sensible man could want in a wife: kind, generous, thoughtful, dedicated to doing good in the world. She was restful, and beautiful, too. She would grace his arm and his bed. God willing, they would make fine children together, children a man could be proud of. It would be a solid, reassuring union. As a woman, she could never be a trusted confidante, of course. Such was the reality of life. In public, they would have to be distant and formal, as their rank demanded, but in private they could be comfortable companions. It was more than he had dared to hope for in a wife.

At this precise moment, however, his body was telling him that a comfortable companion was not what he sought. His purpose now was to introduce Beth—his innocent Beth—to the joys and delights of lovemaking.

At the door he paused to look up at the night sky. No wonder it was so cold. There was not a single cloud. The great upturned bowl, the colour of deepest indigo, was spattered with the points of light he knew so well. This picture was eternal. These same stars would blaze down on Beth and Jon's children, and on their children's children. Nothing would change.

But tonight, everything would change. Children... He had told Beth that he knew the way of preventing conception, but she had not asked him to promise to use it. If Beth were not a virgin, she would never agree to marry him, so he was duty-bound to ensure that no child resulted from what they did together this night. He owed her that. But what if he found that he was holding a virgin in his arms? He fully expected it to be so. What then? She had promised to accept his proposal if there were no risk of bigamy. And the purpose of marriage was children, was it not?

He shook his head. High above, the dog-star seemed to wink at him. "Yes, I know," he murmured, gazing up at it. "I am trying to find an unselfish reason for following my own selfish desires. And yet, the risk of pregnancy could make matters easier, later." He shook his head again, trying to clear his thoughts. This was no time for logic-chopping.

He allowed himself one last glance up at the star-mapped sky. "I will make it good for her, I promise." He turned and opened the door.

She had put back the hood of her cloak and was kneeling on the rug in front of the hearth. Even across the full length of the room, he could see that her shoulders were shaking. Poor girl, she must be terrified. And he had been communing with the stars?

He closed the door quietly, not to frighten her, before setting down his hat and whip and striding across the room to kneel beside her. "Oh, my poor Beth," he began gently, putting a comforting arm round her shoulders.

The face she turned up to him was not stricken, not in the least. It was alight with laughter.

"Beth?"

"Tea." The single word was barely a croak. She was laughing too much to be able to control her voice.

He looked down at the tea tray he had ordered. It was unusual, to be sure, but it had seemed a good idea. Comforting, unthreatening.

"Tea," she said again, on a throaty chuckle.

He was trying very hard to keep his face straight, but he knew he was not really succeeding. "I thought you might be glad of it, after our cold midnight ride."

"And indeed I am, sir. See, I have set the kettle to boil." She had swung the kettle fully over the fire. "But I must tell you that this was not quite what I was expecting."

"Oh?" He raised an eyebrow.

"I had imagined champagne, or something equally decadent."

"You may have champagne, or brandy, if you wish. I have both here. I could even make you hot rum punch if you had a fancy for it."

She shook her head, trying not to smile.

"No, I thought not. Remember that we are friends, Beth. After this night, we will soon be man and wife. And still true friends."

Her expression became more serious, but she did not protest. They both knew the condition. There was no point in belabouring it.

"True friends enjoy each other's company and seek to provide for each other's comfort. In your case, tea seemed to be the ideal solution."

Beth touched her hand to Jon's arm. "You are a good friend, sir."

"No. No, I will not permit that. Not when we are alone. You will not call me 'sir' as if you were an inferior. You are to be my wife, my countess. My name is Jon. Jonathan if you must, but I should prefer Jon."

Her eyes widened and misted for a moment. "Jon," she said slowly, lingering over the sound as if testing it, tasting it with her tongue. "For this night at least, it shall be as you wish."

• • • •

The orange and red of the fire was vividly reflected in her wide, glowing eyes. Her laughter had been infectious, and good to hear, for it meant that she was not afraid. She was doing what she wanted. And with a full heart.

He took both her hands in his—as he had done so many times before—and gently raised her. But this time, there was no chaste kiss on her white skin. This time, he raised first one hand and then the other to his lips and took finger after finger into his mouth, sucking greedily. Reaching her second index finger, he began to nibble her flesh, too.

She gave a little yelp of surprise. Then it mellowed into a sigh of acceptance, and pleasure.

By the time he came to the ring finger of her left hand, he was desperate for more than this. He swallowed it to the first knuckle, and the second, then slowly pulled his mouth away again, in a long drawn out kiss, revelling in the trail of heat and desire he was leaving behind him. On this finger, she would wear his ring. He paused, holding the very end of her

158

ring finger lightly between his lips and stroking its fleshy pad with the tip of his tongue. She tasted wholly delicious.

She groaned, deep in her belly. It was the sound of willing surrender. At last. Jon pulled her into his arms and began to plunder her soft, yielding mouth. She was almost as eager as he, though her lack of experience was as obvious as on that first occasion. She wanted him. She wanted *this*, but she certainly did not know the way of it.

Jon told himself to go slowly, to take her with him every step of the way, to show her how to relish the moment, the touch, the feelings that they would enjoy together. He would make it beautiful for them both.

He drove his hands deep into her hair. From far off, he heard the tinny sounds of metal—hair pins?—clinking on the hearth as her hair tumbled and settled in silken curls around her shoulders. He was holding her head steady for his kiss, but she was avid for him, too. She dug her hands under his waistcoat and round to his back where her fingers gripped and tugged at the fine linen of his shirt, trying to reach his skin.

This was not the slow, gentle seduction he had intended. He forced himself to break the kiss and take a pace back, dropping his hands.

"Jon?" His abrupt movement had loosed her frenzied grip on his flesh. Her face was glowing in the firelight, but with far too much colour now. She was embarrassed again, poor girl. She thought— He did not know what she thought, but he did know he must reassure her.

"We go too fast, Beth." He spoke softly, stroking the back of his fingers soothingly down her cheek. "You are very lovely, but I fear my desire is driving me faster than is wise."

She swallowed hard, but when she looked up at him again, her eyes were defiant. "You forget, sir—" she began proudly. "Pray do not forget, Jon," she repeated, rather more gently, "that I am a willing partner here."

Partner. The word had a good, solid ring to it. He liked it. "Yes, we *shall* be partners. But, for this first time, our partnership should blossom a little more slowly." He smiled down at her and, with careful fingers, began to untie the strings of her cloak. Behind them, the kettle had begun to boil.

With barely a sideways glance, Jon hooked it away from the fire with his boot. This was definitely not the moment for tea.

By the time he had removed her cloak and turned to lay it aside, Beth's breathing had become fast and shallow. Not fear, but desire. She might be innocent—he was sure of that in his own mind—but even an innocent could be overtaken by the human body's natural urges. Jon's task was to fan those flames. The slightest mistake on his part could damp her natural fires and ruin this night for her. That must not happen.

When he turned back to her, he saw that she was starting to undo the neck of her simple gown, in the sort of practical, matter-of-fact way that he had come to associate with Beth Aubrey.

"No," he whispered, laying his fingers over hers. "Pray allow me. This gift you are offering me needs to be unwrapped very, very slowly. It would be generous indeed if you permitted me to do this. Please, Beth."

"I— Oh." She coloured again until her skin was like a ripe peach, its luscious flesh concealed beneath the dark bloom, inviting a lover's bite.

"But if you keep looking at me like that, my dear girl, I shall find myself hard put not to simply tear off your gown." That was nothing less than the truth, for she looked good enough to eat.

"Oh," she said again, but this time with a knowing glint in her eye. Her beautiful blush was fading, and her mouth was starting to curve into a shy but eloquent smile. She slipped her fingers out from under his, teasingly stroking his palm as she did so. She was beginning to understand this game of theirs. And, he suspected, to enjoy it very much.

Jon slowly removed the pins that fastened the front panel of her gown. It fell forward, revealing the simple white chemise beneath and the ties of her skirt. His eyes widened. She wore no stays. There was only a single layer of lawn between his fingers and her breasts.

She read his reaction immediately. "I–I had to be able to dress myself without help," she whispered.

Practical as ever. She could hardly summon Hetty to lace her into her stays at midnight. And yet she was shy of the fact

160

that she had come to meet Jon while less than properly clad. He put his hands to her face and kissed her gently, full on the mouth. Her response surprised him. Her lips opened under his and her sweet breath invited him in.

He moaned and deepened the kiss. At the same time, he dropped his fingers to the ties of her skirt. One single tug, and they were undone. Using touch alone, he pushed the gown off her shoulders so that it slithered down her body to pool at her feet. It made almost no sound, for the fabric was old and soft. One day, Jon would dress her in the finest silks and satins, fabrics that would rustle luxuriously when he peeled them away to reveal the glories beneath.

Glories they were. He could not resist stepping back to admire her. Somewhere, she had kicked off her shoes, for she was now clad in only a chemise and stockings. That thin chemise did nothing to conceal her breasts—small, pert and the delicious colour of cream ripening in the skimming pan. Under Jon's appreciative gaze, her nipples rose and darkened, straining up towards him. It was the most erotic vision he had ever seen.

Jon's body reacted instantly. Shocked at his own callow response, he heard himself groan aloud.

"Jon? Is something wrong?"

Absolutely nothing was wrong. Nothing at all. Except that, if he did not put his lips to those perfect pouting nipples, his body might explode.

He threw off his coat and waistcoat and glanced towards the bed in the corner. No, not there. Here, in the warmth. Here, where every inch of her skin would glow.

He set his hands on her bare shoulders. A fleeting touch. "How beautiful you are there, lit by the flames. Give me a moment."

She frowned, puzzled, though she did not move from her place. But her frown melted away, as she watched him pull off his cravat and then drag the bed out from the corner and into the space in front of the fire. He had tumbled the colourful cushions into a heap in the middle.

"Will it please you to sit, my lady?" He waved a hand towards the bed. Then he held it out to her with exaggerated courtesy.

Beth's stomach lurched. The bed was only two steps away, the two most important steps of her life.

She hesitated for a fraction too long.

"Beth?" He sounded uncertain, troubled.

Beth hesitated no longer. She placed her fingers in his and squeezed gently. "I swear that is a throne you have prepared for me," she said lightly, nodding towards the piles of silken cushions.

It was the reassurance he seemed to need. He did not give her a chance to move. He swept her up into his arms and laid her down on the bed, arranging the cushions for her head and back. She allowed her body to sink deep into the unaccustomed luxury. "Ah, that is wonderful," she sighed, turning her face against the silk and breathing deeply. It had a fragrance of its own, of exotic places where the sun shone fiercely and the sky was too blue to be captured by any painter's palette. She was in a dream. She must be. Such bliss could not be real.

He was still standing, staring down at her, watching her every movement. She stroked the fingers of one hand over the velvet coverlet and purred like a contented cat. "Mmm. How comfortable this is. But a little lonely, I would say. Do you think there is room for two?" She lifted her naked arms invitingly.

"Aye, provided we snuggle together a little." His voice seemed to have become lower than normal.

"That sounds, um, a most practical approach." Beth gave a nervous giggle. Enough. She could not bear to wait any longer. "Would you care to try the experiment? Jon?" She stretched her arms even more towards him.

In a second, he was lying beside her, pulling her close. She could feel the heat of him through the layers of his shirt and her chemise. His heart was thrumming. Or was it hers? It felt like the pulse of a drum, linking their two bodies. But not close enough.

162

She pushed at the fabric of his shirt where it opened at the collar, exposing the deeply tanned skin of his neck and upper chest.

"How shall I explain to my valet if my shirt is ripped off?" he said throatily, putting his fingers over hers.

Beth had enough sense left to appreciate the risk he described. Her chemise must not be torn; nor must his shirt. She took a deep breath and applied herself to pulling his shirt out of his breeches. Unfortunately, her fingers seemed to have forgotten their role. They would not obey her.

Jon laughed and raised one of her hands to his mouth. A kiss, and then the nibbling began again. Beth felt as if her insides were melting, and glowing fit to outdo the fire.

"Let me," he said softly, laying her fingers against his neck while he pulled his shirt free. "And now, what is your will, my lady?"

His shirt was hanging loose and free of his riding breeches. The invitation was obvious, but he was going slowly, out of concern for Beth. He was allowing her to set the pace she wanted.

Oh, how she loved this man. And how she wanted him. Desire was driving her now. All thoughts of missish propriety were long forgotten. With one delicious movement, she slid her fingers under the linen, then stroked up across his chest and shoulders, to push the shirt up to his neck and pull it over his head. "Ah." The single word emerged as half-sigh, half-groan. He was beautiful. And in the firelight, his body was glowing with a golden warmth. Her knight, her golden knight. He would be hers, at last.

His mouth came down on hers, seeking, probing, gently at first, but once she began to respond, he became more demanding. He sucked at her lips and then he nibbled them, just as he had done her fingers, though the sensation was even more arousing on her mouth. Beth closed her eyes and gave herself up to her other senses. Emboldened by the darkness, she touched the tip of her tongue to his and felt an answering groan rippling through his body and into hers. She gasped his name, but it made no sound at all, for he swallowed her very breath and deepened the kiss yet more. Their tongues began to touch and tangle. They were united, in taste, in touch, even in the air they breathed.

When, at last, Jon broke the kiss, they were both gasping like drowning men pushing up to the surface of the sea. But if this was drowning, Beth would gladly give herself up to it. Her whole being was soft and molten, and as pliable as potter's clay. She felt as though Jon's kisses had dissolved her bones, leaving her formless, ready to take some exquisite new shape under his hands. She wanted to be enfolded in his arms once more, to fill the space that his gentle embrace would create.

The silence lengthened. He had gone from her. Reluctantly, apprehensively, Beth opened her eyes. "Jon?" Her voice quavered.

"I am here." He was over by the window. Beth moved in time to see him extinguish the oil lamp. The candle by the door had already been snuffed out. "Forgive me," he said softly. "I did not mean to alarm you, but I thought you might prefer the dark. Now we have only the glow of the fire. Does it trouble you? I can screen it if you prefer."

Without light, Beth would not be able to feast her gaze on her golden knight. "No, it does not trouble me." She swallowed and then added, greatly daring, "Though your absence did." Shocked by her own forwardness, Beth closed her eyes and tried to force herself to relax into the cushions. After a moment, she felt the bed dip as Jon sat down. She thought she could hear him struggling with his boots. And she was sure she heard a muttered curse. She giggled nervously. She could not help it.

"It appears I am quite useless without a valet to pull off my boots." There was laughter in his voice.

"I could help you, if you wish?"

"Good God, no," he exclaimed, still laughing. "I could not cope with the sight of you kneeling at my feet. It is difficult enough as it is."

"Perhaps you should buy boots that do not fit quite so snugly?"

"I may tell you, ma'am, that it is not the snug fit of my boots that is troubling me at this precise moment."

Beth half-opened her eyes and then shut them again hurriedly. Jon was removing his tight riding breeches. In a moment, he would be completely naked. In a moment, he would be stretched out beside her. The tension grew, first in her neck and shoulders, and then spread down through her torso to her stomach.

"Beth." He was beside her again. She could feel his warm breath fluttering across her cheek. "Beth, open your eyes. Please."

She could not resist that pleading note. And when she looked, she saw his face above her, half in shadow, and half glowing red in the firelight. Yet, in spite of the glow, his eyes seemed to be completely black, like fathomless pools. She longed to drown in them.

"Beth. My beautiful Beth. Will you permit me to remove your chemise so that I may see you? All of you?" When she hesitated, he continued hurriedly, "I know you are shy. I ask too much. Forgive me." He stroked his hand down the side of her body, smoothing the chemise into place as if he were trying to restore, rather than remove it.

But that was not at all what Beth wanted. She understood that, even while his fingers slithered over her hip bone and started down her thigh. She wanted him to smooth his hands over her skin. Without the intrusion of petticoats. She laid her hands on his cheeks and ran them gently down over the line of his jaw, his neck, and the taut muscles of his chest. She could go no further, for his body was resting on the bed beside her. She pushed against him with the flat of her hands. "I–I want to see you." Her whisper was barely audible, even to her own ears. "And for you to see me."

He took a deep breath and touched his mouth to the side of her neck, below her ear. "It shall be exactly as you wish," he whispered against her flesh, the words vibrating through her whole being. He kissed his way up to her earlobe and began to nuzzle there. At the same moment, with featherlight touches, he was untying the ribbons of her chemise and pushing it carefully from her body. Soon, she was completely naked, apart from her stockings. A gentle hand lifted away the chemise and began to stroke up the side of her calf, teasing at the weave of her stocking and sending shivers through the flesh beneath.

Beth groaned out his name. He responded with a sound, low in his throat. She had never heard the like before, but she recognised it as male satisfaction, and anticipation. And then his questing fingers reached the naked flesh above her garter. That single touch was electrifying. He stroked his hand round to her inner thigh and let it rest there, while his lips nuzzled a path across her cheek to find her mouth.

"Oh, God, Beth. You are so very desirable."

Her own desire for him was becoming almost impossible to endure. He kissed her, deeply, on the mouth and then continued to kiss his way across her cheek and along her jaw, down her neck to the little indentation at the base. He paused there to flick her skin with the tip of his tongue. Then on, down, to the valley between her breasts. He took one breast in each hand, weighing them reverently, rubbing his thumbs back and forth across her aching nipples until they rose, hard and proud against his touch.

"Mmm." Beth felt the low rumble against her flesh. Then he was rolling one nipple between his thumb and forefinger while he sucked the other with such force that she felt the pull all the way down to her womb. She gasped aloud at the strange, elusive pleasure of it.

Jon raised his head from her breast and murmured something she could not catch, before transferring his mouth to her other breast. This time the sensation was even stronger, as if her womb was contracting in response to his sucking mouth. Was this what it was to be loved by a man? It was almost more than she could bear.

Then Jon was kissing his way down her body, from the crevice between her breasts to her navel, and on, and on. She thought she cried out, but he hushed her and returned his wicked fingers to her breasts, pushing and rolling the nipples until they rose even more.

"Ah, Jon." He had pushed himself down her body until his head was resting between her legs. She could feel the beginnings of his stubble against the tender skin of her inner thighs. And then—

Heavens, he was kissing her. *There*. Oh, it was too much. Building, building, in great waves of feeling that she could not control. It was going to overpower her. She let out a long scream and tumbled into darkness.

Chapter Eighteen

JON DROPPED ONE LAST KISS on her damp curls and pulled himself up to cover Beth's motionless body with his own. He settled himself into the cradle of her hips, making sure he was taking his weight on his elbows so as not to crush her slight form. He found himself gazing anxiously down at her flushed skin, luminous in the firelight. At the moment of ecstasy, she had fainted away. That was almost proof enough that she was still a virgin. Almost, but not quite. Beth herself would never accept it.

For one fleeting second after she had lost consciousness, Jon had been about to take her, to spare her the pain of first penetration. But he had not done it. He could not. He had to allow Beth the chance to refuse him, even now. Anything else would be a violation.

He bent to kiss her parted lips and then the purplish shadows on her closed eyelids. His taut flesh was straining towards the hot, moist entrance to her body, but he would not yield to its clamouring. There would be no union between them unless Beth herself decreed it should be so. No matter what it cost him. He kissed her mouth again and ran the tip of his tongue along the length of her lower lip. "Beth. Come back to me, little one."

It was like a fairy charm. Her eyes opened. She stared up at him, unfocused at first, and then all too knowing. "Was that—?"

"No. No, my sweet Beth. That was ecstasy for you alone."

"Not for you?"

168

"No, my dear. That was for you, to let you feel what lovemaking can become."

"But it proved my virginity?"

He shook his head and touched a finger to her cheek. "I wish— No, Beth. It was not proof."

"But—" She was trying to shake her head. "Jon, that was not our bargain."

"You still wish that?"

"Yes."

He took her mouth then, plunging deep, and insistently, until her response became more and more frenzied, and as feverish as when he had taken her, all alone, to the heights. Only then was he sure that she was ready for him.

"Beth." He pulled his lips from hers and raised his head. "Look at me, Beth." She opened her eyes in response. "Do you trust me?"

She gazed up at him, wide-eyed. "Yes." A whisper, but determined.

Jon drove into her with one long, powerful stroke. It was exactly as he had known it would be. The barrier of her virginity broke before his thrust. A sob rose in her throat and her face contorted in pain. Shocked, in spite of himself, he held himself very still within her, waiting, wishing he could absorb her suffering.

At last, her anguished face relaxed enough for her to look up at him. Even in the dim light, he could see that her eyes were sheened with tears.

"Oh, my poor Beth."

"No. It is done. It is proved. And the pain will never come again, I know. Kiss me, Jon."

He obeyed her, gladly. But as his lips and tongue moved on her mouth, so the rest of his body moved too, driven by ungovernable desire. It was impossible to prevent it, and yet he did not want to hurt her again. He should withdraw. He must.

But it seemed that Beth had other ideas. She wrapped her stocking-clad legs around him and began to kiss him even more passionately. It was too much. His driving thrusts became stronger, until they were both gasping for breath and Beth was bucking against him.

He could not. Oh, God, he must not. In a moment, it would be too late. With his last ounce of conscious control, he pulled himself from her embrace.

• • • •

One moment, she had been soaring. The next, she had plummeted back to earth. Her body felt like an overwound watch spring, brittle enough to snap at a touch. "Jon? I–I don't understand. Why—?"

He took a long shuddering breath, rolled on to the bed alongside her and drew her into his embrace. She felt his hand on her breast and his lips on hers. Skilful fingers trailed down her belly and began to stroke the innermost folds of her hot flesh. She groaned aloud. In an instant, she was soaring again. Soaring. She could see a bright light. Distant. But coming closer.

And then it exploded.

• • • •

When Beth opened her eyes, she was alone on the bed. How long had she been asleep? She had no idea. But she had clearly been dead to the world for some time, since her naked body was now warmly wrapped in the padded velvet bedcover. The crackle of a branch drew her eyes to the hearth. The fire had been made up and was burning fiercely. Where the folly room had been comfortably warm before, it was now becoming rather too hot.

"Jonathan?" He must be here somewhere.

The only response came from the fire, spitting like a snake as it consumed the dry logs. Beth began to shiver uncontrollably, as if she were walking naked under the winter stars. She was alone. Jon had taken his pleasure. And then he had left her.

At least he took the trouble to ensure you would not be cold as well. Her cynical internal voice was back, pecking at her conscience like a raven on a carcass.

That single thought was enough. She refused to lie helpless like a victim. She was her own mistress, and she would take responsibility for everything she had done. Even this. The slight ache in her belly was real enough, a reminder of her own complicity. She would not regret it. After such bliss, she could not. But her reputation must not be lost along with her virginity. She must be safely back at the rectory before first light.

The prospect of making her way across the expanse of Fratcombe Manor park in the dark was daunting. She would have only starlight to see by, for there was no moon. Still, it could have been worse. If the sky had been clouded over, there would have been no light at all.

She sat up, struggling to free herself from the velvet folds. She must find her clothes. Thank goodness she had had the sense to dress warmly.

As Jon had warned her to do.

Had it been his intention, from the first, to leave her to walk back to the village alone? Was he so callous, so calculating?

"Beth." A draught of freezing air swept across the room, turning the flames bright orange.

He is still here. As I should have known he would be. He asked me to trust him and, faint-heart that I am, I failed to do so. I shall not do so again.

"I did not think you would wake so soon." He was beside her on the bed, pulling her into his arms, caressing her hair.

Beth tried again to free herself from the bedcover. She was desperate to return his embrace, to prove to him—and to herself—that she trusted him completely. "Oh, bother, I—" She growled in frustration.

Jon responded by tightening the covers around her, pulling her even closer, and kissing her very thoroughly. Yet he was laughing at the same time. "You must not get cold, my dear," he murmured as he broke the kiss.

"But you—" It was only then that Beth saw he was fully clad. He was even wearing those confounded boots.

She turned her gaze to the fire. "Is it time to leave?" she asked quietly. She could feel the colour rising on her neck. The thought of returning to the rectory, even with Jon's careful help, was reminding her of how very far she had strayed from the path of propriety.

"No, not yet. There is something I wish to show you first."

Beth whipped round to look at him. He looked more relaxed, more at ease, than she had ever seen him. The fine lines on his face seemed to have been smoothed away and there was a slight curve about his mouth. Not a smile, exactly, but a sign that he was content, at peace with his world. Was she, Beth, responsible for that?

He stood up and, in a single powerful movement, lifted her into his arms. Wrapped as she was, she could not resist. In truth, she had no desire to. She did try to free her arms, for she needed to touch him. Very much.

"Don't fight me, Beth. It is too cold for that." He dropped a kiss on her forehead and started for the door.

Beth was too astonished to say a word. Jon shouldered the door open and carried her out into the night. He had been right about the cold. Under the cloudless sky, the air was almost freezing. If Beth had not been so warmly held, she would have shivered. As it was, she sank deeper into Jon's arms. She did not care where he was taking her. It was glorious simply to be held so.

He carried her round to the back of the folly. She heard noises, scuffling movements on the ground, and whiffling. Saracen, of course. He must be stabled somewhere near. To Beth's surprise, Jon ignored the horse and started to climb some stairs. She had not realised they existed.

"Where are you taking me?"

"On to the roof."

"Why?"

They had reached the top of the stairs. Jon strode across to the middle of the roof and planted his feet firmly so that he could adjust Beth's position in his arms. "Look up, and you will see."

She leant her head back on to his shoulder. "Oh. Oh, how beautiful it is." The sky was not black, as she had expected. It was a deep rich colour, somewhere between darkest blue and purple. And the stars were strewn across it like daisies in a meadow—except that these daisies were twinkling and they would never fade and die, as mere flowers did.

"Have you never gazed at the stars before, Beth?"

"N–not like this."

He laughed, and tightened his grip. "It is a little unusual, I admit. But when we are married, we can do it again. Only if you wish," he added, sounding apologetic.

"Is that why you come here? To look at the stars?"

"Mmm. In the wilds of Spain, the night sky always seemed immense, and magical. So I had the folly refurbished as an observatory. I come here at night. And not for the nefarious purposes you suspected yesterday, Miss Prim." His white teeth flashed. He was trying to make his grin look like a leer, but it was not working. He was laughing too much.

"Fie on you, sir. To call me 'Miss Prim' when I am in your arms and we have—" She stopped. Even with their new-found closeness, she could not say the words.

Jon's reply was to carry her over to one corner of the roof where he sat down on a wooden bench and settled Beth on his lap. "From here, you may see most of the park, as well as the stars." He gestured towards a fine telescope and a small stool behind it.

Beth snuggled against him. Was this what their life together would be? He had talked of companionship, but she had never imagined it could be so close, so warm, so trusting. She was right to love this man, even if he would never be able to love her in return.

The back of her head was on his shoulder. His arm was around her, holding her snugly, safely against his body. Then he rested his cheek against her hair so that she could feel his breath on her skin. She closed her eyes to savour the moment. She wanted to remember this for ever.

"I'm afraid that gnarled old tree rather spoils the panorama."

His prosaic comment shattered Beth's reverie. She opened her eyes and followed his pointing finger. "You could always cut it down, if it offends your notion of perfection," she said, a little sharply.

"Oh, no, I could never do that. It is the only tree on the whole estate with mistletoe growing on it. I never saw a single sprig of it in Spain."

"Mistletoe?" Beth suddenly felt very, very cold.

It made no sense. She was as warmly wrapped as before, and quite as secure in Jon's arms. What was it about mistletoe?

"It is my childish fancy, I fear, but I know you will not betray my weakness. An earl is not supposed to feel affection for such things. But, when I was a little boy, mistletoe seemed to be the symbol of Christmas. It was a truly happy time for all of us, especially for Henry and me, as we were so close in age. We played such games together. With Cousin Ned, too, sometimes. We— Sadly, Henry died, and I became the heir. Nothing was quite the same afterwards."

Jon's bleak grimace was telling. In her sudden concern for him, Beth pushed the image of mistletoe from her mind.

"George came later. He and I— He is a great deal younger than me and w–we have very little in common," Jon said in a low voice. "And I'm afraid that you know, from bitter experience, what manner of man he is."

Beth certainly did. But she assumed that all Jon's close family would have to be invited to attend the wedding. Including his lecherous, repulsive brother. "Shall you invite him here?" She could not bring herself to utter the word "wedding". If she dared to assume it was going ahead, some demon might appear and snatch it from her fingers.

"No."

Beth could not believe how much anger there was in that single word. Did Jon despise his brother because of what he had done to Beth? Or was there more?

"No. George no longer comes to Fratcombe Manor." He kissed her hair, breathing deeply. When he spoke again, his anger was leashed. "You will meet him again—and my mother—at King's Portbury. But only after I have made you mistress of it. Which requires a wedding. A very *private* wedding."

"You mean *here*?"

"Why, yes."

"But I assumed your brother would be your best man and—"

"No, not George. Given a choice, my best man would be my cousin, Ned Garway. But he is still fighting in Spain. My cousin Luke, too. So there is no one. My steward will serve. It will be a very private affair, as I said."

"Oh." It sounded almost as if he were ashamed of her. Though he had implied it was to protect her from his own family at King's Portbury. She tried to cling on to that small shred of reassurance. "You have decided everything already?"

"I assumed you would wish the Reverend Aubrey to perform the ceremony. And that it should take place as soon as I can arrange it. Was I wrong?"

She shook her head. She had been wrong about his motives. He had been thinking about her, and about what she might wish. Her throat was too tight for speech and she could feel the beginning of tears in her eyes. To be married to Jon, and by the dear man who had protected her against so much pain and loneliness. It was much more happiness than she deserved.

"Excellent. I shall speak to him tomorrow. Or rather—" he glanced up at the sky, but it was still quite dark "—later this morning."

"What if he will not agree? What if—?"

"He will agree, I promise you."

"But—"

Jon silenced her protests by putting his lips to hers and kissing her hungrily. Soon passion was beginning to consume them both, as it had before. For Beth, everything else was forgotten.

She tore her mouth from his at last. "I need to touch you." She was wriggling within her velvet. "I don't care if I freeze in the process."

"But I do," he said, on the thread of a laugh. He rose easily to his feet and started across the roof, still holding Beth securely wrapped. "Let us return downstairs where it is warm. We have hours yet before I must take you back. A long, long time, Beth, in which I promise I shall let you do exactly as you wish."

• • • •

Jon strode so quickly along the hallway that Mrs Aubrey's little maid was left a long way behind. "I will announce myself," he called over his shoulder. Better to have this done

175

quickly. He rapped on the library door and threw it open, without waiting for the rector to respond.

"Jonathan." Mr Aubrey had been sitting behind his desk, quill in hand, gazing vacantly out of the window. He threw down his pen and started to his feet, smiling broadly. "What brings you to see us so early?"

Jon paused in the open doorway to bow politely, before closing it quickly and coming forward into the small book-lined room. A good log fire burned in the grate, warming the library against the autumn chill, exactly as Jon had warmed the folly room last night.

"Jonathan?" The rector's smile had become a little uncertain.

Jon dragged his wandering thoughts back to the business in hand. This should be a straightforward interview, a matter of plain dealing between two men who knew each other very well. So why did memories of sweet-tasting skin and sighs of ecstasy keep trying to intrude and divert him from his purpose?

Because this was more than a business transaction now. Those last blissful hours holding Beth in his arms, uniting their bodies till they were sated with loving, and yet still yearning for each other. In one night, Jon had learnt that their physical union could be more satisfying than he would have dreamt. *Could be?* Rather, it *would* be, for both of them, provided there was no impediment now.

"Good morning, sir. I have come to ask your permission to marry Beth."

The rector's mouth dropped open. He stared. No wonder. Jon had blurted out his request like a panting, love-sick boy, rather than a grown man. What had become of the Earl of Portbury's hard-won self-control?

The rector cleared his throat and straightened his shoulders. "It is perhaps a little early in the day," he said carefully, "but I think I should welcome a glass of Madeira." He crossed to the little table where the decanters stood. Stopper in hand, he half-turned back to Jon. "You will join me, I hope, my boy?"

Jon forced himself to respond as if this interview were the most normal thing in the world. "Thank you, sir. With pleasure."

By the time the rector had set down the glasses and resumed his seat behind the desk, they had both had time to collect their thoughts. Jon took the visitor's chair opposite the rector's and allowed himself a small swallow of wine. It was only Madeira, but it burned its way down to his empty stomach. After spending the early hours at the folly removing every last trace of Beth's presence there, he had stopped only long enough at the Manor to change his clothes.

The rector set his elbows on the desk and steepled his fingers. "You are asking my permission to marry Beth?"

"Yes, sir. As soon as may be. We hope you will perform the ceremony, too. If you agree, I plan to post up to London for a special licence." He had not said as much to Beth, but it was the only sensible way to proceed. She would accept that. She was nothing if not sensible.

"Jonathan, I— My boy, I do not see that I can give you what you seek. Beth lives here as our adopted daughter, it is true, but I have no authority over her, especially not in something as important as this. She is a grown woman and her own mistress."

Jon nodded. "I am aware of that, sir. And I am proud to say that she has already accepted my proposal of marriage."

"Indeed? You surprise me."

Jon bristled. "May I ask why?"

The rector laid his hands flat on the desk and leaned forward, frowning. "Beth has great common sense, and great delicacy, too. She knows—as you and I do, also—that she is a lady born and bred, but a lady with neither name nor family. A nameless female cannot marry a peer of the realm. I cannot believe that she would have agreed to such a thing."

Jon swallowed his surging temper. This old man was his friend, and Beth's protector, to boot. If the rector could not be brought round to see the advantages of the match, no one else would, either. "Beth has your name, sir, and that is quite honourable enough for *this* peer of the realm. Allow me to be open about this. I may be an earl, but I do not seek another great match, for I have learned how disastrous they can be. What is more, I have seen the available candidates. Believe me, sir, I could not abide any of them for even a week." He forced himself to relax a little, and tried to smile winningly. "Beth and I have an understanding. She will bring me the peaceful, comfortable home I have been longing for and—God willing—the son I need to carry on my line. In return, I will give her my name and the position she has lacked since her unfortunate accident. Once she is the Countess of Portbury, no one will dare to question her past."

The rector's eyebrows rose but he said only, "So it is not a love match?"

Love? Jon shook his head vehemently. "Love is for hot-headed young bloods and simpering misses just out of the schoolroom. No, sir, this is to be a union of wiser heads than that. I esteem Beth greatly. She is a woman of sterling qualities, as she has amply demonstrated during her time here at Fratcombe. She will make me a splendid countess on the public stage. And in private, we shall enjoy the quiet companionship we have both come to value."

"I see." Mr Aubrey sounded a little sad. He was staring down at his hands, avoiding Jon's gaze.

In the end, it was Jon who broke the tense silence. "Will you agree to perform the ceremony, sir? It is Beth's dearest wish."

The rector slowly raised his head. His eyes had lost their usual brightness. They were rheumy, as if he had suddenly aged ten years. "I am sorry, Jonathan. It is impossible. You must see that, surely?"

Jon drew himself up. "No, sir, I do not."

The rector sighed. "I have to know that the couple are free to marry. You are a widower, but Beth— Jonathan, she could be anything, even some other man's wife."

Jon took a deep breath. He was going to have to be extremely frank and trust to the old man's discretion. "I can assure you that Beth has not been any man's wife, sir." He held the rector's gaze, waiting for a sign that the full import of his words had been understood. It came sooner than Jon had expected. The rector's eyes widened a fraction, and his sharp intake of breath echoed in the silence. "I see that you take my meaning, sir. To put the matter beyond doubt, I should perhaps add that there is now every reason to carry out the marriage ceremony as soon as it may be arranged." It was a little underhand to lead Mr Aubrey to believe that Beth might be with child, but Jon found he was prepared to go to almost any lengths to achieve his purpose. Nothing else mattered.

The rector downed the rest of his wine in a single swallow, got to his feet and began to pace. There was precious little room in the tiny library. He had to turn after every three or four steps.

Jon remained perfectly still, watching. There was nothing more he could do until the old man had finished struggling with his conscience.

"You leave me with no choice," the rector said at last, in a weary voice. "You assure me that Beth has been no man's wife, and I must accept your word. Though I must tell you, my lord, that I deplore what you must have done to establish your proofs of that. I would not have trusted you alone with Beth if I had suspected you might fail to behave as a gentleman should." He glowered at Jon. "It seems my judgement of you was wrong."

Jon had risen when the rector began to speak. Now he clamped his lips tightly together. He could say nothing at all in defence of his own honour without impugning Beth's. That he would not do.

"If there is a risk that you have got her with child—?"

Jon looked the rector in the eye but made no other response. He had done enough to hurt the old man. He would not tell him a direct lie.

The rector shook his head sadly. "If she was a virgin when you took her, there is at least no risk of bigamy."

Jon allowed himself a tiny nod.

"And as there must now be a risk that she is with child, I have no choice but to ensure that this, er, irregular union of yours is sanctified in church. You have forced my hand, Jonathan, as I have no doubt you intended." He frowned up at Jon. "Go to London. If you return with a special licence, I will marry you both."

Jon let out a long breath. "Thank you, sir. I–I ask your pardon for the—" His voice trailed off. He could not think of an appropriate word.

"Deception?"

Jon flushed like a guilty schoolboy caught in some childish mischief. "You have every right to be angry, sir, and I admit that my behaviour has been, er, less honourable than you had the right to expect. For that, and that alone, I apologise unreservedly. I hope that I may, one day, regain your trust." He raised his chin. "However, I cannot apologise for what has been done, since there was no other route that could have led to marriage between myself and Beth. That I could never regret, even if it were to lead to a rift with you. Needless to say, I fervently hope that it will not."

The rector's eyes had lost their rheumy cast. They had become thoughtful instead. He nodded slowly, twice. "I doubt there will be any rift, provided— Jonathan, I have one question for you. Tell me the truth of it, on your honour. Was Beth a willing partner in this?"

The question twisted in Jon's gut. The rector was asking if he had taken Beth by force, to ensure she could not refuse him. How could a Christian gentleman think such a thing?

Because he does not know what to think of you now, Jon. The voice of Jon's conscience was strong. He had given the rector every reason to doubt his honour. He must reassure the old man now. But he must not betray Beth. After a pause, he said only, "Beth was a willing partner. Yes."

The rector sighed. With relief, Jon supposed. "Since I have every intention of forgetting what has passed between us this morning, you may be easy now, Jonathan." The harshness of tone was gone. "I shall say nothing to my wife. Or to Beth. Other than to offer my congratulations, of course." His warm smile lit up his eyes. He might disapprove of what they had done, but he was glad for them both, or for Beth, at least.

"You are very generous, sir."

"Thank you, my boy. Shall you live here at Fratcombe, do you think?" It sounded like the most natural enquiry possible. The inquisition was done, and forgotten.

180

"For some of the time, I am sure," Jon replied, relaxing at last. "Beth will want to keep an eye on her school and on the progress of her little ones. I shall endow it on her behalf, of course, so that you may employ a replacement teacher. But I imagine we shall spend much of the year at King's Portbury, my principal seat. May I hope, sir, that you and Mrs Aubrey will visit us? I am sure that Beth will join me in issuing the invitation, the moment we are settled at Portbury Abbey."

The rector cocked his head on one side and narrowed his eyes, though his smile did not falter. After a moment, he said, "That is very generous of you, Jonathan. Mrs Aubrey will be most gratified, I am sure. And speaking of Mrs Aubrey—" he crossed to the fire to pull the bell "—I think it is high time we gave her this momentous news. She will wish to congratulate you both."

He turned to smile wickedly at Jon. "I have not seen Beth yet today. I wonder how she will look? I imagine—don't you?—that she will be blooming like a rose, now that she is, um, betrothed."

Chapter Nineteen

JON GAZED AT THE DYING fire as he savoured the last of his port. Supper had been something of a trial, even though he had dismissed the servants. Beth had seemed subdued, even anxious. Jon could not understand it. Now that they were married, her position was secure. No mere Lady Fitzherbert could harm her. Surely she could not be fearing her wedding night? They both knew that their lovemaking could be glorious.

She would be in her bedchamber now, their private realm. Jon felt his body stirring in anticipation and swore at the flames. He could not endure the thought of backstairs gossip about the master's feelings for his wife. If he was to avoid that, he would have to pay particular attention to keeping a proper distance from Beth. Cool formality was required between an earl and his countess. He had seen it between his parents, even without servants present. It was a lesson Jon had learned very young. It should not be difficult to put it into practice now.

He glanced at the clock. Too soon yet to join her. He would drink another glass of port. Slowly.

He began to make plans for the journey from Fratcombe to London, hoping that it would divert his thoughts from the night's pleasures to come. Gentle, prolonged lovemaking was what they needed, for the early days of their marriage. Unfortunately, travelling so late in the year would not make that easy.

Tomorrow, he would tell his steward to organise Portbury horses at all the staging posts. That would make the journey more comfortable for Beth, and quicker too. The sooner Jon had her installed at King's Portbury, the sooner their comfortable union could truly begin. And then his mother could take over the task of instructing Beth in her duties.

His mother would welcome Beth with open arms, he was sure. He could not promise her an heir yet, but he fully intended to do his best to get one. With Beth, he would enjoy the intimate side of their life. Perhaps, one day, he might even be able to tell her about—

No, there were some things that a gently-bred lady should never hear, even from her husband. In that dark moment, Jon realised that he would not be able to sleep in Beth's bed, however much he wanted to hold her in his arms. He could not take the risk. He must always leave her to sleep alone.

• • • •

This was not a bedchamber, Beth decided. It was paradise.

"Happy, my dear?"

Beth forced her heavy eyelids open. Jon was leaning over her, gazing down into her face. "Mmm." The tiny lines around his eyes relaxed but otherwise he did not move a fraction. He was waiting for her to say something a little more meaningful. "When we were, um, together at the folly," she began shyly, "it was wonderful. I did not think that anything could be— But here, in our marriage bed, it was utterly blissful."

"Ah." He sank back on to the bed beside her and pulled her into his embrace. After a second or two, his fingers began idly playing with a lock of her hair, pulling it straight and watching it spring back into a tight curl. "You have beautiful hair, Beth. I cannot tell you how often I have longed to do that." He repeated the gesture and laughed at the simple pleasure of it.

She was, without doubt, the happiest woman in the world. She had married the man she loved and, while he did not love her in return, he must care for her a little. How could their physical union be so glorious if he did not? He was very formal and reserved in public—far too much so for Beth's taste—but that might change. And, even if it did not, she would have moments like these, when he held her in his arms and they could talk about anything, and nothing. They had all the rest of the night in front of them.

"Will you teach me about the stars, Jon?"

"If you wish it. But that cannot be until we return to Fratcombe, next year."

"Oh." Beth had dreamt of being carried up to the folly roof again, safe in Jon's arms. But perhaps it was for the best. It was truly winter now. They could wait until the summer, when the weather would be warm enough to dispense with clothes altogether. Goodness, what an outrageous thought. It must be the effects of all the wanton things that she and Jon had been doing together. She snuggled a little closer and tried to stifle a yawn. It had been a long, tiring day but she was not yet ready for sleep. Not when Jon's naked body was so tantalisingly close.

He dropped a kiss on her hair and rested his cheek against it. "After London—where our visit must be very brief—we shall be at King's Portbury until after Christmas. In January, I shall have to be in London when Parliament reassembles, but there is no reason for you to leave the Abbey until shortly before the Season starts. We probably shan't be able to return to Fratcombe until the summer. Can you wait until then for your lessons?"

"I…" He had her life all mapped out. And large parts of it seemed to involve leaving her alone in a house where she knew no one, except Hetty Martin. Thank goodness Beth had had the strength to insist that Hetty should serve as her lady's maid.

Jon stroked a finger down her neck and over her breast. His touch was magical. Her body took fire instantly. She reached up to pull his mouth down to hers. "The lessons I need, husband," she said huskily, "are here and now."

• • • •

Jon lay motionless until he was sure that Beth was sound asleep. She was a wonderful bedmate, so generous, so passionate. He would never have believed that a virgin could turn into a seductress in such a short space of time. But she had. If he were younger, and less conscious of his position, he would remain in her bed for a week, at least. But that would shame them both before the servants. He could not do that to

Beth. Their intimacy must be reserved for the hours of darkness.

He allowed himself to drop one last kiss on her curls and slipped out from under the covers. His heavy silk dressing gown was as he had left it, draped across the chair by the bed where he could easily lay his hand on it in the dark. He let it slide over his body. The silk felt cold and stiff compared with Beth's soft, caressing touch. The urge to return to her was incredibly strong. He forced himself to quell it. He had no choice.

He padded barefoot to the connecting door. The way was clear, for he had been careful to ensure there was nothing he might trip over. He had even counted the steps.

He left Beth's bedchamber without looking back.

• • • •

Beth was finding London something of a trial. Since Parliament was not sitting, most of the great families were on their country estates, slaughtering birds. Jon had taken rooms at Grillon's Hotel, in order—he said—to avoid opening up Portbury House. He was also avoiding any formal announcement that the Earl and Countess of Portbury were in town, in order to ensure that Beth could go about the business of acquiring a new wardrobe without having to receive calls from sharp-eyed society tabbies, eager to find new material for tittle-tattle.

Unfortunately, Beth's shopping expeditions had been lonely ones, for Jon would not accompany her. A man was worse than useless on such occasions, he maintained; besides, he had business affairs to attend to. Beth was prepared to accept that his business might be more important than his new wife's wardrobe, but did it really have to occupy every waking hour? Did he have to be so very distant?

After three days with only Hetty for company, Beth concluded her husband was avoiding her. There was no other possible explanation. Why, they had dined together only once, and he had left again immediately, without a word of excuse.

On the fourth day, she woke with a pounding headache and the old familiar nausea. Her nightmares had returned to point accusing fingers at her guilty past. Had she been wrong to let

Jon persuade her into marriage? He had been adamant that her past did not matter, that his great position would place his wife beyond criticism. Yet he himself was now avoiding her. Was he having second thoughts about his hasty proposal and their even hastier wedding?

She tried to push the drumming guilt away. She had not deceived him. She had refused him. But he had ignored her objections and then used wicked—wonderful—persuasion to change her mind. He was still doing so every night.

He could not make love to her with such tenderness if he regretted their marriage. She would not believe that. He was distant because... He was distant because he was always so, with everyone. She refused to believe that he might be ashamed of her. But he certainly wanted to establish her at King's Portbury, and with his family, before they entered London society as a newly-wed couple. Was that also why he planned to return to London alone, in the New Year? He must know that she was haunted by guilt about her mysterious past. He had thrown the protective cloak of his rank around her, but that would not stop the whispering, the malicious gossip. Was it to save Beth from wicked tongues that he was leaving her behind?

But no, that could not be the way of it. He had announced his intentions on the very day of their wedding. It was not out of concern for Beth's sensitivities that he planned to go to London without her. He had not considered Beth's preferences at all.

She was being unfair, and she knew it. Jon was not callous in that way. He simply stood aloof. He was sure of his own judgement and consulted no one before making decisions. He was convinced that Beth would soon find herself very much at home at King's Portbury. Why should his wife wish to exchange such a comfortable situation for the cold and clamour of London in early January? The weather would no doubt be foul, and the roads quite appalling. It would never occur to him that his wife would gladly endure hours of freezing travel, and damp posting-house beds, in return for a few hours a day with the husband she loved.

He did not know. He would not ask.

And she could never tell him.

• • • •

The private parlour was heaped with packages. Poor Hetty was trying to unwrap and arrange the contents in piles suitable for packing, but even so, there was barely space to sit down.

"Good Gad, ma'am. *More* purchases?"

Beth spun round. Jon was leaning against the door jamb, surveying the chaos through narrowed eyes. A thread of anxiety began to uncoil in her stomach but, this time, she refused to let it grow. She was awake, and in control of her doubts. This was Jonathan, her husband, the man who came to her bed and took her to paradise. He was not hostile to her, and he did not seek her humiliation. His public manner was only a mask he wore, to protect them both from the barbs of the gossips, inside or outside their household.

She had learned one way of cracking his mask during these last few days in London. "I have a confession to make, my lord." She bowed her head meekly. "I think I may have bankrupted you."

He roared with laughter and started towards her. Hetty, eyes demurely downcast, sidled out behind him and closed the parlour door.

Beth raised her head again, and gazed at Jon. When he had first appeared in the doorway, she had thought he looked worn, but now he seemed alive again, almost carefree. "This is the last of them." She gestured towards the piles of expensive clothing he had urged her to buy. "We may leave London as soon as you wish."

"Excellent." He reached out a hand to stroke her cheek, but pulled it away hurriedly before it could touch her skin. He flushed very slightly, as if embarrassed by what he had almost done.

Beth held his gaze unwaveringly. She had finally come to accept, reluctantly, that he never made gestures of affection, even when they were alone. It was as if he expected an interruption at any moment. In her bedchamber, it was different, but only there. And he never, ever, stayed with her till morning.

187

"Everything is ready for our journey," he said. "Tomorrow, I think. I have arranged for Portbury horses at all the staging posts, so we should not be delayed."

Beth tried to keep her expression neutral. She disliked travelling in such pomp, with servants bowing and scraping at every turn. She had been surprised that Jon chose to do so. At Fratcombe, he unbent a little, at least with the Aubreys. The moment he left it, he donned this starched-up aristocratic manner with everyone. Sometimes, she was not sure what kind of man she had married.

He was spelling out the route they would take. "We will travel light. Any extra baggage may follow on behind."

"Hetty will take care of it."

"No. Your maid will travel with you, ma'am, in your carriage. The Countess of Portbury does not travel alone."

"Y–you do not accompany me, sir?" Beth did not quite manage to control the tremor in her voice.

"But of course. However, I plan to ride. I have taken far too little exercise while we have been here in London."

He was avoiding her company, even more than on their journey from Fratcombe. It must all be part of that confounded mask he would not discard. But why? What could he possibly be hiding from?

"We shall reach King's Portbury in a few days, if the weather holds. Then, at last, we will be able to settle down to that comfortable, companionable life I promised you, Beth. You will learn to run my household—my mother will instruct you in your role there—while I deal with the business of my estates, and my duties to Parliament. I have neglected both, I fear, since my return from Spain. In the evenings, we will be able to sup together, as a family, and sit by the fire. It is a delightful picture, is it not?"

It was not delightful at all. It appeared that the dowager would be living with them, as well as *instructing* Beth. That sounded daunting enough. Worse was that Jon clearly wished to avoid being alone with Beth, except in her bed, which was simple necessity, for the getting of an heir.

She had thought he valued her, as a trusted friend. She was beginning to suspect that she might have been wrong.

Chapter Twenty

"AH, JON. PUNCTUAL AS EVER." His mother was beaming at him without a trace of artifice. "Do come over to the fire. I know how chilly you find it, here in England."

Jon took his stance in front of the roaring fire and let it warm his back. He glanced round at his mother's cosy sitting room. Soon, she would return to the Dower House and Beth would take over this room. In the spring, he decided, he would offer to have it redecorated for her, in any colour she wanted. She might like new furniture, too. There was no reason why she should have to keep what Alicia had chosen. The memory of his dead wife sent the usual shudder down his spine.

"There, it is precisely as I said. You are still frozen to the marrow. I cannot imagine why you chose to ride when you could have travelled in your comfortable carriage, with hot bricks for your feet."

"I needed the exercise, Mama." A half-truth. After London, he had known it was wisest to avoid Beth's company. "Spain can be cold in winter, too, you know," he quipped.

"I'm sure it can, my dear." She glanced towards the door. "Is your wife not planning to join us? I thought we might have tea, the three of us together. We have had no time for real conversation since you arrived."

"Beth is tired after travelling all day, Mama. I told her to rest before dinner. I knew you would understand."

His mother gave him a very quizzical look. "If she is fatigued, then she must certainly rest. Pull the bell, Jon, if you please."

189

The butler arrived almost instantly with the tea tray. As was her wont, Jon's mother sat silent and immobile until Goodrite had bowed himself out. It was partly from her that Jon had learned the importance of protecting his privacy. Gossip, whether from servants or gentry, could be the very devil.

The dowager calmly poured tea and handed Jon his cup. She had remembered exactly how he liked it. She had always been a consummate hostess. Beth would be learning from the best possible teacher.

"If you are warmer now, perhaps you would sit down? I find that looking up so far creates a pain in the neck."

Jon gave a snort of laughter, but he did as he was bid.

"Your wife looks to be a delightful girl, Jon. You met her at Fratcombe, I collect?" When he nodded, she continued without a pause. "I see now why you were so eager to return there. You said, if I recall correctly, that you were returning to meet a challenge you relished. If Miss Aubrey was the challenge in question, I can quite understand your haste. She has a—a certain quality that would draw a man."

Jon started back, took a deep breath through his nose and let it out very, very slowly. He did not dare open his lips, lest he insult his mother by telling her precisely what he thought of her tasteless remark. Was she actually daring to suggest that Beth had led him on in some vulgar fashion? That she was a practised seductress?

His silent fury must have been obvious, for his mother quickly became contrite. "Forgive me, I did not mean to say anything in her dispraise. She is, as I said at the outset, a delightful young lady. I would not, for the world, pry into the details of your courtship, Jon. It is enough for me that you are married, and content."

"Thank you, Mama." He must have mistaken her meaning, he decided. She would never malign the wife he had chosen. And she would help Beth to find her feet at Portbury, too. "I hope that you and Beth will soon become like mother and daughter. After all, you never had a daughter of your own, did you?" Alicia did not count. She had been a failure as a wife, and also as a daughter-in-law.

190

"No, I did not," she said, with a slightly tight smile. "If your wife becomes like a daughter to me, I should be more than glad."

It irked him suddenly that his mother would not call Beth by name, even though she knew it perfectly well. "Her name, Mama, is Beth."

"Elizabeth?"

"She prefers Beth."

"Then so it shall be." She leant towards him a little, smiling broadly. "By the way, I sent out all the Christmas invitations in the normal way. I knew your wife—I knew Beth would not arrive here in time to do them." She preened a little. "The first guests will arrive in about a week."

Jon swore inwardly. The Portbury tradition of holding a grand Christmas house party was the last thing he wanted to continue. He should have told his mother to cancel it this year, but he had totally forgotten about it. So he could not blame her for what she had done. Indeed, she had been trying to be helpful. He managed to exclaim as if he were delighted. "I had no right to expect such exertions from you, Mama, especially now that I have a wife at my side to act as hostess."

"As I said, there would not have been time. If the invitations had been late, there would have been gossip." She sniffed. She detested gossip about her family. "Everyone has accepted. Except Great-aunt Harriet, of course, who still refuses to move from Devon in the middle of winter. She promises to make a formal bride visit in the spring, however."

That was the only small consolation. Beth would not have to suffer Miss Harriet Garway's acid tongue until she was more secure in her role as countess. Great-aunt Harriet had been known to make even grown men flinch; most servants cowered and fled as soon as they dared.

"It should be a splendid party, Jon. And I was happy to arrange it. Miss Mountjoy helped. In fact, she has made some remarkably useful suggestions."

Miss Mountjoy. He should have guessed. Had Miss Mountjoy put the house-party notion into the dowager's head? It would be subtle revenge if she had. And no doubt, her suggestions had served to increase the guest list and lengthen their stay. The Mountjoy woman was both clever and dangerous, with a slyly malicious tongue, but as long as she was his mother's confidante, there was nothing Jon could say, not even to Beth.

. . . .

Hetty slipped into Beth's bedchamber and crept across to the bed.

"I am not asleep, Hetty. I feel much refreshed and my headache has gone." That was a blessing, since she had misled Jon, saying only that she was weary.

"Miss Mountjoy is here, m'lady. With a message from her ladyship."

"Miss Mountjoy? Here? How very strange. I will come at once." Miss Mountjoy had been introduced by the dowager as a neighbour from the village, yet here she was, running errands as if she were a menial. Moreover, although she did not live at Portbury Abbey, she clearly knew the house intimately. Beth was at a loss to understand what was going on, but good manners prevailed; she slipped her arms into the wrapper Hetty was holding and followed her maid into the sitting room that divided her bedchamber from Jon's.

Miss Mountjoy's eyes widened as Beth came into the room. She stared for several seconds too long, before dropping a brief curtsey. For some reason, it made Beth uncomfortable to be meeting this odd woman when so informally clad. "I am a little cold, Hetty. Fetch my shawl, please."

"Hetty?" Miss Mountjoy said as the maid disappeared. "What a curious name for a lady's maid." She clapped a hand to her mouth to cover a high-pitched titter. "Oh, pray forgive me, my lady. I did not mean to sound impertinent. But I thought— That is, her ladyship said you would be bound to engage a high-class dresser while you were in London. Seeing someone so young and small was something of a shock."

Miss Mountjoy might be the dowager's bosom bow, but she was certainly not going to be Beth's. Insufferable woman. How dare she?

Beth waited for Hetty to wrap the heavy Norwich shawl around her shoulders and return to the bedchamber before she spoke. She was the Countess of Portbury now. She would not be outfaced by a woman like this. "My maid said you had a message from her ladyship. It was not, I collect, about my choice of dresser?"

Miss Mountjoy's nostrils quivered for a second. Then she smiled too broadly. "No, indeed, my lady, I— His lordship's lady mother was concerned to learn that you were so fatigued after your journey, especially after travelling in such extravagant comfort. We thought you might perhaps be, um, ailing. She knows I have some knowledge of attending to ladies when their health is, er, delicate." She raised her chin proudly. "That was before I came to King's Portbury, of course. If there is anything I might do to assist your ladyship…?"

Good grief. Jon's mother was sending this toady to enquire if Beth was breeding. It was beyond insult. It was utter humiliation. Was this how her life was to be at King's Portbury?

"Hetty." The maid appeared instantly. She must have been standing behind the door.

"Thank you for your concern, Miss Mountjoy, but I shall not be needing your assistance." Let her make what she would of that. "Hetty, show Miss Mountjoy out." Without so much as a nod to her unwelcome visitor, Beth turned on her heel and marched back into her bedchamber.

"How much of that did you hear?" Beth demanded when Hetty returned.

"I–I beg your pardon, m'lady. I wasn't trying to eavesdrop, but I knew I should be on hand in case—"

Beth cut off the excuse with a wave of her hand. "We will not discuss Miss Mountjoy's insinuations about my state of health." She swallowed hard, determined to master her emotions, even though only Hetty was there to see. "But her comments about you are another matter."

Hetty reddened and stared at the floor.

"Hetty?" When the maid did not reply, Beth began to suspect there was something more at work than Miss Mountjoy's vitriolic tongue. "We have been here less than a day. What has happened to upset you?"

Hetty did not move or look up. At last, she whispered, "Countess Alicia had a very superior French dresser, according to the housekeeper."

"I see. And she implies that you are not equal to the task?"

"Not in so many words, m'lady. No one does. But there are, er, looks and whispers. Though I might have imagined those."

Beth was fairly sure that Hetty had not been mistaken. And if the servants were gossiping behind Hetty's back about the new mistress's choice of maid, what were they saying about the mistress herself? For Hetty's sake, Beth would find out the truth of all this. And then she would nip such rebellious behaviour in the bud.

"Ignore them, Hetty. Remember that you are maid to the mistress of the house, if you please. For now, it's probably best for you to remain rather aloof. As a superior French maid would do." Beth smiled encouragingly down at her maid.

"I'll do just as you say, m'lady. Your ladyship chose me to serve you and I am proud of the fact, no matter what Miss Mountjoy may say."

"Miss Mountjoy? Has she been sowing mischief below stairs? But how? She is not a servant."

"She used to be, after a fashion. She were Countess Alicia's paid companion for more than ten years, so I were told, m'lady. Now she lives in a fine cottage in the village. His lordship gave it to her, they say."

"Whatever they *say* about his lordship, Hetty, you will *not* repeat."

Hetty blushed an even fierier red than before. "No, m'lady. Begging yer pardon, m'lady." At Beth's nod of dismissal, she fled back into the sitting room.

Beth began to pace up and down the bedchamber. Jon had provided a cottage for his late wife's companion? Why on earth would he do that? She was clearly a mischief-maker of the first order. Sly, too. No doubt the mean backstairs gossip about Hetty had started with her. Beth would have to find a way of countering that.

But in the meantime, she had to understand about Miss Mountjoy and Jon. Years ago, before he went to Spain, the woman might have been an attractive armful for a man with a roving eye. Had she and Jon been lovers, perhaps? Jon was a passionate man. If he could not bed the wife he hated, would he bed her companion instead? Was the cottage given by way of compensation?

It was a hateful thought. Had Jon thought to resume his liaison with her on his return from the wars? Even if that had been his intention, surely he would not pursue it now that he had remarried?

But Miss Mountjoy had a proprietorial air that disturbed Beth a great deal. As if she had power in this house.

As if she knew secrets.

• • • •

The dowager smiled complacently. "The first guests should arrive tomorrow, Jon."

He was struck by a sudden uncomfortable thought. "I take it they do not include the young ladies from your summer party, Mama?"

Her haughtily raised eyebrows were eloquent. No duke would allow his unmarried daughter to attend a house party where there were no eligible male guests. George, even if he deigned to attend, was far from eligible, for he was only an impecunious younger son, and had a reputation as a rake, besides.

"Beg pardon, ma'am. I should have known better than to ask."

Mollified, his mother began to list names, while Jon made mental notes of what he needed to say to Beth about her houseguests. Some of them, sadly, were much too high in the instep to be good company.

The butler appeared in the doorway. "Your ladyship asked to be informed when the countess returned from her drive."

"Ask her ladyship if she will be good enough to join us."

Before Goodrite could bow in response to the dowager's instruction, Jon was on his feet and making for the door. "No need. I will do it," he said curtly.

In the entrance hall, Beth was in the process of removing her heavy pelisse and bonnet. She turned at the sound of his step. Her cheeks were flushed from the chill wind, but her eyes were sparkling. He had clearly been right to send her out to take the air, to restore her bloom after several days of sitting at the dowager's feet, being tutored in her new role.

She smiled up at him. "Good afternoon, my lord," she said formally, though there was nothing in the least formal about the way her gaze softened when she looked at him. It reminded Jon, much too forcefully, of the way her eyes locked with his when they were making love.

One unwary memory, and desire was thrumming through him. He tried to say something innocuous, but he could not find the words. To cover his confusion, he took her hand and bowed over it, hoping that his extravagant gesture would make up for the words of polite greeting he could not utter.

She must have sensed something, for she ran her middle finger across his palm in a teasing caress. The unexpected touch rippled through his whole body. What on earth was she doing? It was the middle of the afternoon, and they were standing in the hallway, watched by the butler and two footmen. He dropped her hand like a hot coal and hurriedly stepped back.

"That will be all, Hetty," she said, calmly nodding dismissal to her maid. "You wanted something of me, my lord?"

Oh yes. I want to carry you up to your bedchamber and ravish you until we are both mindless with passion.

Shocked by his own reactions, Jon assumed the haughty manner he always adopted when he was at risk of betraying his inner feelings. "My lady mother is waiting for us in the saloon. Will you join us, ma'am?" As custom required, he offered Beth his arm, willing his flesh to remain totally numb. He was determined that there would be nothing for the servants to remark upon.

There was something very knowing about the way she smiled and laid her hand on his arm to be escorted to the saloon. For a woman who was only lately wed, she had learned extremely quickly how to drive a man to madness. Was that what it was? Or was he imagining it all?

"How well you look, my dear." Jon's mother smiled in welcome and waved them to the seats opposite her. Behind them, the butler closed the door without a sound.

Jon led Beth to the seat opposite his mother, but he did not take his place beside her. Better to observe her from a distance, he decided, throwing himself on to the far end of the dowager's sofa and trying to appear more relaxed than he felt.

Beth held out her hands to the blazing fire. "We had a delightful drive, ma'am. There was a sharp wind, to be sure, but the sun was shining and the sky was absolutely clear. The park was quite beautiful, even though the trees were bare." She turned to Jon, raising her eyebrows a fraction. "Perhaps, when your business is less pressing, my lord, you might be able to join me, to show me more of the estate? I should so like to know about all the features here. At one point, I thought I saw an old stone building, half hidden by trees. Do you have a folly here, too?"

Minx! Her confidence was clearly growing by the day. She was roasting him. And in front of his mother, too. He ought to be cross with her, but he was finding it increasingly difficult to maintain his austere mask. In truth, he wanted to laugh aloud. And then to kiss her till she begged for mercy. He was going to have some very strong words with the new Countess of Portbury. Later, when they were safely alone.

"Jon and I have been discussing the arrangements for the house guests," the dowager put in tartly. "If the weather continues fine, Jon will be able to entertain the gentlemen with outdoor pursuits. I imagine some of the ladies might like to join them. I recall that some of the younger wives are excellent horsewomen." She turned to Jon, who nodded rather absently. "I imagine that you will prefer to rest quietly here at the house, Beth. In the circumstances."

Beth blushed rosily and turned away to stare at the fire.

"I see no reason why Beth should not go riding if she wishes to," Jon said, rather more harshly than he had intended. "She is a fine horsewoman, too, and she may have the pick of my stables."

"Thank you." Her response was very low and directed at the hearth.

"Hmmph. I should tell you, Jon, that one of a hostess's duties is to ensure that her guests are entertained. Beth may of course go riding, but only if all the other lady guests are doing so. If some of them choose to remain at the house, as I would expect, their hostess cannot desert them. We are agreed on that, are we not, Beth?"

Beth raised her head and turned to look directly at the dowager. "None of our guests will have cause to fault the hospitality in this house, ma'am. Your lessons will not go unheeded."

The dowager nodded slowly twice, as if accepting due homage from an inferior. Jon found himself wondering precisely what had taken place during the last few days when his mother was supposedly helping Beth to assume her duties as mistress of Portbury Abbey. Was there a degree of friction between the two of them? He had blithely told Beth that, once she was his countess, no one would dare to malign her. But his mother, a dowager countess and the daughter of a wealthy and powerful family, had no need to mind her tongue. If she disapproved of Beth, she could certainly turn her life into a trial.

Jon stared across at his wife, trying to read her expression. Poor Beth. She was still far from secure in her new position. She was haunted by fears that ghosts might appear from her past to accuse her of wicked crimes. Sometimes, those fears had become so strong that she suffered appalling sick headaches. They were less frequent since her marriage, she said, but if his mother—

"I must say that you seem to be quite an apt pupil, Beth," the dowager said loftily. She ignored Beth's sharp intake of breath and turned to Jon. "Your wife may have come to us with little knowledge of how to run a great house, Jon, but she is certainly trying to learn. I have no doubt that she will do extremely well. Eventually. Once she has had a chance to put my lessons into practice."

That was exceedingly barbed, and quite unnecessarily hurtful. Jon looked at his mother with new eyes. He had thought her the pattern card of ladylike behaviour, but this? What on earth did she have against Beth? His mother was a great lady, but she clearly lacked Beth's kind heart and generosity of spirit. Beth did not deserve to be the butt of his mother's sour tongue.

"Beth, you are beginning to look rather pale," the dowager continued, in slightly friendlier tones. "Are you sure you are quite well? Miss Mountjoy told me that she found you laid upon your bed last week. She had concerns that your health might be, er, delicate. She is quite experienced in such matters, of course."

In the space of seconds, Beth's slight pallor had changed to a fiery blush. She made to speak, but no words came out.

Jon was shocked and angered by his mother's sly hint that Beth was not in robust good health. Apart from the occasional headache, she was blooming. He would not permit his wife to be tormented by Miss Mountjoy's malicious insinuations, even at second hand. Equally, he could not rebuke his mother in front of his wife. "I am surprised to learn that Miss Mountjoy took it upon herself to venture up to my wife's bedchamber. She is no longer employed here. As a visitor, she does *not* have the run of my house," he finished firmly, looking directly at his mother.

The dowager raised her chin a fraction and glared back at him. "I understood that Beth had invited Miss Mountjoy upstairs."

Jon did not believe that for a moment.

Beth was shaking her head. "I fear you have been misinformed, ma'am. I did no such thing. Nor would I," she added, with unusual vehemence. "Miss Mountjoy told me that you yourself had sent her to offer me the benefit of her, er, experience."

The dowager clamped her lips together. Her eyes were flashing angrily.

Jon knew exactly where to place the blame. Miss Mountjoy was capable of almost anything in pursuit of her hatred for Jon. This time, he would certainly have to deal with her, but first he had to prevent a rift between his mother and his wife. "Beth, my dear," he said gently, crossing to where she sat and raising her to her feet, "I am truly sorry there appears to have been a misunderstanding over this. But Mama is right, you do look a little pale. May I suggest you rest this afternoon? You have been working so hard, preparing for the house party. And you will have precious little time to yourself once the guests start arriving." He clasped her hand firmly and led her to the door. She did not resist, of course. She was too well bred to argue with Jon in front of his mother.

"I will deal with this, I promise," he murmured into her hair, as he ushered her into the hall and stood watching while she made her way towards the stairs. He tried to ignore the sway of her hips, but the motion was exceedingly attractive to the eye. It was partly his own fault, since he had encouraged her to buy that expensive velvet carriage dress. Its every movement reminded him all too vividly of the body concealed beneath.

He was shaking his head when he returned to the saloon. He must stop enjoying his wife's attractions and start thinking about how to deal with his mother's apparent antipathy to her. What on earth could be the cause of it?

"Was there something in particular you wished to discuss, Mama?" he began innocently, taking the seat that Beth had vacated. "In relation to the guests?"

His mother seemed to have relaxed now that Beth was no longer in the room with them. "No, nothing in particular. I merely wanted to impress on your wife how important it is for this house party to pass off well. It is, after all, her first experience of acting as hostess since she became your countess. She has some rather, er, quaint notions of how to go on."

Jon swore inwardly, but schooled his features into neutrality. "Indeed? I'm afraid I must have missed those, for I have seen nothing amiss. As a mere male, of course..." He allowed his words to hang in the air, like a fly dancing on the surface of the water for the fish to bite.

His mother rose to the bait. "No, you would not. Men never do, I'm afraid. Your father was as bad." When Jon said nothing, she continued, a little hesitantly, "I am hoping that your wife will come to appreciate the difference between her guests' dressers and her own maid. I do not see that a chit from the workhouse, or wherever that girl came from, is at all

200

appropriate to serve as lady's maid to a countess. *You* understand what is needed. Your own new man knows exactly what an earl's consequence requires." The dowager was starting to sound much more confident. "I wish your wife would take her cue from you and engage a proper dresser."

Jon nodded curtly. "Thank you for your advice, Mama. I will ensure the matter is dealt with." He paused a moment to bring his seething anger under control. First Miss Mountjoy, and now this. "Was that the only thing you wished to discuss with me, ma'am?"

His mother looked for a moment as though she were about to make some other comment, but there must have been something in Jon's expression that warned her to take care, for she pursed her lips and shook her head.

Jon smiled tightly. "I must thank you for all the help you have given Beth since we arrived, Mama. I am sure that, thanks to your tuition, she will do very well in her role as mistress of the Abbey. I know that you have found it irksome to be acting as my hostess over all these months, but I am very grateful. I imagine you will wish to return to the peace of the Dower House now that you have helped Beth to settle in?"

"I...um..." There was a tiny hint of a flush rising on the dowager's neck. She swallowed. "That is very considerate of you, Jon," she said tightly, "but I think it would be unwise for me to leave your wife alone quite yet. I am sure she will appreciate having a more experienced female at her side to act as, er, co-hostess. After all, she has had no chance yet to practise everything I have taught her."

"Quite so, quite so," Jon said, nodding. "And there will be other benefits of having two ladies to act as hostess. For example, you will be able to remain here at the house to entertain the older ladies, while Beth rides out with the younger ones, will you not?"

"I—" For once, the dowager looked nonplussed.

Jon leaned across to pat his mother's hand. "It is very good of you to do this, Mama, and I know Beth will appreciate the extra freedom you are giving her. As do I."

His mother nodded. She was clearly outmanoeuvred, but she was much too proud to say a word.

Jon rose and bowed. "I must ask you to excuse me, Mama. I have urgent letters to write and some other business that must be discharged today." With his jaw set, he made his way out into the hall where the butler was hovering. "Have a message sent to my land agent, Goodrite. I will see him here, in one hour." Without waiting for an acknowledgement, Jon made for the stairs. Dealing with his agent was important, but there was something else that had to be done first.

Chapter Twenty-One

WHEN JON ENTERED THE SITTING room that he shared with Beth, he was surprised to find it empty. There was no sound at all, not even the crackle of a fire, but the door into Beth's room stood partly open. He paused, wondering. He knew Beth was quite sharp enough to have understood the meaning underlying her mother-in-law's words. Would he find her weeping in her bedchamber?

He stole forward and peeped round the half-open door. Beth was lying on top of the bed, fully clad, but with her eyes closed. The maid, Martin, was sitting alongside, stroking Beth's face and— No, the girl was bathing Beth's forehead with lavender water. The subtle scent was unmistakable. And it meant Beth had the headache again. No wonder, perhaps, after that nasty confrontation downstairs. Jon took a silent step into the bedchamber.

The little maid must have sensed his arrival. She looked over her shoulder and frowned at him. Then, pert little madam, she dared to put a finger to her lips and motioned to Jon to leave.

Jon's first impulse was to reprimand her for her impudence, but one more look at Beth's peaceful face choked the words in his throat. If she was now sleeping, he should let her rest. He could deal with the maid without waking his wife. He would simply retreat to the sitting room and wait.

After a few moments, Martin emerged, closing the door very quietly behind her. Only then did she remember to curtsey. "Her ladyship is asleep, my lord."

"So I saw. Is she...?"

"She had the headache, and a little nausea, my lord, but she was quite determined that no one should be aware of it. Sh– she made me promise not to tell you."

"And if I had not seen, you would have said nothing?"

"No, my lord. I–I could not betray my lady's trust. I–I am sorry." She looked up at him, unafraid, in spite of the implicit challenge in her words. Hetty Martin might be still very young, but there was no doubt of her devotion to Beth. Love was shining in her eyes. Love for Beth.

Jon's few remaining doubts evaporated on the spot. That sort of devotion more than made up for any lack of dressing skill, or French genius with ointments and potions. He doubted that any of the top-lofty dressers arriving with his mother's guests would show even a fraction of Hetty's loyalty and commitment.

"I would not wish you to do so, Hetty," Jon said quietly, noting how the maid's eyes widened at his use of her given name. "You are her ladyship's dresser and personal maid. Your loyalty must be to her. And only to her."

Hetty curtseyed again.

"I am truly sorry that my wife is unwell, Hetty. I think I know the cause, on this occasion, and I will deal with it. However, if–if she should be upset in the future, or–or afraid, I should like you to come and tell me. Will you do that?"

Hetty stared at the floor, shaking her head.

"What do you mean, no?" Jon snapped. "If my wife needs help, who should provide it but I?"

The maid was still shaking her head. "I could not betray my lady's confidence," she whispered. "Not even to your lordship. Not to anyone." She continued to stare at the floor, like a prisoner waiting for sentence.

No wonder Beth had braved the dowager's disapproval to keep her own maid by her. This girl was a pearl beyond price. "I am not asking you to betray your mistress, Hetty," Jon said, more gently. "I only ask you to use your common sense. If my wife should need help, should need a friend, please encourage her to come to me. Or come to me yourself."

She glanced up, surprised. For a moment, she seemed to be considering his words. Then, at last, she nodded.

"And whatever should happen, I thank you for your devotion to my wife." With that, he nodded her dismissal and strode into his own bedchamber.

"Is there anything I can do for your lordship?" Vernon, the valet, slipped into the room, soft-footed as ever. Did he feel a fraction of the loyalty that little Hetty was showing to her mistress?

"No, Vernon. I shan't need you until it is time to dress for dinner." Jon glared balefully at his valet until the man bowed himself back into the dressing room. Then Jon sat down at the small desk under the window to make the most of the remaining light. He would not know for a few days whether his plan was going to work. All would depend on the response to this letter.

He pulled out a sheet of his embossed writing paper and dipped his pen in the standish. It took only a few minutes to complete the short letter and seal it. Devotion was worth more than rubies. And this would prove whether he had earned it, as Beth had.

With a shrug of his shoulders, he rose and made his way downstairs, dropping the letter on the silver salver in the entrance hall. He would have to be patient until a response could come. And in the meantime...

Jon smiled to himself and strode down the corridor to his library. By now, his agent should be waiting for his new instructions.

• • • •

Beth woke early and lay staring up towards the silken canopy. She could see nothing in the gloom. And she was alone again.

Jon had been a little hesitant about coming to her bed this last time. He had enquired, obliquely, if she wished to sleep alone. Of course she did not. She wanted to sleep in his arms all night, but she could not tell him so. The most she could do was to encourage him to come to her, even if only for an hour or so.

Instead of ignoring the dowager's hurtful remarks, Beth had stupidly let them prey on her mind. So the headache had been her own fault. She must simply accept that her mother-in-law did not like her, or trust her. But the dowager's power in the household would diminish as Beth became more secure. She must do what she could to hasten the process. She had managed to respond with spirit, on occasion. She would cling to that. The Countess of Portbury must not cower, or flee.

She strained her eyes towards the shuttered windows. Soon it would be dawn. She thought she could already hear the servants stirring. This late in the year, they could not wait for daylight to begin their chores, especially as the first guests were to arrive soon. To her own surprise, Beth found she was not at all anxious about dealing with Jon's friends, or even the dowager's. Beth had learned during her time with the Aubreys to handle all sorts of people, from the highest to the lowest.

And in the weeks since her marriage, she had even begun to learn how to deal with her husband.

She smiled up into the darkness. She was beginning to understand him. A little. In public, he was the essence of the aristocrat—distant, austere, mindful of his duty, and polite to a fault. Some of it was assumed, though not his concern for his duty. He had inherited that from the old earl, who had valued duty and rank above all else. Beth fancied he had not been a loving father to Jon. There was no doubt, however, that even though the dowager did not approve of her son's choice of second wife, she did love Jon very much. For that alone, Beth would endure any insult that her mother-in-law might voice.

Beth shrugged against the pillows. There was precious little she could do to remedy the dowager's poor opinion of her. Jon had married Beth out of hand, without introducing her to anyone first. Had he been determined to have his ring on Beth's finger before his mother could object to a penniless woman of no family? Had he—?

"Oh, fiddlesticks!" she said aloud. She was the Countess of Portbury now, and Jon was her husband. It was up to her to make this marriage work. And that included the task of running this vast mansion. Beth was sure she would have the measure of it soon. Somewhere in her past life, she imagined, she must have been taught the way of managing servants, for it came naturally enough. Beth fully intended to demonstrate how much she had learned from the dowager, too. If she could make Jon's mother proud of her, it might ease the tension between them. She would make Jon proud of her, too, if she could.

If only he would stay with her at night. If only he would spend more time with her in the day. Sometimes, she was sure he was deliberately avoiding her company. But why? He did not come to her bed merely for the getting of an heir. Beth might have been an innocent before that astonishing night in the Fratcombe folly, but she could tell that the passion they shared was very special. Jon could not make love to a woman he did not esteem. His first wife had repelled him. With Beth, there was desire, and passion, and rapture for them both.

She laughed softly, remembering. Each time was different, and yet the same. He still explored her body with a sense of wonder, as if he were uncovering something magical. That reverence almost made up for being left to sleep alone.

Almost, but not quite. There must be a way to persuade him to stay, if only she could find it. If she continued to tease him, in private ways that only the two of them understood, he might eventually unbend.

Had his mother noticed that second of shock on his face when Beth had asked about a folly at Portbury? That tiny flicker of response had been utterly delicious. She hugged the memory to herself. Teasing him in public, ever so subtly, was the way to ensure he remained aware of his wife.

All the time.

It was a good plan. And she would use it again. She had half expected to be well scolded once they were alone together, but Jon had been too concerned about her to do any such thing. He was a truly considerate man. And, heaven help her, she loved him to distraction. If only he—

She shook her head, vehemently. Jon did not love her. Perhaps he had never loved any woman? Perhaps he never could? She had seen precious few signs of attachment to anyone, or anything, apart from his duty. It would have to be enough that Beth loved him without reserve. One day, God willing, she would put a son into his arms and see him gazing down, with love, on a child of their joined flesh. Perhaps that would be enough.

In the meantime, she would do everything in her power to prove that she was fit to take her place by his side. Let the dowager judge as she would. Beth was going to show Jon that she could be a worthy countess.

• • • •

A fine carriage was bowling down the drive towards the house. Beth automatically took half a step back from her sitting room window, even though she knew that the passengers could not possibly see her up here. She did not know which guests these were, and she could not go downstairs to find out. The dowager's instructions had been absolute on the point. Her house guests expected to be shown to their bedchambers, so that they could refresh themselves and change their dress before they came down to greet their hostess.

Beth moved closer to the window in order to see down to the sweep where these first guests were about to alight. She had to stand on tiptoe and crane her neck to catch even a glimpse of what was happening.

As she stretched, warm breath shivered across her taut skin. The scent of horse and leather and warm man surrounded her, creating vivid, sensual pictures in her mind. Her body came alive instantly, tingling at the prospect of being touched. She felt herself softening, waiting.

"Good morning, my lady," Jon said softly, his breath caressing the back of her neck. He was standing just behind her, almost kissing her skin with his words.

Beth took a deep breath, reminding herself sternly that Jon would not be feeling any of the excitement that was coursing through her veins. Outside her bedchamber, he was always perfectly correct and infuriatingly distant. She fixed a polite smile on her face and turned. "Good morning, my lord. I did not hear you come in. Did you enjoy your ride?"

Her movement forced him to take a step back. "I—" There was something in his eyes, a hint of sparkling mischief, that Beth had not seen before, but his smile was as polite as her own. "Yes, it was splendid, thank you. The weather is

remarkably fine for so late in the year. Indeed, you could—"
He stopped short.

Had he been going to ask Beth to ride with him? Her heart began to beat even faster.

A noise from below caught his attention. He ushered her closer to the window so that they could both see down. "Your first house guests, my dear." His voice was neutral, matter of fact. As it always was in public.

A small, rotund gentleman climbed down from the carriage, and turned to help an even smaller, rounder lady. They made for the door without waiting for the third passenger, a much younger lady who stepped down and stood for a moment, gazing round her. She was tall, but she lacked the elegance of movement that Beth always associated with tall ladies. In fact, there was even something a little awkward about her.

"Sir James and Lady Rothbury, and Miss Rothbury," Jon murmured.

"They have only the one daughter?"

"Yes, but there is also a son. Rather wild. He declined the invitation. I will admit that I was glad to hear it. As it is, we must make do with the daughter who is not, I fear, the sharpest needle in the box."

Beth stifled a shocked giggle. Goodness, he was becoming quite free with his opinions, even thought it was broad daylight and they were standing in the sitting room. Was this progress at last?

"Look." Jon pointed down the long drive. In the distance, a second carriage could just be seen. "More guests, thank goodness. At least you will not have to entertain only the Rothburys, my dear. On their own, they can be something of a trial. They—" He stopped to clear his throat. "Well now, if I am to help you to greet them all, I had better go and change my dress." He bowed slightly to Beth. "Excuse me. I shall be down to join you shortly." He strode through the door into his own bedchamber and closed it behind him. The confidences were at an end.

Beth hesitated for a moment. Should she wait for Jon? No, best to go downstairs so that she was already waiting in the drawing room when the first guests came down. The Rothburys might be the kind who could get changed in a couple of shakes. It would not do for them, or for any of the guests, to find their hostess missing from her place.

She walked calmly into her bedchamber to check her appearance in front of the glass. Yes, she looked very well in her elegant silk morning gown. Jon had not commented upon it, but Beth knew the simple style suited her. Was that what had brought that stray sparkle to his eyes? Impossible to tell. She shook her head at her reflection, picked up her brightly patterned shawl and made her way along the corridor and down the sweeping staircase to the entrance hall.

Her timing was as wrong as could be. She arrived in the hallway as the latest guests were shown into the house. How on earth had they arrived so quickly? They must have sprung their horses all the way down the drive. For a second, she stood stock still, horrified, searching for an avenue of escape. There was none.

"My woman will direct the unloading of the luggage and— Oh!" As the butler moved aside, the new arrival caught sight of Beth, marooned at the foot of the stairs. This rather gaunt lady lifted her chin, narrowed her eyes, and looked down a very long nose at Beth before dropping the smallest of curtsies. "Lady Portbury, I presume?"

Beth returned the newcomer's tiny curtsey. She added a polite smile, too, since this unknown lady was her guest. "Welcome to Portbury Abbey, ma'am. I shall not attempt to detain you, for I am sure you will wish to rest after your journey. Goodrite will show you to your chamber."

"Thank you, my lady. We shall be—" The newcomer frowned suddenly and pursed her lips. "How strange. Forgive me, ma'am, but have we met before? I was told not and yet— You seem familiar, somehow."

It was all Beth could do to maintain a semblance of composure. Did this woman come from her past? If so, what did she know? Beth forced herself to glide forward a few steps and to smile condescendingly. "I think not, ma'am. I hope I should not have been so impolite as to have forgotten you if we had." She shook her head a little, to complete the effect.

210

"Er, um, no. Of course not. Forgive me, I was clearly thinking of someone else. Pray excuse me, ma'am." She hurried towards the stairs.

Goodrite turned to one of the footmen. "Bring Mrs Berncastle's valises to the yellow bedchamber," he said deliberately, ensuring that Beth would hear the lady's name. "And be quick about it."

Beth walked along the corridor to the morning room, trying not to look as though she were escaping. Berncastle. An unusual name, to be sure, but it seemed totally unfamiliar. Oh, why could she not remember? And what did Mrs Berncastle really know?

Quite possibly nothing at all, for where would Beth have met such a rich society lady? Beth had certainly been poor before she arrived in Fratcombe. Poor women did not mix with the likes of Mrs Berncastle.

Should she warn Jon? No, she would say nothing of this to anyone, for even if Mrs Berncastle had some lingering suspicions, she would never embarrass her hostess by giving the least hint. Such an insult could lead to a speedy departure for the guest in question, and a scandal, besides. Mrs Berncastle had come to enjoy a Christmas house party. She would never take the risk of being asked to leave.

Beth resolved to put the encounter behind her and to spend the rest of the day concentrating on welcoming more of her guests.

Chapter Twenty-Two

"YOUR LADYSHIP, I HAVE such news," Hetty gasped. She dumped the ewer of hot water by the basin and turned, her face full of animation.

Beth straightened the wrapper over her nightrail and assumed a stern expression. "Do you mean *news*, Hetty, or gossip? You know that you are forbidden to spread gossip in this house."

"No, truly it *is* news, m'lady." Before Beth could say a word more, Hetty burst out, "His lordship has given notice to Mr Vernon."

Beth tried to frown the girl down. What, after all, was so exciting about the departure of Jon's top-lofty valet? Now that almost all the guests had arrived, Hetty should have better things to do. Beth certainly did.

"But that is not the *real* news, m'lady. His lordship has sent for his old army batman to take Mr Vernon's place. I'm told that her ladyship—his lordship's lady mother, I mean—is fit to be tied."

"Now *that*," Beth said sternly, "is definitely gossip." It was, indeed, but Beth recognised that it was also likely to be true. On Jon's return from Spain, the dowager had urged him to take on a top-o'-the-trees valet. Jon must have shared her view, for he had paid off his army batman, and engaged Vernon. It seemed that he had now changed his mind. But what did it mean?

No doubt the servants knew, but Beth could not possibly question Hetty, not after giving the girl such stern warnings about the evils of gossip. Did she dare to ask Jon himself? Well, why not? They were man and wife, after all, and he had asked Beth to run his household. He should have told her that he had engaged a new valet. He should have told her.

Since it was still very early, he would be downstairs in his library, working. Later, once the guests' breakfast was over, he would be spending his time entertaining the gentlemen, but for the moment he would be alone.

She would finish dressing and then she would go downstairs to Jon's library and ask him what he had done. And why.

• • • •

The weak morning sunshine was struggling to illuminate Jon's library. If his desk had not been near the window, he would have needed candles in order to work. At least there was not much correspondence to deal with. Possibly the last two days' bad weather had delayed the post?

The door opened to admit the butler. "Miss Mountjoy has called and begs the favour of an interview with your lordship. She is waiting in the yellow saloon."

So soon?

Jon continued to write. "Let her wait. In fifteen minutes' time, you may invite her to join me here." He glanced up in time to see a flicker of surprise cross the butler's face. No, it was not how the Earl of Portbury was wont to treat a lady guest, but Jon was not at all sure that Miss Mountjoy deserved either title. He hurried to finish the instructions for his steward at Fratcombe. There was still much to be done there to remedy the damage done by his brother. George had a lot to answer for.

After some minutes, Jon sanded and folded the paper ready for dispatch. He checked the time by the long case clock. Any moment now.

Seconds later the door opened. "Miss Mountjoy to see your lordship," the butler intoned.

Jon rose politely but did not acknowledge his visitor. Instead, he held out the letter. "See that this is sent to my steward at Fratcombe Manor immediately, Goodrite. That will be all."

213

As the door closed, Jon turned to Miss Mountjoy and favoured her with a cursory bow. "There was something you wished to discuss, Miss Mountjoy?" He waved her to the chair opposite him. With a swift curtsey, she crossed the floor in an angry swish of silken skirts and took her seat. Jon leaned back in his chair, calmly steepled his fingers and set his facial expression to bland. Then he waited.

"I imagine, Lord Portbury, that you were expecting me to call? In the circumstances."

Jon raised an eyebrow. Otherwise, he did not move. The loud tick of the long case clock was the only sound to be heard in the room.

"I have come to tell you, Lord Portbury, that I will not be abused and manipulated in this outrageous fashion."

"Outrageous, is it?"

"You know very well that it is. When you settled that annuity upon me, and gave me the cottage to rent, it was in response to your wife's last request. It was a sacred trust, yet now you would renege upon it."

Jon allowed his hands to drop softly to the desk. "I have reneged on no promise, Miss Mountjoy," he said carefully. "Your annuity remains in place. Your cottage, however, was a mistake, about which I was not consulted. It is worth a rather higher rent than you are paying. Therefore, as my agent informed you, the rent will increase from the next quarter day."

"To a level which you know I cannot afford."

"That, ma'am, is not my concern. You have your annuity. You may always move to cheaper accommodation."

"You have ensured that there is none available, Lord Portbury. You take me for a fool, but I know you intend to force me to leave the district."

"If you know it, ma'am, why are you here?" Jon said silkily.

"I have come to tell you that I have no intention of quitting King's Portbury," she snapped, "or the cottage I am renting from you. If you try to force me out, I shall fight you. I am not without ammunition, as you should be aware."

Jon leant forward a little and allowed a sardonic smile to curl the corner of his mouth. "Indeed? Perhaps you would enlighten me? I do *own* your cottage, after all."

"I cannot stop you from evicting me, but I can ensure that your reputation, and that of your house, is destroyed if you do. If you proceed against me, I shall tell the whole world about your first wife's preferences and why the Earl of Portbury was unable to sire an heir."

Jon leaned back once more and sighed theatrically. "What a fascinating piece of gossip that will make, especially once your own role, as my late wife's *paramour*, is made plain to all. I fancy your reputation might suffer at least as much as mine. Do you imagine you would be received after that?"

"It is a price I would gladly pay for a victory over you, my lord. After all, I could always remove from the district later, perhaps even change my name. You, the great Earl of Portbury, have no such escape route. Once the world learns that Alicia preferred me to you, you will be the butt of every scandal sheet in the land."

Jon nodded slowly, as if considering her threat. "Do tell me about this escape route. If you move to another district, precisely what will you live on?"

She smiled then, for the first time, a confident, knowing smile. "Unlike the rental of my cottage, you cannot change my annuity, my lord. It was my deathbed gift from Alicia, a token of her regard. You merely executed her wishes. I find it gratifying that, even if I ruin your reputation, you will still be obliged to maintain me."

"Ah, I see. You believe your annuity renders you invulnerable." He pushed back his chair and rose. With one fleeting sideways glance at her, he strode across to the window and stood staring out at the garden with his hands clasped behind his back. "You know, Miss Mountjoy," he said evenly, "you really should read legal documents with more care." He heard her sharp intake of breath, but he did not turn. "If you had done so, you might have noticed the character clause I inserted in your annuity. It states, quite clearly, that if the beneficiary should lose her character, whether by criminal conviction or otherwise, her right to any payment will cease. I would wager a considerable sum that a woman who admitted to having a lewd relationship with the late Countess of Portbury would forfeit her character in the process." He turned slowly. "Shall we put the matter to the test?"

Miss Mountjoy's hands had become claws, gripping the arms of her chair. Her face and neck had turned grey. In the space of moments, she had shrunk from a handsome woman to a desiccated husk. "You are a devil! I hope you rot in hell!"

"And you are—" He gave a snort of mirthless laughter and shook his head. "No, we will not discuss that. So... What do you propose to do now?"

"What choice do I have?"

"None."

"You wish me to leave King's Portbury?"

"I do."

"Very well. I will go. I will leave before the next quarter day."

"That seems an eminently sensible solution. And the other matter?"

She seemed to shrink even more. "I will say nothing. You leave me no choice."

"Quite so, ma'am. Let me add, however, that if any rumours should arise, from any quarter, about the conduct of my late wife, the annuity payable to Miss Louisa Mountjoy—wherever she is and whatever name she may trade under—will cease on the spot. Do I make myself clear?"

"Yes," she said, in a small, crushed voice. "There will be no rumours, and no gossip. I shall not trouble you again."

Jon crossed to pull the bell, but thought better of it. His first marriage had been a disaster, largely because of Louisa Mountjoy's liaison with his wife. But, even so, he could not parade her defeat before the servants. "You are distressed, ma'am, which is understandable." He could not help his icy tone. The woman would have ruined him if she could. "I will leave you here to regain your composure. My butler will return in a quarter of an hour to show you out. I suggest we do not meet again." With a curt nod, he strode to the door and left her.

In the corridor outside, he almost fell over his wife. "Beth, I–I did not expect to see you down so early." She was looking remarkably alluring, in a gown of palest pink trimmed with flounces. Another one of those expensive fripperies he had encouraged her to buy in London. They all became her much too well.

She dropped him a curtsey. "Good morning, my lord. I wonder if I might have a word with you?" She sounded unusually determined.

Jon wondered what had caused her change of mood. Last night, when they had been together in her chamber, she had been so soft, so yielding. Not at all like this stern young matron.

"Might we go into your library? Where we may speak in private?"

That pulled him up short. "Er, no. Not the library. It is not— That is to say, Miss Mountjoy is in there."

Beth stiffened and grew a little pale.

"We were discussing a–a matter of business. She will be leaving in a few moments, once she has—" This would not do. He was tying himself in knots, and for no good reason. He refused to feel guilty about what he had done to Miss Mountjoy. She deserved it all, and more.

Jon smiled down at Beth and tucked her hand under his arm. "The library is too gloomy this morning. Let us leave it to Miss Mountjoy. We can be private in the conservatory, and make the most of the light, besides. Madam, will you walk?"

• • • •

Beth held herself a little apart as they walked through the house to the conservatory. She did not remove her hand from his arm—that would be much too confrontational—but she certainly could not relax into his touch.

Miss Mountjoy. He had been alone in his library with Louisa Mountjoy. What on earth had they been doing at this time of the day? And why did she have to be left alone there? To recover? From what?

The pictures racing through Beth's imagination were far from comfortable. Although she had no reason to suspect that Jon and the Mountjoy woman were lovers now, she could not banish the suspicion that they might have been lovers once. Had she come to see him this morning, by appointment, before any of the guests was about? Before his wife was about? It did not bear thinking of. Beth fancied Miss Mountjoy was capable of anything, even seducing a married man.

In total silence, they walked through to the conservatory where Beth let Jon usher her inside. He had been right. By comparison with the rest of the house, it was full of light. It was warm, too, but the myriad of green leaves made it seem cool, and very restful to the senses. Jon pushed aside some of the overhanging branches and led her through to a small clear space where they could be private. There was a white painted bench to one side, but he did not invite her to sit. He simply stopped and faced her.

Now that they were alone, and the moment had come, Beth felt her courage ebbing away. How had she ever thought she could challenge Jon? She struggled to put a simple sentence together, but no words came.

"You asked for a private word?" His tone was gentler than she had expected. Was that because he was guilty about Miss Mountjoy?

The thought of that obnoxious woman in Jon's embrace gave Beth a degree of courage that surprised her. "I understand you have engaged a new valet, sir." The words came out in a rush. "As mistress of your household, I should have preferred to learn of such a change from you, rather than from the servants."

He flushed. "Good God. First my mother, and now my wife. Since when do I need permission from the women of my household to decide upon my own manservant?"

He was angry. Yet Beth was beginning to know him well enough to suspect that this show of temper was partly a cover for his embarrassment. He must know he was in the wrong over this.

"Might I ask why you have decided to make the change, sir?" Beth asked innocently.

Her tone had its effect. He took a deep breath and, when he spoke again, his anger had been replaced by gruffness, as if he were explaining a lesson to a rather stupid child and working hard to control justifiable impatience. "I no longer have need of Vernon's skills. He should serve a single man, the kind of employer who wishes to cut a figure in society. All well and good when I was just returned from Spain, but no longer."

He reached for Beth's hand and, to her surprise, raised it to his lips for a gallant kiss. Was that by way of apology for his show of bad temper?

"Now that I am married, I plan to spend more time in the country." His voice was almost normal again. "There is much to do here, and at the other estates. A country gentleman has no need of a man like Vernon. Joseph's skills will be more than adequate, even when I am in town."

"You call him 'Joseph'?" Beth said, surprised into betraying herself. Was Jon's relationship with Joseph as close as Beth's with Hetty?

He shrugged. "We spent a long time together in the Peninsula. For some reason, everyone there used his given name. I fell into the way of it. I accept that it is improper, but— Well, let us see what happens once he has arrived."

• • • •

Jon watched the play of emotions crossing Beth's expressive face. She was clearly intrigued by what he had done and would want to learn more of his relationship with Joseph. What would she think if she learned he had done it for her? His mother had taken it almost as a personal insult. She had even accused Jon of abandoning his station in life. But Jon's plan had worked. The dowager was now training her fire on Jon rather than on Beth. Her disdain for Beth's choice of lady's maid had been forgotten in her anger at her son's deliberate flouting of the standards she had instilled in him.

Jon allowed himself an inward smile. He had promised he would deal with the situation. And he had.

At that moment, he became aware that he was still holding Beth's hand. Shocked at his own weakness, he dropped it. Too abruptly.

Beth flinched as if from a blow. "Is Miss Mountjoy ailing?" Beth's voice was cold. "Perhaps I should offer my help if she is feeling unwell?"

"I am sure she will have recovered her composure by now." That was the truth, but it was not enough to restore Beth's confiding mood. If he wanted that, he would have to unbend a little. He sighed. "I must tell you frankly, Beth, that I do not think she would welcome an offer of assistance from either of us." There, it was done.

Beth's eyebrows rose and her eyes widened in apparent disbelief.

In for a penny. "I do not wish to malign the lady. She was Alicia's friend and they had, um, a great regard for each other. However, I find Miss Mountjoy's continued visits here excessive."

Beth glanced up at him in surprise and then quickly looked away. Strange. Surely Beth did not actually like the woman? There had been no sign that she did. Given the woman's history with Alicia, Jon would much prefer to keep his wife and Miss Mountjoy as far apart as possible.

He drew himself up and said, "Miss Mountjoy will be leaving King's Portbury before the next quarter day. I— She has decided that this area is no longer to her taste." He had betrayed himself, he realised. There had been too much venom in his voice.

But perhaps not? Beth's shoulders were no longer so tense, and there was the beginning of a smile on her delicious mouth. The temptation was altogether too much, especially in a place like this where they could not be observed. Jon dragged her into his arms and began to kiss her.

She stiffened, but only for a second. Then she melted into his embrace and returned his kiss with more skill than he had thought she possessed. This was not the innocent nymph of the Fratcombe folly. His wife had become a practised and eager seductress.

He knew he should break the kiss, put her from him so that they could resume their proper, public relationship, but her response was so passionate that he could not. Just a little longer exploring her luscious mouth, stroking her hair, her skin, the curve of her breast... Just a little more of the scent and taste of her...

She groaned from deep in her belly and put her hands to the waistband of his pantaloons, fumbling for his buttons. In a moment, there would be no going back.

"No, Beth." He did not recognise his own voice as he pulled away from her. Since the day of their marriage, he had been telling himself to keep his distance from her. Closeness made a man vulnerable, and weak. And closeness to a woman was the most dangerous of all.

She had blushed scarlet. The fingers that had been trying to undress him a moment ago were now twisting together in embarrassment. She was mortified by what had happened between them.

It had been his mistake as much as hers. "Sit down, my dear," he said, as gently as he could.

She crossed a little unsteadily to the bench and took her seat. She looked up at him expectantly. Did she think he was about to join her? Poor Beth, marriage had taught her much, but she did not fully understand what drove a man.

He smiled and shook his head. "No, best if I stand," he said, keeping his tone light. He would focus on practical things until this interview was over. And then he would avoid Beth for the rest of the day.

"Now that all our guests are here," he began, but stopped when she shook her head. "I beg pardon. I thought that—"

"The Reverend and Mrs Aubrey will not arrive for a few days yet. Do you not recall? The rector wanted to be sure that his curate was not taking on too much of the Christmas burden."

Jon had completely forgotten the Aubreys. Extraordinary that he should have done so, when he owed them so much. His preoccupation with his wife must be affecting his brain. He took a deep breath and began again. "Now that *almost* all the guests are here, we can direct the servants to bring in the greenery to decorate the rooms. The Yule log will wait until Christmas Eve, of course, but there is plenty of mistletoe to amuse the younger guests. We shall not participate, of course, as I said before."

Mistletoe. The word hit Beth like a blow. It registered vaguely in her mind that Jon was still talking to her, but she could no longer hear what he was saying. *Mistletoe*. The word was pounding in her head like the crack of doom. With mistletoe in the house, something terrible would happen. She could not explain it, but she knew, for a certainty, that it would be so.

She sprang to her feet and ran for the door.

"Beth? What on earth is the matter? Beth?" Too late. She was gone in a flurry of pale pink skirts. Jon slumped on to the bench where she had been sitting moments before and tried to piece together what had just happened. He had been talking about the Christmas festivities, the Yule log, the mistletoe. He had warned her again that he would be avoiding the mistletoe. Their kisses could easily become too passionate for any room but a bedchamber. It had happened here, only moments ago. If it happened in front of their guests, everyone would be mortally embarrassed.

Had she run from him because he refused to kiss her in public?

Chapter Twenty-Three

FROM HER PLACE NEAR the centre of the drawing room, Beth let her gaze travel round, counting heads. It was almost six. Nearly all the guests were assembled for dinner. Only the Berncastles were not yet down. For the first few evenings, they had been only a small group and conversation had been rather difficult. But tonight there would be twenty people sitting down to dinner. With so many guests, they should make a merry party, surely? And better still once the Reverend and Mrs Aubrey finally arrived.

Beth was trying to avoid looking up at the chandelier in the middle of the room and the large sprig of mistletoe that hung there. It seemed to draw her eye, even while it horrified her. It was full of sinister pearl-white berries. Their pallor was waxy, like the skin of a corpse. The very sight of them made her feel nauseous, and strangely guilty.

But why should she feel guilty at the sight of mistletoe? What did it mean?

She shivered a little and backed away a step, straight into a man's arms. She knew immediately, without turning, that this was not Jon. This man's touch, and his scent, were repellent.

The man was not about to let Beth go. "A kiss under the mistletoe, sister," he cried gleefully, pulling her under the chandelier. It was George, of course, Jon's disreputable brother, who had arrived only two days before. Although he had quickly made a formal apology for his attempted assault at Fratcombe, he clearly had not mended his lecherous ways. The mistletoe was giving him too good an excuse.

Beth tried to slide out from his embrace without seeming to struggle, but it was useless. He was quite determined on his prize. His mouth descended on Beth's, his lips thick and wet. Where Jon's every touch was wonderful, George revolted her.

She began to struggle in earnest, but George was holding her so tightly that she could not even pull her mouth away from his. Then his tongue tried to force its way between her lips. She clamped her jaws and teeth together as tightly as she could. She would not allow this beastly invasion.

At last, defeated, he let her go.

"A great institution, mistletoe," he said with a lascivious grin. "Gives a man—and a gel—a chance to see what they have been missing."

Beth could not suppress a shudder.

"I think you should perhaps ensure your partner is willing before you indulge in such activity, brother."

Beth whirled round. Jon was standing in the doorway. He was white with anger. For once, he had ignored the presence of the other guests. He was challenging George directly.

But George was not in the least put out by Jon's public rebuke. He casually reached up to pluck a berry from the sprig of mistletoe. "Plenty more where that came from, eh, sister? And plenty more kisses for us both to enjoy, too, I'd say." He dropped his voice to murmur in Beth's ear. "Don't want to give 'em all to my prude of a brother, you know, m'dear."

Beth gasped.

Ignoring her reaction, George turned to face Jon. "The ladies will have kisses a-plenty, for I have rarely seen mistletoe with quite so many berries. It is an invitation to Christmas mischief, and merriment for all."

For a moment, Beth fancied that Jon was going to floor his brother on the spot. There was a stunned silence in the room. But then Miss Rothbury broke it, stepping under the chandelier and reaching up to pluck mistletoe berries, one after another, counting them into her hand. "Look, Mama." She beckoned to Lady Rothbury who was standing by the fire, slack-jawed in astonishment. "They are just like jewels. I do like jewels so much, don't I?"

Her mother rushed forward to grab her daughter's hands and hold them still. "Enough, my dear, enough. The berries are to be picked one at a time, one for each kiss. And when they have all been picked, there can be no more kissing under the mistletoe. That is the tradition, you know."

"I may not pick them?" Miss Rothbury sounded like a small child, deprived of a favourite toy.

Beth stepped forward to join the pair. "I am sure we can find plenty more sprigs of mistletoe if you like them," she said gently. "Shall we put a sprig in your bedchamber?"

Miss Rothbury's beaming smile was all the answer Beth needed. She nodded to the butler, standing impassively beside the door. Goodrite would see to it. For now, Beth needed to distract her guests from these odd happenings until dinner should be announced. She sensed Jon's large, reassuring presence only a few paces behind her. Yes, she could do this.

"Ladies and gentlemen, shall we decide now on what we wish to do after dinner? Since it is Christmas, his lordship—" she nodded towards Jon "—has a predictable fancy for telling ghost stories, but we would be happy to accept more energetic suggestions. Charades, perhaps?"

• • • •

With a feeling of relief, Beth shepherded the ladies along the corridor to the drawing room. The dinner had gone remarkably well, helped by Jon's excellent and plentiful wine. One or two of the older ladies were swaying a little and would probably soon be asleep in their chairs. No matter. The younger ones could play games at one end of the room while the older ones dozed.

How long would it be before the gentlemen joined them? Beth rather hoped they would not play charades after all, for drunken gentlemen could be difficult during such games. George had been downing bumper after bumper. That kiss under the mistletoe had been bad enough. What might he do now?

She told herself that Jon would ensure his brother behaved. If necessary, Jon would throw him out until he had sobered up. At least, she hoped he would.

225

When Beth entered the drawing room, she saw that Mrs Berncastle was holding forth from the centre of the room. She too had taken rather a lot of wine. She was not drunk, of course. No lady was ever drunk. But she had certainly become more and more talkative and uninhibited as the evening wore on. Some of her earthy comments had put Beth to the blush.

At Mrs Berncastle's side, Miss Rothbury was giggling, pointing up at the chandelier. Beth tried to ignore them and especially the mistletoe she so dreaded. Surely Goodrite would bring in the tea tray soon?

"Mistletoe is lovely," Miss Rothbury crooned. "The berries are like the finest pearls, don't you think, ma'am?"

For a moment, Mrs Berncastle looked thunderstruck. "Mistletoe! Of course, *that* was it!" She spun round and pointed accusingly at Beth. Her arm wavered slightly, but her voice was steady enough and full of outrage. "I *knew* you were familiar. I recognise you now. Under all that finery, you are nothing but a dirty little thief. You are that Clifford woman, who was companion to my great-aunt Marchmont. You stole her priceless mistletoe jewels, and then you fled the county to avoid being hauled off to gaol and hanged, as you deserved."

Beth stood like a statue, transfixed by that accusing finger. Clifford! The name pounded in her brain. The barrier cracked. Her name was Clifford. Of course it was.

The room and everyone in it seemed to melt into a hazy, indistinct blur. She felt she was floating, revolving in a cloying mist. It was a mist of memories, and guilt, and unbelievable pain. A moment later, the mist dissolved as if drenched by a shower of sheeting rain.

She remembered it all now, every last mortifying moment of it. She could feel the shivers convulsing her body as if she were still ploughing on through that freezing, howling gale. She closed her eyes for a second, but when she opened them again, nothing had changed. She was still freezing, still shivering. And the house guests were still staring at her as if she had sprouted devil's horns.

Near the open doorway, Jon stood frozen, his face ashen. He must have heard it all. He had learned he was married to a thief, and the revelation had shocked him to the core. Such an honourable man would surely never touch her again.

Beth could not blame him. She was to be an outcast. All over again.

Pain engulfed her. The familiar tunnel began to close in.

She picked up her skirts and fled from the room while she could still see.

. . . .

The headache had lessened but Beth had not slept.

She swung her bare feet to the floor and crept across to the window to peep out. Still much too dark. In half an hour or so, perhaps. At least she would not have to climb out of the window this time, as she had done from old Lady Marchmont's house. This time, the key was on Beth's side of the locked door. For the moment, she was still in control of her life.

She returned to the bed, checking yet again that everything was ready. She had laid out her simplest, warmest clothes. Her stout boots were on the floor alongside. And her little valise contained the few essentials she would need. She could dress in these clothes without Hetty's help, and she would be gone long before anyone in the house was aware of it. Hetty would mourn, of course, and not only for the loss of her place. The girl had tried so hard to help and console Beth last night, even though she had not understood the cause. She would understand everything by now. The news of the mistress's disgrace must have spread like wildfire below stairs.

And Jon? What was Jon thinking?

It had been cowardly to lock him out of her bedchamber, to refuse to see him or speak to him. But truly, Beth had been unable to bear the thought of it. Jon had been plainly horrified to learn that his wife was a fugitive from the law. By now, his horror would have turned to disgust, perhaps even hate. Beth knew she could not remove the slur from her name. Nor could she undo their marriage. The most she could offer him was her absence, in hopes that, eventually, the scandal would die down and the gossips would leave him in peace. He would remain bound to her, however, and the brother he so distrusted would be his heir. He would blame Beth for that. Rightly. She was guilty of so much.

But she had not known. She would never have married him if she had known the truth of her own past. She had tried so hard to warn him, but he had refused to listen. He had been so sure that the rank he offered was enough.

She dropped her head into her hands, but the cold metal of her wedding ring jarred accusingly against her skin. Why was she wearing it? She was taking almost nothing that Jon had given her. Her fine clothes remained in the dressing room, and her jewels were in their cases. He would have no cause to reproach her there. She would take a little money, but only enough for her journey. Her wedding ring, however…

She turned it on her finger. Last night, she had taken it off and laid it aside, but then she had put it on again. She had told herself that, if she was claiming to be a poor widow, she would need a wedding ring to prove her status to the world. But of course that was not the whole truth.

She twisted it off once more and laid it by the letter she had written to him. She had asked him not to follow her. But why should he want to, after all she had done? More likely that he would be glad to be rid of her.

There was no time now to start composing another letter. This one had taken hours, and many tears. With a sigh, she picked up the ring and slipped it back on to her finger. She could not leave it behind. It was the only thing she would have from him.

Time to dress now.

Soon, it would be time for her to go.

• • • •

"Could you please cease this pacing, Jon? You are making my head spin."

Jon sank on to the end of the chaise longue opposite her bed. "I am sorry, Mama, but I have to talk to someone about all this, and there is no one else but you. Beth has locked herself in her bedchamber. She refuses to admit anyone. I have been pacing my own floor for hours and it is driving me to distraction. I cannot think straight."

His mother sighed. "You saw what happened, my dear. We all did. Beth fled from her accuser, without saying a word in her own defence. That had all the appearance of guilt."

Jon ground his teeth. He had come to ask his mother's help for Beth, not to hear yet more condemnation. He believed—no, he was certain—that his wife was innocent, but everything was so confused that he was incapable of working out how to defend her. "Mama, I—"

"In the end, it may be for the best," his mother continued quietly. "Indeed, you would be better off without her, were it not for the child. You could—"

"What do you mean *child*, ma'am?"

"There is no need to play the innocent with me, Jon. I know that she is breeding. And I know that she used it to entrap you into marriage. It is a sorry business, and if the child should prove to be a girl after all..."

For a moment, Jon was struck dumb. Then he began to laugh. He laughed until his whole body was racked with pain. His mother looked by turns indignant and then hurt. Jon ignored her. At last, when the pain became too much, he dropped his head into his hands. His laughter cracked and stopped dead.

Jon felt the brush of his mother's silken wrapper against his leg. Her soft hand reached out to cover one of his. "Jon?" Her voice was low, the thread of worry clear. "I do not understand. It is as if you were bewitched."

Jon flung himself to his feet and began to pace again. He could not endure her touch. There was only one touch he needed now.

"Jon?"

He stopped abruptly and turned to face her, planting his feet firmly and his fists on his hips. "You are wrong, ma'am. You could not be more wrong. You tell me that Beth is breeding, that she seduced me into marriage." He gave one last shout of bitter laughter. "If only you knew the lengths I had to go to, in order to persuade her to accept me."

"I do not understand." Her usual confidence seemed to have left her.

"Beth did not entrap me into marriage, Mama. What made you think such a thing? It seems you have a very low opinion of my character."

"I am sorry, Jon. All the physical signs pointed to pregnancy—her tiredness, her sickness. Miss Mountjoy was quite sure of it."

Jon clamped his jaws together. Miss Mountjoy again. But she was dealt with. He would not lecture his mother about her now.

"And the fact that you, who are so very conscious of your position in society, should have rushed into marriage with a woman with no name and no family. How else could I explain it, but by your need for a legitimate heir?" When Jon did not reply, she swallowed hard and added, in a small voice, "I have tried to like her, Jon, but I found it impossible to overcome my disgust of what she had done to you. Except that now you tell me it was not so?"

"No, Mama, it was not so. She refused me." The dowager frowned up at him. "Twice," Jon added, with deliberate emphasis. "And when she was finally persuaded to accept me, she added onerous conditions that I had to fulfil. If there was entrapment, ma'am, it was my doing, not Beth's."

The dowager let out a long breath. "Then she is not breeding?"

"She was certainly not breeding when I took her to the altar, ma'am," he responded stiffly. "The symptoms you mentioned are a great embarrassment to her. She feels— She felt guilty about her missing past. That, and open hostility, can bring on the headache. Sometimes, she can barely see, and she has to take to her bed. That, not the guilt you thought you saw, is why she fled. I am sure of it." He held his mother's gaze for a moment before turning away to stare out of the window.

"Your ladyship!" The dowager's dresser rushed into the room without knocking, followed closely by Hetty. "Miss Martin says—"

The dowager's gasp of outrage was drowned by Hetty's anguished cry. "She has gone, my lord. In the dark. She will die out there, my lord."

Jon spun round. He ignored the tears coursing down the girl's pale face. "How long ago did she leave? Where is she going? Tell me what you know, Hetty. Quickly now."

The girl seemed bewildered, and Jon's barked questions were not helping. He would have to coax the information out of her. He forced himself to curb his impatience and ask one careful question at a time. Her mistress, Hetty offered at last, must have fled at some time during the night. She had taken only a small valise. She had left everything else behind— clothes, jewels, money, everything. And a letter.

Jon snatched it from her hand, dismissing the two servants with a stern warning about discretion. Without even a glance at his mother, he turned his back and tore open the letter. It was barely three lines. She was leaving him in order to purge the stain on his honour; she would never return; and Jon should not try to seek her out. That was all. There was not a word about her guilt or innocence.

He crumpled the sheet in his fist and stared out into the darkness. There was no moon, but the sky was clear. It wanted more than an hour till sunrise and, even then, it would still be exceedingly cold. Beth was alone, somewhere, fleeing in order to protect Jon's honour. She had nothing, and no one, to protect her. She might freeze to death out there, without ever knowing how much Jon loved her.

The realisation shuddered through him. What a fool he was. What an arrogant fool! He had been in love with her almost from the first, but he had convinced himself that she was simply a friend, a restful companion, a willing participant in their mutual passion.

Because of Jon's failings, she might die, out there in the dark. Alone.

He groaned aloud. A red-hot blade was twisting in his gut. He deserved every shred of the pain that knifed through him.

A gentle hand touched his upper arm. "Jon? What is it, my dear?"

"I love her. And I have driven her away." The words were torn out of him against his will, as if they had a power all their own. In that moment, staring vacantly into the far distance, Jon understood that he loved Beth more than life itself. If he did not find her, if he did not bring her back, warm and alive, his own life would be worthless.

He glanced down at his mother. He wanted to shake off her restraining hand, to berate her for the mischief she had done. But one look at the pain in her face chased all those angry notions from his mind.

She stroked her fingers gently down his arm and dropped her hand to her side. "Will you go after her?" When he nodded, she said crisply, "Let me deal with your guests. And with everything else here. What matters is that you should bring your wife—your Beth—back safely." She was trying to smile encouragingly.

Jon's mind was tumbling, racing, planning for action. "Make sure that none of the guests leaves while I am gone, Mama. And no letters, either. There must be no scandal-mongering. As for this wicked accusation against Beth, I will deal with it when we return. In the meantime, let no one know we are gone."

His mother nodded. "If I may be allowed one word of advice before you go…?"

Jon pulled himself up very erect and frowned forbiddingly. He did not want any advice from his mother. Her coldness and hostility had led Beth to believe she was friendless in this house.

His mother's eyes were glistening. "When you find her, tell her that you love her," she said hoarsely. "It will make you vulnerable, like baring your breast to the sword and saying 'Strike here'. But love cannot be demanded, it can only be offered. If you want to win Beth's love, you will have to risk your own."

Jon was shocked into immobility. His own mother, the starched-up dowager Countess of Portbury, believed in love?

She laid her hand on his arm once more. This time, she pushed him towards the door. "Please bring her back, Jon." There was a catch in her voice. "When you do, I promise that I will welcome her as the daughter I never had."

Jon needed no urging. He already knew he had not a second to spare. He must ride out after Beth, the woman he loved. He must bring her home.

Chapter Twenty-Four

IT WAS COLD. SO VERY cold.

Beth bent her body into the wind and trudged on. This time, there was no sheeting rain to soak her. This time she was more warmly clad, and better shod. And this time there would be no knight in shining armour to rescue her from the beckoning darkness.

There must be no rescue at all. Jon was noble enough to come after her, but he must not find her. He would expect her to walk the eight miles to Broughton to board the coach for the first stage of her journey. He would assume that she was making for Fratcombe. He would be wrong.

In truth, she had no idea where she should go, except that it must not be Fratcombe. The Aubreys could not be asked to harbour a thief. Besides, they would be bound tell Jon where she was. No, she must go somewhere she was not known. Bristol, perhaps, or even Cornwall.

The wind was whipping at her skirts. Did she dare to follow the second part of her plan? To her left was the long flat road that would bring her, eventually, to Broughton and the coach office. To her right was the two mile path up over the moor. There was light enough now for her to see her way. And no one would think to look for a countess there.

Beth's little valise had been getting heavier. She transferred it from one hand to the other and began to climb the lonely path. The slope was easy enough, at first, though the air swirling around her seemed to become colder with every step she took. She continued doggedly. She could endure worse than this. Before Fratcombe, her life had been very hard. As Lady Marchmont's companion, she had been no better than a menial, wearing cast-off shoes and gowns that even Jon's servants would have rejected. Lady Marchmont was exceedingly rich, but her household lived like paupers while she hoarded her money and her jewels. Especially her jewels. That mistletoe clasp—intricate, heavy gold for the stems and leaves, and berries made of priceless pearls—had been the old witch's pride and joy. Until the day it vanished.

Lady Marchmont's maid had claimed to have seen Beth sneaking into the mistress's bedchamber. On such flimsy evidence from a jealous servant, Beth had been pronounced guilty by Lady Marchmont and all her guests. Including the Berncastles. If Beth had not climbed out of that locked room, she would probably have ended up on the gallows.

The path seemed to stretch ahead for ever, steeper than she recalled. No matter. It was only the first of many challenges she would have to face. At least the wind seemed to have dropped. It was no longer cutting through her cloak and biting at her skin. She tried to smile up at the sky. She would cling on to her innocence, and to her love for Jon. She was doing this for him. She would cherish the memories of their times together, of how he had held her, and kissed her, and loved her. Nothing could deprive her of those.

She plodded on with even greater determination, clutching the memory of him like a talisman. She might find another village that needed a schoolmistress. She would be Mrs Clifford, the poor widow of an army captain tragically killed in the French wars. There were many such. One more would not be noticed.

She was shivering again. It was not the wind this time, but cold, penetrating damp. She glanced up at the sky. Was it starting to rain?

She could not tell. She could not see the sky. Suddenly, there was ghostly grey mist swirling all around her. It had come out of nothing. But it hid everything. She could see barely a yard in front of her feet.

She refused to allow herself to panic. She had no cause. The path over the moors was straight enough. She had only to keep going and she would soon reach Broughton. She must not allow herself to be afraid.

She stretched her free hand out in front of her, in case there might be some obstacle in the path, and continued to walk into the forbidding grey wall, though she could not prevent her steps from becoming shorter, and rather timid. Surely she had already passed the halfway point? She must reach her goal soon.

The path was becoming much more uneven. She stumbled to a stop and strained to make out the way ahead. Were there loose rocks here to make her lose her footing? She must take care. If she were injured here, no one would find her.

The mist had become so thick now that she could barely see her own feet. She took a few steps more, but stopped. She could see nothing. She was no longer sure she was on the path at all. Perhaps she should sit on the ground and wait until the mist lifted? But if she did so, she might freeze. Besides, she would lose precious time. She must reach Broughton, and catch that first stage before anyone from Portbury discovered her flight. She dare not delay. She must keep on, in spite of the mist.

Taking a deep breath of the thick air, she made to stride out again.

A hand caught her waist from behind. She screamed. But the sound was swallowed up in the swirling mist. Then another hand clamped across her mouth. She was pulled sharply backwards into a man's body. It reeked of sweat. The hand on her mouth was so filthy she could taste it. She fought to free herself, kicking and stamping with her heavy boots.

Her captor was too wily to be outfoxed by such feeble female struggles. He held her fast and dragged her backwards into the enveloping mist.

· · · ·

Jon had succeeded in leaving the Abbey without being seen by any of the guests. The grooms were quite another kettle of fish. They had stared, goggle-eyed, at the pistols holstered by his saddle, and the extra rolled-up cloak tied on behind. They had not dared to ask questions, of course, and the grim set of the master's jaw should have warned them not to gossip.

He would make everything right again, once he had brought Beth home. But where was she now? He slowed Saracen to a walk while he checked the time by his pocket watch. He had covered barely two miles of the Broughton road. Beth had several hours' start on him and, even on foot, she would probably reach the town before he could overtake her. A stage was due to depart in less than half an hour from now. What if Beth was on it? Whatever he did then, he was bound to create a scandal. And he could hardly demand they stand and deliver his wife.

Saracen sidled a little, nostrils flaring in response to the wild scents of the moorland. "You want a gallop, boy. And you are right. If we go this way, we can save at least four miles. We might even reach Broughton before Beth's stage leaves." He turned the big horse towards the moors and cantered up the slope.

What if Beth had come this way, too? What if she had already caught the first stage out of Broughton?

He shook his head in exasperation. Surely it was much too dangerous, especially at this time of year? But she had done dangerous things before and nearly died in the process. That thought worried him so much that he turned Saracen on to a side path after only half a mile. The diversion would not take him long. And it might yield valuable information. He eased the big horse down the slope until he could make out the barren field at the edge of his own estate. Yes, the travellers from Fratcombe were still there. They were known to keep a close eye on everything that went on around them. But would they be able to tell him anything about Beth?

Jon covered the remaining distance at the gallop and put Saracen at the wall. The big bay cleared it easily and cantered across to the cluster of caravans at the far side. From nowhere, a shrivelled old man appeared and held up a commanding hand. He must be the leader here. Behind him, curious faces peeped out from painted doors and windows. Dirty tousle-haired children crawled out from behind wagon wheels to stare at this latest arrival.

"What d'ye want?" The old man scowled up at Jon.

"I am the Earl of Portbury and you are on my land. By my leave." The man's scowl softened but he still did not allow Saracen to pass. "I have come to ask for your help in— Good God! Beth!"

He was sure he was not mistaken. He had glimpsed Beth's face in the half-door of the furthest caravan. She was here, with the gypsies. Had they taken her by force?

He snatched a pistol from its holster and levelled it at the old man. "You have my wife. Give her to me, or I swear I will shoot you down." Slowly and deliberately, he moved his thumb to cock the weapon.

Before he could do so, the pistol was struck from his hand.

A merry laugh broke the sudden silence. Jon half-turned to see a darkly handsome young gypsy lounging against the side of the nearest caravan. He was holding another throwing knife loosely in his hand. Judging by his success against Jon's pistol, he knew exactly how to use it.

"What right have ye over this woman?" the old man demanded. "We rescued her from death at the Devil's Drop. She do belong with us now." He glanced over his shoulder. Beth had emerged from the caravan and come to stand behind him. She was dirty and dishevelled. Her cloak was torn and her boots were thick with mud. She was the most beautiful woman in the whole world.

Jon gazed longingly at her. "I rescued her from death, too, a full year ago now. So her life was always mine." Beth nodded warily, as if to confirm the truth of Jon's words.

Another tiny sign. It gave him hope.

"She be safer here. In your household, she be cried a thief. Leave her where she be valued. Or was you wanting to deliver her up to the noose?"

"Of course not. She is no thief, but even if she were, I would still defend her, with my life if needs be. She is my wife."

The old man shrugged. "So we do both have a claim on her. But my son here do hold the knife. Why should he give the woman to you?"

Jon let his hands drop, displaying empty palms. "Because I love her," he said simply.

Beth's gasp echoed round the camp. The young gypsy hurled his knife, point first, into the earth, just as Beth started to run towards Jon. In what seemed like only a second, Jon had thrown himself from Saracen's back and his precious wife was in his arms.

"You love me?" She was gazing up at him with wide, glowing eyes.

"More than life," he groaned, and began to kiss her.

They clung to each other, oblivious of everything. Their bodies seemed to melt together, while their lips sought and their tongues danced. When at last they broke apart, gasping for breath, they found they were alone but for Saracen, cropping the grass by the half-buried knife.

Jon bent to draw it out of the ground. He ran his thumb along the blade with a grimace. It was wickedly sharp.

Beth clasped her own cold hands round his to hold them still. "I am no thief, Jon. I swear it."

Jon freed a hand to cup her chin and gazed deep into her eyes. "I know that. You are the essence of honesty and goodness. You could never have been a thief. Together, we will find a way of proving it. But first, we must go back and face them down. Can you do that, my love?"

"With your love to strengthen and support me, I can do anything."

He threw the knife back into the ground and picked up his pistol. "Come then."

"Wait." The young gypsy had appeared again, as if by magic. He retrieved the knife and offered it to Jon, hilt first. "Take it. Use it on the black heart of any man who would harm your woman. She be worth a life."

Jon stared. Then he took the knife and tucked it into his boot. "Thank you. And be sure that, as long as I am Earl of Portbury, your band will always be welcome on any of my estates."

• • • •

Beth leaned in to Jon's beloved body. Even through the heavy cloak he had wrapped her in, she could feel the heat of him reaching out to her. He loved her. He *loved* her. She sighed out a long breath and allowed herself to relax even more. They had not ridden together since their night in the folly. That memory made her insides glow even hotter.

Jon nuzzled her ear. "What on earth were you doing at the Devil's Drop, love? It's nowhere near the Broughton path."

She shuddered. "I must have wandered from the path when the mist came down. That young gypsy pulled me to safety, though I didn't realise it at the time. I kicked him quite hard." Jon's deep chuckle vibrated against her cheek. "They said that, if I needed sanctuary, I could have it with them. I–I was going to stay."

His arm tightened round her. "But you changed your mind."

"Yes," Beth whispered. "Because you said you loved me."

"I did. I do," he replied earnestly. "Though I did not realise it until I thought I had lost you." She felt him swallow hard. "Beth, could you ever—?"

She reached out from her cocoon to press a finger to his lips. "You know, for a leader of men, you are remarkably unobservant." He tried to catch her finger in his teeth, but she was too quick for him. That was for later. "I have loved you since that first time you lifted me into your arms."

"Ah. At the folly."

"No, you noddy. When you rescued me from the storm."

His eyes widened. He shook his head a little, as if trying to cope with a momentous new idea. Then, after a long silence, he said, on a choke of laughter, "I can see that I have a great deal of catching up to do. May I say, ma'am, and darling wife, that I expect it to be a pleasure?"

• • • •

Jon leaned back against their sitting room door and let out a long sigh of relief. Beside him, Beth put her hands to her burning cheeks. She must have been terrified she would be caught, stealing back into the house looking like a filthy vagrant.

He could smile now the danger was over. "Chin up, my sweet. We are safe now. Only Hetty and my mother's woman knew you were gone, and mama will have made sure that no one suspected a thing. You may trust her, you know. She has promised to support you. So hurry and get changed into something appropriate for a top-lofty society hostess."

"Your mother will support me? Are you sure, Jon? She does not like me above half. And if she—"

He stopped her worries by the simple expedient of kissing her again. "My mother's mind was poisoned against you, I am sorry to say, by Miss Mountjoy. She detests me, and would do anything to injure me."

"Because she is your discarded lover?"

"Good God, no!" he exclaimed, though her new-found daring delighted him. "What made you—? Ah, Beth, you could not be more wrong. In truth, Miss Mountjoy, er, loved Alicia very much and blamed me for her unhappiness. Now that Alicia is dead, the Mountjoy woman seizes every opportunity for mischief-making. But she is leaving Portbury soon. She will not trouble us any more."

"Poor woman. She must be very unhappy." Beth was shaking her head sadly. "And lonely, too, without Alicia," she added.

"She is your enemy and yet you think kindly of her?" He was thunderstruck. He had known Beth was generous, but this?

"Ask the rector when he arrives. He will tell you that we are to love our enemies."

Jon stared at her in stunned silence. He would never be able to match her generosity of spirit. And he did not deserve such a treasure. "You must hurry now, love," he said gruffly, leading her towards her bedchamber door. "And while you are preparing to face your guests, I shall have an interview with Berncastle. I guarantee that his wife will be begging your pardon before the day is out. She will admit she mistook you for a woman named Clifford. Since she was foxed at the time, you will graciously forgive her, will you not?"

She let out a gasp of embarrassed laughter.

He used the moment to pick up her left hand and touch the ring. "You left everything behind but this. It gave me hope." He kissed it reverently. Then he patted her on the bottom and pushed her through the door before he changed his mind.

Chapter Twenty-Five

THERE WAS TENSION IN the atmosphere of the drawing room. Although Mrs Berncastle had publicly avowed her mistake and apologised to Beth in front of everyone, Beth knew perfectly well that not one of them believed it. Soon the tale-bearing letters would go out, and the gossip would start. Poor Jon. How would he bear it?

Beth forced herself to ignore that horrid thought and threaded her way through groups of laughing young men and formidable dowagers to join Lady Rothbury by the fire. She smiled down at her. Poor woman. The high-waisted fashions were far from flattering on her, for she was as round as an apple. "Your daughter is joining us, I hope, ma'am?"

"Oh, yes, Lady Portbury. Indeed, she says she plans to surprise me this evening." She cocked her head on one side, like a fat, black-eyed robin. "I fancy she is going to come down to dinner in her new evening gown."

"That will be splendid," Beth said kindly.

"Why, Miss Rothbury," Mr Berncastle exclaimed at the same moment. "How fine you— Devil a bit!" He rocked back on his heels and grabbed a chair to recover his balance. "I mean, beg pardon, but ain't that the missing mistletoe jewel?"

The whole room gasped as one and turned to stare at Miss Rothbury. She was dressed in figured green silk. And on her shoulder she was wearing a huge clasp of wrought gold and pearls in the shape of a bunch of mistletoe.

She smiled round innocently at the company and straightened the folds of her skirts. "I told you I should surprise you, Mama. Is it not beautiful?" She stroked a finger over several of the pearls, and then down the golden stalk.

Lady Rothbury rushed forward to grab her daughter by the shoulders. She was almost weeping with embarrassment. "Child, child, what have you done? Where did you get this?"

Miss Rothbury looked confused. "I think I have always had it. Have I not, Mama? You know I have always loved pearls."

Mrs Berncastle pushed her way to the front. "You must know, Lady Rothbury, that this jewel belongs to my great-aunt, Lady Marchmont. It was stolen from her last year." She glanced along the line of astonished faces and paused, like an actress. "We were both in the house at the time, as I recall. As was your daughter."

Beth was gripped with boiling fury. How dare the woman make such accusations? There was no malice in Miss Rothbury, none at all, but Mrs Berncastle was clearly determined to have her revenge for that humiliating public apology. Well, Beth would not allow it. She strode across the room to stand between Miss Rothbury and her accuser. "Mrs Berncastle, I am sure you would not wish there to be *another* misunderstanding over this. Would you?"

Faced with the grim challenge in Beth's face, the woman paled and took a step back. After a moment, she shook her head.

"Miss Rothbury must have picked up the jewel by mistake," Beth said flatly, daring Mrs Berncastle to contradict her. "She is fond of such trinkets and would not have thought it wrong. I am sure her mama will see that it is returned to Lady Marchmont with a suitable apology."

"Quite right, my dear," Jon said firmly, taking his place by her side and dropping an arm round her waist.

Bless him. She needed him and he was there. They had their proof now, but at the cost of poor simple Miss Rothbury's reputation. It felt so wrong. "I hope," Beth began, fixing each of her guests in turn with a stern glare, "that I may rely on everyone here to say nothing at all about this incident?"

"I am sure they will not, my dear," the dowager put in quickly, smiling warmly at Beth. "For it would be such a shame if there were to be no more invitations to Portbury Abbey, would it not? And all because of a little scurrilous gossip with no foundation. No foundation at all."

Miss Rothbury was still looking bewildered and stroking her pearls. Then, seeing the dowager's encouraging smile, she began to laugh.

Slowly at first, and then with increasing mirth, the rest of the Portbury guests joined in, until the room was ringing with laughter.

Jon was not laughing. Instead, he squeezed Beth's waist and pulled her into the centre of the room. He was looking down at her in a very serious way. Had he changed his mind? Was he thinking she had done wrong to support Miss Rothbury?

"It is Christmas," he said, not attempting to lower his voice. "And at Christmas, a man may kiss his sweetheart under the mistletoe."

Beth's gasp of astonishment was caught in a long, delicious kiss that went on and on, until her head was swimming and her legs were like jelly. Her distant, austere husband was content to kiss his wife before all the world. Under the friendly mistletoe. Love was truly a wonderful thing.

"The Reverend and Mrs Aubrey!"

At the sound of the butler's announcement, Jon broke the kiss. Beth fancied he did so reluctantly. For herself, she would not have cared if it had gone on for ever.

"My, my," the rector said, coming forward with both hands outstretched. "Now *that* was certainly worth travelling all this way to see."

• • • •

Jon pulled out the last pin and watched with obvious satisfaction as Beth's hair tumbled down. He stroked a curl back from her cheek. "You know, you are a remarkably good woman, Elizabeth Portbury. I swear you do not have an unkind fibre in your whole body."

"I—" She could feel herself blushing all over. It was not helped by the fact that she was wearing nothing but a pair of silk stockings and her unbound hair. Jon had the advantage of her, for he had not yet removed his dressing gown.

She tried to make a dash for the bed, but Jon caught her up into his arms and stood looking down at her with very male appreciation. She wriggled, but he held her fast. "You will be allowed to hide under those sheets later, my dear Elizabeth. For the moment—"

"But my name is not Elizabeth!" she burst out. For a second, she thought he was going to drop her, but he strode across to the bed and set her down. She squirmed between the sheets. That was better. She could not think straight if he was gazing at her with so much desire in his eyes.

"Explain, please," he said curtly. Suddenly, he was frowning.

Oh dear. She should have told him before, when they came back from the gypsy camp, but they had had so little time alone. And then the furore over the mistletoe clasp—and that very public kiss—had pushed all other thoughts from her mind. "My name is—was Bethany de Clifford. I was always called Beth. Don't you see, Jon? They were searching for a missing Elizabeth. It is no wonder that they never found a missing Bethany."

He shook his head and then he laughed. "And you remember everything now, do you? Parents, a family? Now I think of it, I seem to know the name, de Clifford."

She nodded. "Sir Humphrey de Clifford was my father's grandsire. Papa was a younger son with no prospects. When he eloped with my mother, who was only a poor curate's daughter, the baronet cast him off. Lady Marchmont always told me I was lucky to have any position at all, after they died, for I was barely a lady."

"You are more of a lady than she could ever be." He leaned over her and ran his fingers through her hair. "And now that you are a countess—*my* countess—you are above censure. You may do exactly as you like."

"*Exactly* as I like?" she enquired innocently. She watched his eyes widen and darken as she slowly pushed the sheets down, starting to uncover her naked body to his gaze once more. Then she reached out and pulled his belt undone with a single sharp tug. She let her gaze travel down his splendid body. He was fully aroused. For her.

244

She flipped the sheet away so that she was totally exposed. And so that he could not ignore the empty space beside her. "What I should like, my lord, is a little, er, energetic male company. Of course, if you are not in the mood to provide it, I could always—"

He was beside her, and kissing her, before she could say another word. They had been passionate before, but this was different. This was passion between lovers who were no longer afraid, lovers who had at last recognised that, together, they made a single perfect whole.

Jon was holding her in his arms as though she were as delicate as a snowflake and as likely to melt away. But she would not. She was strong now, and lusty, and she wanted to love him with her body as well as her heart. "Love me," she whispered, wrapping her legs around him and pulling him close. "Love me. I am yours."

• • • •

Beth rolled over sleepily and reached across the pillow. "Jon?" she murmured. She wanted to be in his arms again, rejoicing in his touch.

He was gone.

She was jerked fully awake. She sat up. No, she was not mistaken. Jon's side of the bed was empty. He had loved her. And then he had left her. But surely it made no sense now? Why would he not stay?

She scrabbled about for the tinder box and lit her bedside candle. What was she going to do? Tonight, she had been so sure he would stay that she had not even asked him. She must ask him now, this minute, or she would never have the courage to do it. Then she would be condemned to sleeping alone for the rest of her life.

She swung her feet out of the bed and dragged on her wrapper. She could not find her slippers. No matter, she would go barefoot. After all, she would be returning to bed very soon.

She lit a branch of candles, leaving the first one by her bed. Then she crept out into their shared sitting room. It was silent, and dark. The fire had gone out long ago. She set the candles down on the little table by Jon's door and put her ear against it.

Still silence. She took a deep breath and eased the door half open.

He was lying on his back, asleep. She could hear his deep, even breathing. She pushed the door a little wider and reached for her candles.

"No! Stop! Release her or I will shoot you down. Oh, good God, no, no!"

Candles forgotten, Beth raced across to the bedside. Yes, he was still asleep, but now his breathing was shallow and rapid, and there was sweat on his brow. A dream. No, a nightmare. Something terrible. For a moment she stood frozen, wondering whether to wake him, or leave him.

She did neither. She let her wrapper slide to the floor and slid into the bed beside him. He was shaking. And muttering. Tentatively, she reached out to place her palm on his naked chest. After a moment, his shaking stopped. She slipped both arms around him and allowed her body to stretch down the full length of his. He groaned and tried to pull away, but then his whole body relaxed and he returned her embrace.

Beth smiled against his skin. She would wait.

"Beth?" It had taken several minutes for his body to emerge from that nightmare and for him to realise that she had joined him in his bed.

She touched a kiss to the line of his jaw. In the dim light from the sitting room, she could see his profile, but little more. "You were having a terrible nightmare." She understood only too well what they could do. She took a deep breath. It had to be now. "Is that why you insist on sleeping alone? Because of nightmares?"

He groaned. He started to push her away, but then he pulled her back into an even closer embrace. "I— Yes. I had hoped you would not find out, love. It was—" He shuddered.

The dark might help, Beth decided. "Tell me. Perhaps if you speak it aloud, here in the dark, the memory will stop tormenting you."

After a long silence, he said, "Very well. It was after Badajoz. I was in the town, with two young ensigns, trying to restore some order. It was impossible. The men were all roaring drunk, thieving and— One group had a woman, an innocent Spanish woman. They were going to rape her. I tried to stop them. I–I shot at the ringleader, but my pistol misfired and then the blackguards struck me down. My companions carried me back to camp. They were too young and too frightened to do anything else."

Beth closed her eyes against the horror of it. "And the woman?" she said in a tiny voice.

"I found her body. Later, after the looting had stopped. My only consolation was that the rapists were also dead, killed by their comrades' wild shooting. There was so much death, so many innocent women raped…"

"It was after Badajoz that you sold out?" She had to know it all.

He nodded against her hair. "The men left their wounded comrades to bleed for two days while they drank the town dry. It was sickening. So when Mama wrote about George trying to ruin the estate all over again, I took it as an excuse to resign my commission. But I should have saved her. She died because I failed."

Beth did not have to ask what he meant. She stroked his hair back from his damp brow and snuggled against him. "You did all you could, my love. You risked your life for her."

"Wellington should have stopped it. He knew the horror of it all, and he did nothing. For two whole days, he did nothing."

It was no wonder Jon had sold out after such disillusion. But Beth would not say that, not ever. She would simply hold him while he slept, until the nightmares subsided.

"Come back to bed with me, love." She took his hand and sat up, pulling him after her. "You have nightmares here. In my bed, we have only love and passion. Come, sleep with me till morning. The memories will not dare attack you there." She smiled at him, even though she was sure he could not see.

"Darling Beth, I swear your love could heal anyone, and anything." He caught up his dressing gown and, together, they padded across the floor and back to their marriage bed. Soon they were peacefully asleep in each other's arms.

• • • •

It was Christmas Eve at last. Jon felt more contented than ever before. His beloved wife was by his side and, thanks to her, he

247

had spent his first undisturbed nights in months. He owed her so much. Yet, when he had offered her the moon, she had asked only for a chance to drive his horses.

He waited until the curricle had come to a stop and the groom had run to the horses' heads. She really drove extremely well. He reached across and squeezed her fingers gently. "Perhaps you would like to tool the curricle round the lanes for ten minutes or so and then return for me? I have business with Miss Mountjoy, but it will not take long."

"I am flattered that you should trust me with your precious horses," Beth chuckled.

"More to the point," he responded with a grin, "I am trusting my horses with my precious wife."

They both laughed, though Beth was blushing, too.

Jon climbed down. "Go with her ladyship, Sam. She is going to drive around the lanes for a short while." He watched until the curricle was out of sight before marching up the path and knocking on the cottage door.

"Lord Portbury," Miss Mountjoy gasped as she opened the door.

"May I come in, ma'am?"

"I—" She stood back and dropped a polite curtsey. "Very well. It is, after all, your house."

Jon ignored that and walked into the neat parlour. "Miss Mountjoy, I have come to enquire about your future plans."

She drew herself up very straight. "Our meeting at the Abbey was to be our last, you said. Or have I misremembered?"

"Forgive me, Miss Mountjoy, I should much prefer it if we did not repeat the substance of that last interview. Harsh words were spoken, on both sides. And on both sides they are better forgotten."

She frowned, puzzled.

"Miss Mountjoy, much has happened since our last meeting. I have come to realise, and to regret, the cruel way I treated you then. I do still think that you should leave King's Portbury—partly for my family's sake, but for your own sake also, since there must be many unhappy memories here for you. I cannot comprehend your feelings for Alicia, nor hers

248

for you, but I do understand—now—that they were sincerely felt. I know that love is a gift, wherever it strikes. I should like to change the terms of our agreement."

A slight shudder ran through her frame. She was afraid.

"For the better, Miss Mountjoy." He drew out a sealed document and offered it to her. "This is the lease on a cottage by the sea. It is on the south coast, a long way from King's Portbury, but it is a delightful house. If you wish, you may have it for the rest of your life for a peppercorn rent. I ask for nothing else. I am certain that you will respect Alicia's memory and keep her counsel, for I know the bond between you was very strong. I do not suppose that death can break it."

"There are no other conditions?" she whispered, in disbelief.

"None." He set the lease down on the table.

"Lord Portbury, this is more than I deserve after what I tried to do to you. In return, I–I should warn you to beware of your brother. He— It was he who encouraged me to poison your wife's reputation. He hoped that you and she would part. That there would be no heir. I am sorry." She hung her head.

Jon took a deep breath. George had been the cause of all this? His brother? Jon knew he had every right to have George thrown into the gutter for such wickedness. But he knew, too, that he could not do such a thing. Not any more. He would threaten George with penury, and do his best to make sure he believed it, too, but that would be all. "Thank you, Miss Mountjoy." She looked up, surprised by his tone. He smiled at her. "I wish you a long and contented life in your new home. Let everything else that has passed between us be forgotten."

She did not speak but her face cleared. As she picked up the lease that guaranteed her future, Jon fancied that her eyes were shining. There was nothing more to be done now. He bowed.

She sank into a deep curtsey.

"I will show myself out. Goodbye, ma'am." Jon closed the parlour door gently and made his way out into the fresh, crisp air of the winter morning. He felt as if a huge weight had been lifted from his shoulders by an unseen hand. Alicia was gone. And all the heartache that had been part of his first marriage was gone too, washed away by Beth's love and the generosity she showed to everyone around her. Jon would never have a fraction of his wife's goodness, but he would try to learn from her example. Today's gift to Miss Mountjoy had been his first small step on that hard road. Meting out justice to George would be the second. George would have justice, certainly, but tempered with mercy.

Jon walked through the cottage gate to see his curricle approaching at a fast trot. He held up his hand, waiting to judge how well Beth was handling the ribbons. She halted her pair very successfully, but not before they had gone a good thirty yards beyond him. He marched down the lane until he stood at the side of the curricle, arms akimbo, and shaking his head. "Dear, dear. Is that the best you can do, Lady Portbury?" He climbed up beside her and held out his hands for the reins.

She ignored him, smiling wickedly. "You were clearly much in need of the exercise, sir. As to what I can do…" She rearranged the reins in her gloved fingers and tightened her grip on the whip. Then she grinned. "Watch!"

Seconds later, the Countess of Portbury was springing her horses with such vigour that her husband was thrown back in his seat and robbed of the power of speech.

His laughter was echoing round the lane as the curricle disappeared from sight.

THE END

Dear Reader: from Joanna

If you enjoyed *The Mystery Mistletoe Bride*, I'd be really grateful if you could leave a review at your usual online store or on your favourite reader website. Your review can help other readers to enjoy my books. *Thank you!*

One other request. I've done everything I can to ensure this ebook is free of errors, but even the best of proofreaders can miss things. If your eagle eye spots a mistake, please do let me know, via email to joanna@libertabooks.com so that I can correct whatever has gone wrong at my end.

In case you were wondering, the old Joanna Maitland website is no longer available. Information about me and my books is now at libertabooks.com/joanna.

• • • •

Competitions, Free Short Stories, Giveaways and More

For news, free stories, competitions and giveaways, please visit the multi-author website at Libertà Books where you can have your say on the weekly blog, or maybe write a love letter to a favourite novel.

Do come and join the fun in the Libertà hive where readers and authors chat and laugh about books, films, history, costume, the craft of writing and much more.

The Libertà hive tweets @LibertaBooks

You can find us on FaceBook/libertabooks too.

251

Feuding Families Series

Feuds within families, feuds between families.
Can love triumph across the divide?

MY LADY ANGEL
Passion and Strife in Regency England
Can a noble widow and a mysterious stranger find love while
a family feud threatens to ruin her?

THE SOLWAY BRIDE
Flight and Abduction in the Scottish Borders
A runaway bride rescued by a lovelorn soldier. Is Gretna
Green the answer?

STAR CROSSED AT TWILIGHT
Can a Scottish Romeo and Juliet find love?
Robert loves the fairytale atmosphere at Caerlaverock Castle,
though he's never seen any fairies there. Until now…

www.ingramcontent.com/pod-product-compliance
Lightning Source LLC
Chambersburg PA
CBHW020359210626
46816CB00006BB/2041